FATAL ALLY

FATAL ALLY

Tim Sebastian

This first world edition published 2019
in Great Britain and the USA by
SEVERN HOUSE PUBLISHERS LTD of
Eardley House, 4 Uxbridge Street, London W8 7SY.
Trade paperback edition first published
in Great Britain and the USA 2020 by
SEVERN HOUSE PUBLISHERS LTD.

British Library Cataloguing in Publication Data
A CIP catalogue record for this title is available from the British Library.

ISBN-13: 978-0-7278-8952-2 (cased)
ISBN-13: 978-1-78029-614-2 (trade paper)
ISBN-13: 978-1-4483-0231-4 (e-book)

This is a work of fiction. Names, characters, places and incidents
are either the product of the author's imagination or are used fictitiously.
Except where actual historical events and characters are being described
for the storyline of this novel, all situations in this publication are
fictitious and any resemblance to actual persons, living or dead,
business establishments, events or locales is purely coincidental.

All Severn House titles are printed on acid-free paper.

Severn House Publishers support the Forest Stewardship Council™ [FSC™],
the leading international forest certification organisation.
All our titles that are printed on FSC certified paper carry the FSC logo.

Typeset by Palimpsest Book Production Ltd.,
Falkirk, Stirlingshire, Scotland.
Printed and bound in Great Britain by
TJ International, Padstow, Cornwall.

NEW YORK

Three teams would do it. One in the fast, smart SUV. A second with motorbikes by Gramercy Park. The third on the corner of East 20th Street and Irving Place as backup.

And then there's what you can't see.

Two ways to get out. The short route via the Lincoln Tunnel and the New Jersey Turnpike – the longer one, twenty-six miles, but fast and straight along FDR drive and out over the Willis Avenue Bridge.

Two separate arcs north of Gramercy Park, heading for Teterboro airport across the New Jersey line; the Embraer Legacy 600, fuelled and cleared for imminent take-off; customs and immigration, in the way of such matters, bought and paid for in advance.

They had rehearsed most of it in other countries – but never as a team. In the hills above Beirut, near the village of Baa'bda. On a baking, dirt track outside the Uzbek city of Andijan, where government forces had shot down unarmed demonstrators in the main square and then meticulously put a bullet in the head of anyone still breathing. And then, for real, in piercing daylight, with crowds of passers-by screaming their heads off in the Petrozavodskaya suburb of Moscow.

They liked an audience.

In their head, all the training was reduced to a single mantra. Surprise equals shock equals power. You hit hard and loud and nobody moves. A thousand people can watch, but nobody sees *you*. They're mesmerized by the streaking image, the racket of engines like chainsaws, blaring horns, figures in bright colours.

To them you're simply invisible. Because you're slow, methodical, head down, hiding in the middle of the chaos, doing the business.

Twenty minutes on standby and then real life stumbles into the picture.

The police are towing a truck along East 21st Street. A van decides to unload. There's a crowd of nuns from God knows where doing God knows what.

But you've only got a single shot, so you do it anyway.

The bikes go first, white and yellow, buzzing like giant hornets, rearing up on one wheel, screeching around the square on the sidewalks, dodging passers-by, pushchairs and dogs. They are theatre.

As they ramp up the noise, the SUV pulls slowly out onto E.20th. It's black with blackened windows, shiny and immaculate.

You can't be that bad if you've got a clean car.

And the couple leaning against the railings of the park, turn almost lazily to watch, still smiling, still chatting, showing no sign of alarm.

The bike riders are glorious acrobats, the crowd in awe. No one can take their eyes off them.

They don't see that the SUV has moved around the square, right behind the couple. And the two of them don't see it either.

They're both young. Exploring, chatting. Early days because the shyness is still there. Hands touching from time to time, not holding.

They could have had a chance at something. It looked that way.

From the back of the SUV comes an effortless performance from a balding man in chinos and trainers. A janitor, a plumber perhaps. Baseball cap with illegible logo, epaulettes on a blue shirt. You see a million of them every day and you won't recognize a single one.

The crowd missed the cosh in his hand as he brought it down hard on the back of the woman's head. They missed her fall, missed her companion, mouth open, walking straight into a hypodermic needle. As he loses his footing, there's another blue shirt to catch him and between them, they carry him, as if it's the most normal thing in the world, to the back of the SUV and lay him gently on the floor.

No rush, just the practised, unhurried movements of the two professionals. Seen but not seen, easing the SUV slowly, so very slowly into the afternoon traffic.

It was the smell that hit her first. The disinfectant. Sharp and invasive. Then the rattle of distant trolleys, whispered voices. She opened her eyes, taking in the white hospital gown, white bed, white walls. A room for all purposes. Recovery one day – if your luck held; departure the next – if it didn't.

Clawing at the bedside phone, she dialled her emergency number. 'It's Mar . . .'

She stopped mid-croak and tried to swallow.

'I'm Margo Lane.'

'Yes, I know. You should stay where you are until the morning.'

'And you are who?'

'Duty assistant. We'll be in touch.'

'Is that so? How did I get—'

But the man had hung up.

The Service, she recalled, had a habit of hiring charmless graduates, devoid of social graces. Like machines they were programmed to use the minimum number of words and ensure they were meaningless to anyone who might overhear them.

And frequently to everyone else as well.

Margo found a button beside the bed and called the nurse.

'What time was I admitted?' she asked her.

'About four hours ago . . . you were really out of it.' She stood at the end of the bed and pointed to Margo's head. 'Does it hurt?'

'Now you mention it. How did I get here?'

'Ambulance. I don't deal with that part.'

'Who's paying for this?'

The nurse rearranged her pillows. 'You had some visitors not long after they brought you in. Nice couple. Said they were colleagues. Wouldn't leave their names though . . .'

'Did they say if they were coming back?'

The nurse shook her head. 'They didn't really say much of anything.'

She fell in and out of sleep.

She remembered bursts of sunshine through the trees in Gramercy Park, the two of them thinking aloud with long, silent intervals; the nuns on the other side of the square, offering by their presence an unspoken and utterly false assurance that everything would be fine.

After all the training you still see what you want to see – still arrange the dots in the wrong order, open the wrong doors.

It would fall into place – some kind of place – but not a happy one.

Two *visitors* had come to see her while she lay unconscious. They hadn't waited, hadn't identified themselves. Left nothing behind. She had been observed and discarded.

Which meant that it was over.

For everyone, except her.

LONDON

Y ou move on, Margo told herself. Course you do. The Service had designed a whole range of rituals and cliches to get you through those occupational inconveniences. Like abduction. Or killing.

And if you needed it, there was an anonymous outhouse of men and women, who smiled just a little too frequently, spoke in very low voices and wondered, in between long silences, whether she was coping and how things were going at home.

On her return to London Margo had spent a day with them, enough to avoid the label 'uncooperative'; she had drunk their milky tea and told them with all the conviction she could muster that 'it was just one of those things'.

Grimaces all round. Nodding heads. Murmurs of regret.

There had been one final debrief. Gentle. Far too gentle, she thought. One of the Service's so called 'elder statesmen', way into his sixties, had been sitting at the wooden tea table beside the apple tree in the garden. He had risen stiffly to greet her. Not there to interrogate. But in a kindly, almost disinterested way, to enquire how she had processed the events in Gramercy Park and what she would do next.

Processed?

Did she have any idea why her contact had been abducted in broad daylight in central New York? Had he been careless? Said too much? Or did the leak come from somewhere else?

Replaying the conversation, she had no doubt what they were doing. The questions were superficial, almost academic. A far cry from the forensic inquisitions she had attended when other operations had failed and the Service had dug savagely into its own gut, determined to gouge out the truth, wherever it lay.

This time the Service wasn't digging for the truth or anything else.

The file was being closed.

* * *

Much later, when they acquired the CCTV from the New York police, it seemed that the two men in blue shirts had been complacent, almost lazy.

The whole thing too pat, too slick.

The police too slow.

The airport too easy.

As if everyone had let it happen.

But no one said it.

My friend.

She could see him on that spring day they had met in Manhattan – both at breakfast in the Astro Café on Sixth Avenue, both laughing at the rudeness of the waiters and the size of the omelettes.

They were crammed together at the bar and somehow they had tried to scramble out at the same time and fallen against each other, and laughed some more. She from embarrassment – and he? Well, he had planned it that way. Of course he had. That had been London's view. Almost certainly a trap.

And yet he had never stopped surprising her. A week later he told her that he worked for Moscow, that his cover was part of a trade delegation, that he was a specialist in artificial intelligence.

Ten days after that he'd given her a name and address that produced near-catatonic excitement in London.

By mid-June, three months to the day since their first meeting, he had been seized as he stood next to her amid the trees and sandwich eaters and the wide-eyed, ever-smiling nuns in Gramercy Park. No contact was ever made with him again.

Mikhail.

At least give him his name.

'Why are you doing this for us?' she had asked him. 'Taking such risks . . .'

An afternoon without end in Central Park.

'Feels right,' he said and his smile broadened suddenly as if he just wanted to play. 'Who knows, maybe I'm doing it for you.'

And in that moment she had wanted to break every rule in the book and tell him: *Don't say that. You can't do this for me. Do it for all those cringing abstracts like 'freedom' and 'world peace' that only Americans can say with a straight face.*

*Do it because you hate your boss, or you didn't get promotion
or you're greedy and want the cash.*

*And if you can't think of anything else, do it because you want
to live one day in a place where the rain is soft and the winters are
mild and the skies are cast in a dozen colours, all at the same time.*

Just don't do it for me.

He had smiled again as if he had read her thoughts.

'You think too much,' he said.

It had taken months to find out what happened. Manson, long labelled
the Service's 'shit in residence', had gone over to Washington to
get a briefing. But they didn't tell him anything.

So he had trawled the European services for almost a year, begging
bowl outstretched, until a new Russian defector who had fallen in
love with Rome and short skirts – one in particular – came over to
London to recount what he had seen and heard.

Turned out that an American agent had been arrested in Moscow
and to get him back, the CIA had thrown Mikhail to the Russians.
If they could extract their man from Moscow, the KGB would be
allowed to lift theirs from New York.

A deal that apparently suited everyone – 'except Mikhail and of
course us'. Manson leaned back in his chair. Even though it was
early morning, his suit was creased as if he'd slept in it.

As he talked, he leafed through a light-blue file. Inside it she
could see a cascade of handwritten notes, marked and annotated in
several colours – the patchwork story of a man traded and sold for
slaughter.

Mikhail had been executed in Moscow's Lefortovo prison a
month after his arrest, but not before they had extracted everything
they wanted. Contacts, methodology, motive. The usual list.

There had been no trial. No family visits. No last requests. He
had been quite alone.

'Fuck the Americans,' Manson had said with characteristic
economy.

Margo remembered him looking at her quizzically across his
desk. 'You're very silent about all this.'

'Perhaps I think too much,' she told him.

MOSCOW

t's only when you see the very old weeping, she thought, that you confront true despair.

The kind that had sat inside them for decades, spawned by unimaginable evil.

Wherever she looked there were fresh tears on wrinkled, mottled skin; old eyes, struggling to focus in the harsh daylight, hands clasping scuffed and faded photographs.

They didn't cry for nothing, such people. Not here.

Margo had broken orders to make the trip; Manson's warning flung at her back as she had marched out of his office; made her own arrangements, dismissed the risks.

Saunders from the Moscow Embassy had met her at the airport, tweed jacket and a bad temper to signify that his weekend had been interrupted and he'd had to give up a lunch party at the *dacha*.

'I'm Margo Lane,' she told him.

'I know who you are,' he replied. 'They told me you're only here for a few hours. Wasn't necessary, you know.'

She was going to answer him, but thought better of it. The little creep didn't know, couldn't know why it meant something to her, why she'd fly, at some appreciable risk, all the way to Moscow to visit a cemetery, when you couldn't even be sure who was in it.

'Wait in the car,' she told him, when they arrived. 'I won't be long.'

Past the gates of the Donskoy Cemetery and they were huddling in small groups. Some, she felt sure, had been coming every weekend for most of their life, drawn by the separate and collective tragedies that had touched them all.

No lost or faded memories in this place. No sleeping, gentle souls at rest under the fir trees. Everything raw and bitter, just as it had been.

In its heyday, during Stalin's purges of the 30s, the crematorium had despatched some 500 souls a night – a charnel house, way out beyond the reaches of the civilized world.

Margo could feel the anger that lay just below the surface. The same anger that had brought her from London.

Move to the left of the main door, they had said. A hundred metres down the main path between the endless gravestones. Left at the dark grey monument and then you will see it.

It's probably the place where his remains have been left. Probably.

Only then did she let herself think of him.

She stood in front of the central plaque. Mass grave number three. Ahead of her the statue of a woman, half-kneeling, arms across her chest, head bowed forever, frozen in stone.

Close by, a single urn in memory of the lost, the unknown, perhaps even the unloved.

'*Nevostrebovanniye prakhi*'. Unclaimed ashes.

They would have brought him here in darkness, she thought, when the cemetery was closed. Nameless, state functionaries, sweating and swearing. And in the long grass behind the gravestones, they would have dug a small hole, shoved the container with his ashes inside and covered it over. Amazing, that they had bothered at all.

And yet they would have seen it – and enjoyed it – as ritual humiliation. A shabby final act, without prayer or mention, as if Mikhail had never existed.

Two days after returning from Moscow she had gone to see Manson. Even on a bright day his presence had made the room seem dark and unhappy.

'You shouldn't have gone to Russia.' He didn't look up from his papers. 'You disobeyed a direct order.'

'I had my reasons.'

'Which were . . .?'

'What do you think? He was my agent.' She sat down uninvited. 'I want to re-open his file.'

Manson stopped writing and slowly lifted his head. 'I'm happy to have a conversation with you, Lane – but not that conversation. OK?'

'No it's not. He was betrayed and you did nothing about it. The file was opened and closed on the same day. I know what a real investigation looks like – and this was a sham.'

Manson raised a single eyebrow. 'There's no point going down this road because there's nothing at the end of it. No compensation. No revenge. No resurrection. Just a fucked-up relationship with an awkward, angry ally who *we* need, more than he needs us.'

'Thank you for making the situation so clear.'

'You can take that tone if you want to, but it doesn't change anything. Leave the Americans alone. Understood? Move on, Lane. You lost a man who could have been saved. Should have been saved. But it's over.'

She made for the door but Manson called out after her. 'He didn't belong to you. You know that, don't you? Agents don't belong to anyone. They drift in and out . . .'

'That's bullshit. Try some other cliches.' She was angry, didn't mind if he saw it. 'They're human beings. Mikhail was a human being. Remember what *they* look like?'

He got up and stood by the desk, suddenly tired, ill at ease. She could see his eyes fighting to stay open.

'What happened to you?' She shook her head. 'All these years here. All those grand ideals? Or did you just decide it was easier to lie in your basket and piss where they told you to?'

He looked down at the floor. 'Forget it, Lane. I wish there was another way, but there isn't. For all our sakes, forget it.'

She had crossed Vauxhall Bridge, turned right along the Embankment and as the city left work and fumbled its way home, she found herself on a bench in St James's Park.

It was autumn and a gale blew sudden gusts of leaves across the damp grass.

A few people glanced at her – caught the strong jaw, the short blonde hair, a little spiky on top where the wind had played with it.

Her coat hid a slim figure – one size *too* slim, according to the common view. Ever since she could remember, there had been someone in her life, wanting to feed her more.

Had the passers-by been closer, they might have seen the slow movement of her eyes, absorbing, recording, not rushing pointlessly from object to object, but calm and grounded, just as they had been on the day she was born.

Her parents remembered a birth without tears. In Margo's first seconds on earth, her eyes had fixed on one face then another, but without surprise or distress. Born with questions, said the specialist. *Who are you people and what are you doing here?*

Default expression became a lukewarm smile, never far away – except today. A smile for all seasons and moods. The kind of smile you can hide behind because it tells nothing to the rest of the world.

No easy boxes to fit Margo Lane.

Day one at school, she'd been told to take off her coat – refused point blank – drew herself up to her twenty-five inches and invited the teacher to remove her own coat if she chose but she, Margo – child of irrepressible convictions – had no such intention.

She had sat there the whole day with the coat clasped around her, having proved a point for life. No one, but no one, could ever make her do anything she chose not to.

So place her in a group, and as the years passed she would emerge most often as the conductor in an orchestra of voices.

The one who can start them speaking and the one who stops them dead.

The one who led her schoolfriends through forests and over streams, always pushing on up the next hill to the next tree, to the next signpost, the next corner, the next brick wall – and then a bit further. Just to see what was there.

No wonder she had been unable to resist the collected curiosities at Vauxhall Cross – the men and women who clutched at secret straws, who went looking for threats and dangers and sometimes didn't return.

Margo pulled her coat tightly around her. The cold wind had sucked tears from her eyes and she wiped them away with her glove.

She remembered what a colleague had told her soon after joining the Service. 'There are no happy endings in this building. That's not the business we're in. But there can and there should be fitting tributes to those who sacrifice themselves for what we do.'

Fitting tributes?

More like pompous crap.

She thought of Manson telling her to forget it.

Mikhail deserved better.

MOSCOW
THREE YEARS LATER

There were four of them around the table, playing cards, with the beer and the vodka chasing each other and their voices rising in the clammy, overheated flat off Leninsky Prospekt.

Arkady Mazurin had been drunk half the day, long before the others arrived; a mangy, fat dog of questionable pedigree across his knees, the screams down the phone of his lunatic, long-divorced wife, still in his ears, and his luck draining away.

It had been all right until one of them had talked politics. Said how much better it had become under the new man. How the spies now controlled everything. Not like the old days when the Party hacks kept trying to interfere. Now Security was back on top where it belonged – ruling the roost.

He'd grown first bored, then angry and then he'd let them have it. All about how rotten the system was from top to bottom, how the best and brightest were leaving, how the vast state of Russia was like some broken-down truck by the side of the global highway, going nowhere.

'What's the matter with you?' one of them had asked.

He pulled himself up and stood over them. 'We were brutal, and stupid and we ruined millions of lives – and the new crowd has learned nothing.'

It was Grishin, who had spoken up, like the little rat he'd always been, playing everyone off against each other. 'My dear Arkady, none of us was perfect.'

'You talk of perfection?'

'I only meant that we served—'

'We served ourselves . . . remember? We of the glorious Committee for State Security. He shook his head. 'And you talk of perfection?'

Grishin produced an oversized handkerchief and blew his nose.

'I was going to say that it's no good drinking to forget the past. What we did was—'

Arkady crossed the room and stood right in front of him. 'I don't drink to forget the past. I made my peace many years ago with what I did. No, my friend' – his nose was centimetres from Grishin's – 'I drink because the present is so fucking horrible.'

Nothing was said for at least a minute. Far below them they could hear the traffic, grinding slowly through the fresh snow.

And Arkady knew he'd said too much.

He remembered the surprise, registering on Grishin's plump, greedy face. He also remembered that special Russian movement of the eyes. A tiny swivel. Barely visible. But you know so well what it means when you're in Moscow. You know that the man has registered what you said. And before long, when it suits him, when he can use it for maximum personal benefit, when he can sell you for the right price, he will tell someone else. At which point – slowly, or even not so slowly – the incriminating tale will begin its climb through the State's ineffably tedious catalogue of citizens' misdeeds, until one day, in an office far, far away from anything resembling civilization, an alarm bell begins to ring.

Arkady knew how it would go. The bright new technocrats would open a big, fat file, probe his decades-old reports and messages, look at his absences, go after things that didn't quite add up, weren't quite true, couldn't be backed up by facts. Contact reports, surveillance, bank accounts.

If they really went for it, it wouldn't take them long. Not if they had him in the frame.

And then?

And then they would send the car to bring him in.

Used to be the grey Volga with the curtained rear windows – room for three in the back, so that the other two could beat him up if he became difficult.

He rubbed a hand across his face and pushed the dog onto the floor.

After that, it was all too clear. He had no friends left in high places. Hadn't attended the stupid reunions, the retreats, the whisky parties where old spies lied about their failures and inflated their successes. Hated the self-righteousness and all the talk of serving 'otechestvo' the Fatherland.

So there would be no one to take his call.

Outside the window another winter had lain down across the city. As he peered through the grimy, frozen glass he could see the lights burning in a hundred buildings way out into the suburbs. Shapes moved, screens flickered. Everyone was out there. Just as they always were in Russia.

Everyone and no one.

Arkady shut his eyes. I'm fifty-nine, he told himself. I could still have a life somewhere.

LONDON

Margo wished she hadn't told him about her job.

But they were getting married in six months, or a year, or sometime – so it seemed only fair. Let him take a quick look over the fence, a glimpse of the secret world. And then they could go back to their spaghetti and forget about it.

When she said it, Jimmy had given her one of his quizzical looks. 'You serious?'

'It's not the kind of thing to joke about, is it?'

'I wouldn't know.' He looked back at her over his shoulder. 'We've been engaged half a year and you never thought to mention it.'

'It just didn't seem important . . .'

'Christ, Margo. You didn't think it important to tell me what you actually do? I thought you were a researcher at the Foreign Office, writing briefs for ministers on arms control, proliferation, up to your bloody eyes in target selection and throw weights.'

'It doesn't change anything . . .'

'Of course it does. You lied to me, lied to my parents and friends . . .'

'Just hang on a minute' – she could hear her voice rising – 'I'm not free to blurt this kind of thing out to anyone I feel like. Ever heard of rules? Procedures?'

They didn't speak much after that. She cleared dinner with most of the pasta going into the bin. Jimmy turned on the television and sat resolutely in front of it.

Hours later when he climbed into bed she could feel the silence pushing its way between them.

'Why did you tell me today?'

'I thought you should know . . .' She turned to face him in the darkness.

'But why today?'

'It seemed like it was time.'

'Just a gut feeling? Thought I could finally be trusted?'

She reached for his hand but he pulled it away. 'I always trusted you. I wouldn't be with you if I didn't.'

If the truth were known, she thought later, perhaps she hadn't trusted him after all. The very things she loved about him – his openness and spontaneity – made him unsuited to keeping secrets. She couldn't tell him that. But she thought that soon she would have to take a different tack with him, remind the middle-class public schoolboy with the badly-cut hair, that it was time he grew up, that some things were more important than being open. That she operated for the public good, in a pretty hostile world and that people like her had to make some sacrifices if that carefree, pub-centric, have-a-great-day crowd that he hung around with weren't going to have their sleep disrupted by stray bullets or bombs.

And he wouldn't take it well. Not a lesson like that. So the questions would keep on coming – buried one day, dug up again the next. But always dropped back in her lap. The way a dog delivers a bone.

He put out a hand and touched her hair. 'What happens if I get a phone call one day from someone I've never met and never heard of, who says you're not coming home, because something happened somewhere that he can't tell me about? Is that how this ends, Margo?'

She hadn't prepared for that one. Hadn't put herself in his shoes.

'Did you hear what I said?'

'I don't know what to tell you, Jimmy.' She turned away in case, even in the darkness, he could see her expression. 'I just don't know.'

WASHINGTON DC

'I need a favour, Vitaly.'

'Delighted, Harry – Russia is full of favours. Which one would you like – a holiday by the Black Sea, a trip to a ball-bearing factory?'

Harry Jones smiled across the crowded Georgetown restaurant. Long before becoming national security adviser to the president, he had studied Russian, been attached to the US embassy in Moscow and eavesdropped on some of the Kremlin's most secret radio transmissions. Russians – and especially their ambassador to Washington, Vitaly Yanayev – were never dull.

'How are things at the embassy, Vitaly?'

The ambassador smiled. 'You tell *me* – you listen to everything we say from morning till night. From the noises we make in the bathroom, you calculate what we ate for dinner the night before. You analyze the bedtime stories we read our children, in case they contain coded messages. And in return we keep hundreds of your people employed following us all over America in our mundane daily lives. How do *you* think we are?'

Jones grinned. 'We only have your best interests at heart . . .'

'You're too kind.' Vitaly pushed his plate away and poured himself another glass of wine. He was immaculate as ever – just a shade more immaculate than a diplomat on a state salary has a right to be. The tie, a little too expensive, the jacket, an inch too sculpted. He liked his clothes, liked himself in the mirror, but he knew that his vanity was a weakness and that Harry didn't share it. Two years ago he had written in a cable to Moscow that Harry Jones always dressed like a liberal arts professor from the Midwest. A bow tie, tweed suits, strong, practical shoes. 'Harry Jones, doesn't do Armani,' he told them, 'but he does do power. And he is comfortable using it. Do not underestimate him.'

That was language Moscow understood. Harry Jones had their respect.

Vitaly raised an eyebrow. 'You mentioned a favour, Harry. What can I do for you?'

Jones shifted slightly in his chair. 'We have a package we need to locate in Syria and bring home.'

'Of course you do. We too have packages there from time to time. A human package?'

'You could say that.'

'And you want me to suggest an exit.'

Harry took off his glasses and rubbed his eyes. 'I'll get the check. A little cold air might do us some good.'

They emerged onto M street and headed down the icy hill on Wisconsin Avenue towards the Potomac. A taxi was struggling to make it up to the traffic lights. Tiny snowflakes danced around them. Harry thought that in an hour or so the storm would hit the city and shut it down for the night.

'Moscow weather,' he told Vitaly. 'Pretty much the same there today, I guess.'

The ambassador took his arm as they crossed the road gingerly towards the Watergate Hotel.

'So will you help on this one?' Harry stopped and stared straight into the Russian's eyes. 'You've access to the government there and assets on the ground that we haven't.'

'And the package is in government hands?'

'It may be – certainly within their sphere of influence. We're talking about the "Shabbiyah" – the paramilitaries. That's why I came to you. You're the only ones Damascus will talk to.'

'Who is this package, if I may ask?'

'One of our coordinators.'

'I see. Coordination is such a risky business these days, because there is so little way of knowing who to trust. Someone you buy one day, may be bought the next by others for a bigger sum.' He grimaced. 'But you know that better than I do.'

'This may have been the problem we've encountered.'

Yanayev thought for a moment. 'And do you know the location of the package?'

'Rough area. No more. Our information could be out of date now by several days.'

'And it's critical that you find this man . . .'

'It's a woman, Vitaly.' He saw the ambassador raise a single eyebrow. 'And yes, it's critical that we find her.' Harry looked up and down the street but there was no one else nearby. 'Will you help?'

'I'd like to, my friend.' He paused and wiped his runny nose. 'But you don't have much credit these days in my capital. They don't like the interventions in the Middle East, they don't like your games in Georgia and Ukraine, or the little stunts in Congress on human rights. There's not much appetite to make life easy for you.'

Jones could feel the cold seeping into him through his bald head. He had forgotten to bring a hat. Vitaly was better equipped, sporting a flamboyant fox *shapka*.

'This one's important. I wouldn't be here otherwise.'

'I know, Harry, and I'll send the message through, but I also know what the answer will be.'

The ambassador's black sedan slid abruptly to a stop beside them and Harry realized that it must have been close by since they left the restaurant.

'This is my ride.' Yanayev slapped him on the back. 'Can I drop you back to the White House – or would that look bad?'

'It wouldn't – but I could do with the walk.'

Yanayev got in, but then stopped midway and turned back to face the American.

'Give me a gift, Harry.' He extended a gloved hand. 'A big one, an expensive one that I can take to Moscow to buy you your favour. That's the only way this is going to work. Cash on delivery. Needs to be something impressive. And it needs to be soon. Without it' – the wind grabbed at his shapka – 'without it, they'll turn you down.'

Vitaly Yanayev loved America. But as Russia's ambassador to Washington he rarely admitted it. Still less did he admit why.

He had confided once to his wife, Lydia, that it was because the US was a land of infinite variety and unpredictability. 'In Moscow,' he had told her, 'I will always be stabbed in the back. Except when they miss or hit me in the hip or, God forbid, in the buttocks. But in America I never know. Sometimes they will stab me right in the chest, in the middle, and stare straight into my eyes with love and adoration while they do it. It's so refreshing, so different . . . you just never know what to expect.'

He couldn't help recalling that conversation as his car inched through the afternoon traffic back to the Russian embassy.

Harry Jones hadn't lied when he said he needed the fresh air. He hadn't slept for thirty-six hours, not since the cable had come across his desk – the one from State, followed by comments from Langley. But he'd known it anyway. She hadn't replied to any of his messages in more than a week. The ones he'd left on an ordinary gmail account, opened by someone else a world away with a name that meant nothing to anyone. He always used a different internet point. Different times of day. And now there was silence.

As he walked, he could see her face the day they had said goodbye. She had never cried. When things got to her, she would always bite her upper lip, the way she did that day at the airport in London, as she boarded the flight to Istanbul.

'Harry, we need to get a grip on this. It has to end here.'

'Not for me, it doesn't.'

But his words didn't seem to reach her. The small elfin figure was already turning away, the long dark hair sweeping around her neck, a wave in constant motion, her ancient black leather jacket on her arm.

She had smiled at him quickly, just once – a sudden shard of light in a grey sky – and then she was gone.

And in that instant Harry knew she had breached his defences, crossed the line, set by reason and duty. A line and a code he had lived by for so long. His love of country, his patriotism and loyalty. The oath he had sworn to the president. He had told himself to step back, excise her from his consciousness, even as he had realized the impossibility of doing it.

He reached the White House gate, nodded to the guards who scanned his pass and strode to the side entrance and his office in the West Wing. Once there, he was never more than a step away from the most powerful man in the world, with unfettered access to his military might, his secrets and those of his allies right across the world. He could engage, at will, the assets of the most extensive spy service the world had ever seen – its satellites in orbit, its ground stations, its undersea listening posts in the furthest reaches of the globe. If it moved they saw it, if it spoke they heard it. Task the machine, throw money at it and it would deliver almost anything you wanted.

But Harry Jones wasn't thinking of any of that. His mind was focused and crystal clear.

She was missing in the civil war in Syria and he would do whatever it took to get her back.

LONDON

M argo Lane's day had begun badly – cold silence from Jimmy in the flat – wet streets outside, sleet and snow promised for later.

The phone had rung at seven which hadn't pleased either of them – especially since she had gone into the bathroom to take the call.

She had reached the fifth floor conference room ten minutes ahead of schedule but Manson was already there at the head of the table.

'What's so urgent?' She hung her coat by the door.

'I've ordered coffee.' Manson looked up from the file. 'We'll wait for everyone to arrive. Don't want to say it all twice.'

She took a seat furthest away from him and stared out of the window. Conference Room D. Same place where her first interview had been held. Not the initial greeting in the drab little house in Camberwell Green, nor the informal chat in the café in Victoria. But the first recorded session where they had told her it was time for a decision. She didn't have to sign the papers. She could go off and become a lawyer, or head for the City and retire at forty-five with a yacht in the Caribbean and a chalet in the Alps.

Nothing wrong with that.

Alternatively, she could embrace a life of intermittent, but incalculable risk, and the prospect of unending, lonely hours with a bunch of people, far more fucked-up, they said, than she was, stretching away into an ill-defined future.

Leave now, though, and we'll never bother you again.

As they spoke, every instinct was screaming at her to turn and run. But she couldn't do it. Sat there, expressionless, on the grey steel chair, with the black plastic cushion, just sipping her tea.

Raincoat and umbrella on the floor beside her. Poppy in the lapel. *I come from a normal world*, it all said, but she knew that she'd left normality at the door. And if she simply stood up and went off down the corridor, handed in her visitor's badge at reception, headed for the Tube and the journey back to Hampstead, where Mum and Dad and the Labrador were living happily ever after, *her* life would never be so interesting ever again.

Much later, she told herself, it was like watching a giant killer wave, listening to its savage, roaring advance and then calmly walking towards it.

Twelve years ago – and now this.

'Morning everyone.' Manson's eyes took in the four people at the table. 'I'm giving you copies of a signal that came in from Moscow overnight – please read it.'

He pushed a grey file, containing a single sheet, towards each of them – Forbes from the Russian section, Silverton from C's office, Halstead from Legal. Margo knew them by sight – all younger than her, not long out of training, fresh meat for Manson to bully and manipulate. She wondered if they knew his real function: to be a pain in everyone's arse.

Manson turned away from them and stared out at the Thames. Rain was spattering the windows. A light mist had spread itself along the north bank.

'Right. Let's get on with it.' He swivelled back to face them. 'Yesterday afternoon a man called Arkady Mazurin – who used to be our most valued asset in Moscow – surfaces after five years of total and complete silence and calls a crash meeting with our station chief Robert Evans. They met in a bookshop near the Lubyanka. Mazurin was apparently drunk – but lucid. Bottom line: he wants out.'

Margo leaned forward. 'Why? The signal doesn't say.'

'Says he's got something special for us. Wouldn't say what. And anyway we promised we'd get him out when the time came.'

Margo closed the file and pushed it back towards Manson. 'What's the real reason?'

Manson shrugged. 'How the fuck do I know? Apparently a previous employee of ours in Moscow made him a half-baked, half-promise more than twenty years ago, that if he ever wanted out, we'd make it happen. Now he's cashing it in.'

'Yes, but why now . . .?' Forbes from the Russian section seemed suddenly anxious to get involved.

'Work it out for yourself,' Manson shot back. 'Why do agents leave places in a hurry? They're in trouble. Money, women, or they're blown. Whatever it is, he's not going to tell us the truth. Bad boys don't tend to run straight home and tell Mummy what they've done.' He raised an eyebrow. 'Or do they?'

Forbes blushed. 'I still don't get it. Why not leave years ago? He's been retired more than five years . . . why now?'

Manson reached down to his briefcase on the floor, removed a bigger file and began flicking through it. He didn't bother to hide his irritation. 'He has a wife . . . an ex-wife.' He gave Forbes an unpleasant look. 'Don't you people read files in your section these days?'

Margo caught Manson's eye. 'You said before that Mazurin is no longer any use to us. Is that true?'

'According to the file, we gutted him some years ago. But maybe he held something back for a rainy day. Wouldn't be the first time. Or . . .' He paused and looked up at the ceiling. 'Or he just wants us to try that little bit harder to get him out.' He put the file back in his briefcase. 'Thoughts?'

Margo looked round the room but nobody spoke. Forbes was staring down at the table, licking his wounds. The two others were buttoned up tight.

'OK . . .' Her eyes fixed on Manson. 'We don't have much of a choice here . . . if he has something of value, we want it. If not, we still made a commitment and unless there's a pressing argument for breaking it – which none of you seems to have – we need to deliver.'

'Agreed.' Manson didn't bother with the others.

Margo gestured towards the grey file. 'According to the signal Mazurin still has a diplomatic passport. After all, he was in the Soviet delegation – there undercover for almost ten years. In my view, it's best if he flies direct to New York. We arrange to have him invited to some meaningless ceremony there – something to do with one of his old colleagues – or his old department. The Russians always bought into nonsense like that – flattered them, made them feel important. We'll do the same again. It'll arouse less suspicion.'

'And the embassy?'

'Tell them to leave it for a day or so, then make contact and let Mazurin know the invite's on its way. He'll have to apply for an exit – all KGB, serving or retired, have to do that. If he gets clearance, then we'll know he's got a good chance of making it.'

'And if he doesn't?' Halstead, turned ninety degrees to face her. The prospect of failure seemed to stir his interest for the first time.

Margo rounded on him. 'Then I'm sure he'll be grateful for your prayers.'

She was surprised at how little emotion she actually felt.

'You'll have to take charge of this one, Lane . . .' Manson had gestured to the others to leave. He got up and shut the door behind them.

'Why me?'

'Why not you? You've worked in Russia, you also understand' – his voice hovered over each syllable – 'the Americans – if memory serves. It would seem to have your name engraved all over it.'

She stood up.

'Just a moment.' Manson returned to his chair and dug back into his files. 'Mazurin was one of the best we had in Moscow. Our man. He'd only work for us. Christ knows why. Getting him out – even if he just sits on a plane and farts for 10 hours – is a major undertaking.'

'What are you worried about?'

'I worry about the things we don't know . . .' The arrogant, hectoring tone had suddenly softened. 'Man comes back to us from the dead. Tells our agent that he has something we need to see.' Manson shook his head. 'How did he get it? Is it ancient or modern? Is it about them – or us? What's he leaving out.' He sighed. She could see the dark pools under his eyes. He wouldn't have slept since the signal came in overnight. 'And then of course there are the Americans to deal with. Always wanting a slice of the pie . . .'

'Do we warn them?'

Manson sniffed as if the thought were somehow unpleasant. 'That he's coming out? No choice. If we don't tell them – and something goes wrong, they'll shit on us from a very great height. Spiteful bunch, these days – and they have more ways of showing it than we do.'

He got up. 'As for whether he has some sparkling new gift for us . . . we'll keep that to ourselves.'

MOSCOW

Arkady played over the meeting a hundred times. What the Englishman was wearing, cufflinks instead of buttons, mauve tie, dull suit, dull shirt, dull face – where did they find these people?

But what had he expected – a Vaudeville act? A caricature of the British spymaster of old, with half his lunch congealing on his jacket, and a waistcoat and watch chain? They didn't make them like that anymore. Probably never had.

The man had been under forty and knew his business. Came out of nowhere, browsed the bookshelves and spoke faultless, unaccented Russian. So they weren't playing games. The Englishman had treated him courteously, but without sentiment or warmth. Arkady imagined that he belonged to the brand new breed, fed on statistics and psychometrics, with bottles of mineral water on the desk in front of them and forms to fill in every time they went to the lavatory. They'd all save like good boys and girls for their pensions, check their cholesterol once a year and dutifully mow the lawns of England at weekends. Or would they?

He didn't know. Didn't know anything anymore.

All he knew was that the man came from somewhere else – *iz-za bugra* – literally from beyond the hill. He had an inner sense of calm and certainty that nobody in Russia can possess. He'd grown up without the danger of random attack, without being called to apartments where husbands had pickaxes sticking out of their foreheads, or children had knifed their mother in the back, or strangled granddad, or where the tramps – the *bamzhi* – fell asleep in the basements of blocks of flats only to have the radiators burst and drown them where they lay.

So he would know nothing of the extremes of ludicrous, limitless, domestic violence that Russians lived with, grew up with, day after day. He would have lived in a place governed more or less by the rule of law, instead of the irredeemable kleptocracy that reigned over Russia. He would have read what he wanted, travelled

where he wanted and never had to fear that the system might run
him over, if he got in its way.

The conversation had lasted less than a minute and a half. Casual
not hurried. Arkady had said his piece – amazing, he thought, my
life in forty-five seconds and my hopes for the future. The Englishman
had asked five questions and said he'd return in less than a week.
Same time, different bookshop. A mobile phone had been passed.

Four of the questions had been easy – only the fifth had kept
him thinking all the way back across Moscow to the flat.

Do you have something urgent to tell us?

He had whispered the reply in the bookshop and now he whispered it again to himself.

In the living room Arkady had reached automatically for the whisky
bottle, but this time he stopped himself. It wasn't a day for drinking.
Tonight he had made his move. Climbed back into the danger zone
where all his faculties were needed. A clear head and a set of plans
inside it. Contingencies. Fallbacks, escape routes. That's what he
needed. The whole kit of parts that would get him out of Russia
alive and land him somewhere safe. Maybe.

He sat in the chair and let the memories approach him, silently
like wild animals emerging slowly from the darkness of the forest,
teeth bared.

Arkady shut his eyes.

Seven p.m. on a housing estate in Leningrad, fly-blown, dingy,
half-dead. And the monthly deal was being sealed.

Six of them crowded into the tiny living room: the deputy mayor
and all his associates from the City Administration. Round the table
there were glasses of tea and some dry biscuits. Someone had
brought a bottle of Georgian brandy but it was empty now and the
voices were getting louder.

Time had come to put the stakes on the table. So they began as
they always did, reaching into their pockets, dragging out the wads
of cash and pushing them across the table to the boss.

That little smile on his face. Like he'd won it.

But this time something was wrong. Only four of them had
handed over their stake.

And that smile had suddenly disappeared.

'What is it, Fyodor Ivanovich?' The boss's voice was smooth, untroubled.

The big man at the opposite end pushed his chair away from the table. 'I can't do this anymore. I thought I could but I can't.'

'What worries you, my friend?'

'What worries me?' The big man laughed. 'What worries me is what should be worrying you.' He pointed a finger at the boss. 'Each month we come here. We, the important and most respected heads of department at City Hall, all of us trusted colleagues of yours, Mr Deputy Mayor. We drink, we talk and then we hand over our official pay packets to you. You put the money in your pocket and nothing is said. We each get back in our cars and go our separate ways to our allotted districts where – in return for the stake we gave you – only we may take bribes from our citizens.' He shrugged and looked around at the other faces. 'And so it goes. We take bribes from the police, from the crooks, from honest businessmen and from the corrupt – from whoever and wherever we can extort it. And we turn up at the city parades and accept the grateful thanks of the people for doing our Socialist duty.' He bit hard into his lower lip. 'And you ask what worries me . . .'

There was absolute silence in the room. Silence outside. For a moment it seemed to Arkady as though the rest of the world had simply died and the six of them were the only survivors.

'I can't do it any longer, my friends.' Fyodor Ivanovich got up and reached for his coat, draped over the back of the chair. 'I strongly suggest that we end this practice before someone finds out about it . . . but that is your choice.' He nodded. 'I've made mine.'

Another four steps and he would have made it to the front door, from there onto the dark stone landing, down the three flights and out to his car, a tatty Volvo that sat rusty and inconspicuous in the parking lot.

But he took only one.

Arkady didn't remember who moved first; didn't remember who tripped the man, sending him crashing to the ground; who hammered his head on the bare boards; didn't remember who produced the wire flex or who pulled it tight around the big, fat neck; who sat on his body as it jerked wildly or who shoved a rag into his mouth to stop him screaming.

But he did remember the eyes looking up at him, shot with blood, pleading for help.

He remembered the coins falling out of the man's trouser pocket and clattering noisily on the floor, the blood congealed around the wire flex, glistening in the naked light.

And he remembered how the little smile had returned to the deputy mayor's face. How he'd picked up the phone, his hand rock steady, and spoken of a terrible accident requiring the immediate despatch of a team to take care of it all and make it go away.

He remembered the man's calm and confidence – the certainty of a regular, practised killer.

It was dark when the five of them had trouped out into the car park.

Still dark when Arkady had returned to collect the black and white film that a KGB unit had carefully installed in the ceiling, to use or not to use, depending on who ended up in power.

The way it was always done in Russia.

Arkady sat up and rubbed his eyes.

That film from Leningrad would, he was certain, buy him his ticket to London and ensure he was treated with the respect his talents deserved.

Not because the British would be interested in a sordid murder thirty years before in Russia's second city – but because the deputy mayor, pictured in that film, had done so surprisingly well in his subsequent career.

He'd exceeded all expectations. Really, the man had been a marvel.

And now, his photo had been shown around the world, and he was about to take the most ambitious step of his life.

Arkady could hardly believe it himself.

If Russia's elections went as planned in three months' time – and why wouldn't they? – the former deputy mayor of Leningrad – would acquire nothing less than the ultimate political prize in the Russian Federation.

Just one rung left on the ladder – one step away from the Kremlin.

In the kitchen Arkady's dog Vasya snorted himself awake in his basket, shuffled into the living room and slumped down across his feet. He wondered what would become of the animal. Perhaps he could take him to Yelena, who would scream and protest that she had never wanted a dog even when they were married, and certainly didn't want one now.

He stroked the dog's head and Vasya shut his eyes, trusting, at peace. Normally Arkady would whisper to him, a few words of nonsense, soothing and affectionate. But suddenly he felt embarrassed. He didn't know what to say to the creature, whose trust he would soon betray.

LONDON

Dean Anderson had reached the age where he was irritated by most things. Irritated by the 'kids' at the CIA station in London, irritated that his advice to them was apparently of such little value, irritated that his pension, due in six months' time, was considerably less than he had hoped. Irritated that day, because MI6 wanted to meet in some 'fucked-up country house park' in North London, instead of the secure embassy room, where you could get your drinks with ice and didn't have to sit in traffic for half a day to get there.

Why did Brits always play games?

He shivered a little as he made his way over the gravel to the grand, white house. It reminded him of parts of Virginia – the old estate, home of the once-landed British gentry, with its wide lawns, dipping down to the lake, shrouded in forest.

He'd read the blurb before coming. A century earlier, they were fighting duels out here, killing each other before breakfast because their honour had been slighted.

Honour? To Anderson, no one got killed anymore for honour. You got killed because you might have seen or heard something – and you weren't clever enough to forget it.

Honour was a flag on your coffin.

As he walked, a cold easterly wind shook the bare branches of the trees and the soft rain settled over him. Not an American cold – not that block of ice that slammed into you when you walked outside. But something more gentle, more insidious.

Be careful of Britain, they had always said, back at Langley. It's never what you think.

He passed a woman being pulled along by an impatient dog; a pensioner, wrapped in an old college scarf; two guilty lovers, hand in hand, dressed for the office where they should have been.

Around them, the dying light of a winter afternoon.

Margo Lane was waiting for him at one of the tea tables in the corner of the old converted kitchen. He had met her a handful of times, thought her offhand and socially inept, but he couldn't help admiring her instant recall, the clear blue eyes and the look of innocence so totally at odds with the mind inside.

'Dean.'

'Margo.' He put his coat over the back of the chair and sat down opposite her. A quick glance round the room confirmed that the elderly of London were out for tea. He waved a hand in their direction. 'Friends of yours?'

She smiled. 'All ex-KGB. We look after theirs, they look after ours.'

He laughed for the first time in two days.

'That fellow Manson still throwing his weight around at your office?'

'If he didn't, it'd be someone else. Office life.' She picked up her purse and stood up. 'You protect the table while I'm gone – and I'll bring tea. I take it you're armed.'

He watched her join the queue and suddenly remembered he was still smiling. She returned with a tea tray and poured him a cup. 'In fact I wanted to talk to you about Russia . . .'

'Still there last time I looked.'

'An old Moscow friend is coming out in a week or so. He did good service for us over a number of years. Retired from the Russian Security Service five years ago. Now he says he's had enough and it's time to leave.'

'High-level?'

'He was once.' Margo leaned forward. 'We just want him to get safely to New York and we'll take him from there. I'd be grateful if you didn't lay on a reception committee. Fewer people who know about it, the better.'

'I see.'

'Idea is that he attends a leaving party for one of his old colleagues at the UN. They were close many years ago. Party is going to be in two weeks' time.'

Anderson sipped his tea and replaced the cup carefully on the table. 'If he was high-level, our people are going to want to get a crack at him. Forty-eight hours minimum.' He saw her eyebrows rise. 'For Chrissake Margo, there's a lot of loose ends going back over the years.'

Margo shook her head. 'We gutted him when he left. Gave him a holiday in Germany, spent two weeks getting everything he knew. We passed the file to you . . . you've had it all.'

Anderson bit into his bottom lip. 'There's always more. Depends how you ask for it.' He could see her wince.

'Then you can have another go at him when he's here. Give the man a break, Dean. He wants to get out in a hurry, he'll be fragile, probably in a lousy mood and he won't be very co-operative. We'll spoil him for a couple of weeks and then the conversations will be more productive. You can have some time with him then.'

'Listen to me, I know the way Langley thinks and if a fish this size swims into our waters – even a former fish – they'll reel him in. That much I can tell you for free.'

'So you won't oblige us on this one?'

'Help, yes. Oblige no.'

'You owe us, Dean. You know that . . . three years since you fucked us over in New York . . .'

'Wait a minute, wait a minute . . .'

Around them, the elderly men and women were getting ready to leave, hunting for gloves and sticks, pulling on their hats. Margo wished she could go with them.

She pushed away her cup. 'I'll tell the office what you said – they're not going to like it. Maybe we'll find another way.'

Anderson stood up and struggled into his coat. 'Up to you. And as for what happened three years ago . . . we did our best. Your guy got caught in a terrible situation . . .'

'Of your making?'

'Think what you like.' He took a note from his wallet and threw it on the table. 'By the way, what the hell did you bring me all the way out here for? We could have had this conversation in the centre of town.'

She stayed where she was. 'It's a beautiful place, Dean. Peace, quiet, a little classic British architecture. Look around. I hoped some of it might rub off and we could behave like civilized human beings.' She stood up abruptly. 'Seems it was a waste of time.'

WASHINGTON DC

Vitaly Yanayev was proud of his wife. The thick chestnut hair that she'd had since he'd first known her, the tall, statuesque figure, her easy manner at receptions and the quick sense of humour.

She was, he realized, quite unlike the normal Russian dumptruck that most of his colleagues squired on the diplomatic circuit. Which in turn led to jealousies and malicious gossip.

But he wasn't worried. Lydia was pure gold – the only person in his life whom he had ever trusted completely.

She was already eating breakfast when he arrived in the panelled dining room of the Residence – and she instantly spotted his frown.

'What is it, my dear? You look concerned.'

Yanayev sat down and poured himself coffee. 'Right now I've no reason to be concerned, but that could change.'

She said nothing, not wishing to push him.

'The Americans want a favour from us – and it's one that Moscow will be reluctant to give them. That's fine . . . it's their decision. But the favour would buy me a useful lever. If the White House can give us a downpayment of some kind . . . it would strengthen my argument.'

Lydia smiled, got up and went over to her husband. She kissed him on the forehead. 'You'll do what's right. You always do. Now I shall be late for my music lesson. I'll see you tonight.'

Yanayev was right in assuming his wife had inspired jealousy within the embassy. Some of the other wives bitched about her handbags and shoes and joked that her hair made her look like a bear who'd just woken up after the winter.

And then there was the fact that she was Jewish. Among Russians, that always brought with it another complex prism through which to be judged and criticized.

Some Jews, of course, did well in Russia. After all, Stalin's security apparatus had been headed by one. But the country's latent xenophobia and bigotry always meant that Jews had to try harder than everyone else.

And Lydia had tried very hard indeed.

At school she had excelled as a Pioneer, showed calm and resourcefulness, obedience to authority. Her teacher's first grudging report to the local Party hack had commented on her knowledge of Communist doctrine which, he added cattily, 'had gone some way to counteracting the negative aspects of her family background'.

It had indeed. She rocketed up through the Komsomol – the Communist youth movement – securing minor positions of authority and getting noticed by some of the bigger local players.

All the same, at any point in her trajectory, the State could have marked her card – a question mark would have sufficed – and shunted her off into a provincial Party siding to die of boredom.

But it didn't. Was it the playful manner, the quick wit or the young woman's irrepressible enthusiasm for life – or was it that someone had spotted a use for her?

After all, a reliable Communist – from a respectable – and so far spotless, Jewish family was a rare commodity among cadres. No doubt there were things she knew and things she could find out. Whatever the case, someone in a position of responsibility and blessed with half a brain, had decided Lydia had potential.

And that was why they began to watch her. But they weren't the only ones.

Not long after she had been accepted into the Engineering Faculty at Moscow State University, she had been befriended by Sam who was short with tight curly hair and talked like an express train.

The first time they were alone in the student canteen he told her he was Jewish and that his father owned a furniture shop.

'That's nice,' she had said.

'No, it isn't,' he replied. 'The problem is, you don't know "fuck" about the country you live in. First of all it's a piece of crap. Everyone spying on everyone else. The second thing is, if you have any talent at all, then they want it. Look at all the special schools:

one for skiing, one for German, one for knitting, one for chess, or
carpentry. They're only just realizing that in the 1920s and 30s they
shot everyone who knew anything. So now they're fucked and they
know it. Gotta find some talents. You could be one of them.'
      She looked at him contemptuously. 'I *am* one of them.'
      He downed his tea in a hurry and took a quick glance over his
shoulder. Sam did everything in a hurry.
      'I know that. And you're pretty pleased with yourself as well.'
He chuckled.
      She frowned back. 'You shouldn't be speaking like this. And I
shouldn't be listening to you.' She got up, but he touched her arm,
not roughly, and yet with sufficient pressure to make her hesitate.
      'How many Jews do you know here in Moscow?' he asked.
      'Why do you want to know?'
      'Just curious.'
      'My family, that's all.'
      'Well, now you know one more. You see, we're already a little
community. You help me and I'll help you.'
      'And supposing I don't want to help you?'
      He laughed. 'Why would you not help your own people? You're
a Jew . . . I'm a Jew. We rise or fall together. We're a package deal.
That's why we've lasted thousands of years. You'll see.' He patted
her arm. 'One day I'll buy you a glass of tea in Jerusalem.'

When she thought back, years later, Lydia remembered that this
was the first time she had really thought about the Jews – least of
all being one of them. Her parents never talked about it – '*Luchay
net*,' said her father. 'Better not to.'
      '*Nye nado*,' said her mother. 'It's not necessary.'
      So for many years being Jewish had seemed like wearing secret
underwear. You knew it was there, but you hoped no one else did.
You didn't flaunt it, didn't advertise it – and eventually you stopped
thinking about it all together.
      Life lived in watertight compartments, the Soviet way.
      Only Sam changed that. Sam and the friendship he had given her.
      And his little community.
      It was 1983, the year before Gorbachev came to power and Lydia
remembered a hot afternoon in Park Dubki, near her parents' apartment. She was in her final year at university and had gone there to

read one of her engineering books before an exam. But when she glanced up after an hour Sam had appeared from nowhere, whispering her name, beckoning her from the shadow of a tree.

'What is it, Sam?' Even as she looked at him, she could see something was desperately wrong. He was sweating heavily, there was dirt on his chin and one of his cheeks. His hands were shaking.

'Sam, talk to me.'

'I don't have time. I'm finished.'

'What do you mean?'

'They raided my dorm this morning, found some Jewish literature – bit of politics, bit of religion – nothing important but it's illegal. Someone tipped me off that they're waiting to arrest me. But there's nowhere to run. In an hour or two I'll have to go back and face them. No choice.'

Lydia felt the colour draining from her face, a stab of fear deep down in the stomach. 'I'll talk to the Komsomol people I know. We'll sort it out. Don't worry, some of them are friends of mine . . .'

But he didn't want to hear it. 'Listen to me very carefully. You can't afford to speak on my behalf. You need to denounce me and you need to do it today. Say you always had doubts about me. Say I was always weird and talking nonsense, but you took no notice. And when they tell you about the leaflets, say you're horrified and that it's a serious crime against the State, and you hope I'll be put away for years.' He grabbed her hand. 'You have to do this. Promise me . . . please . . .'

'But why, Sam? I don't understand. Why do you want me to say these things?'

'I have to go. They may be close by. I don't have any more time. You need to do this because you're going places in this system, you've been noticed, they're going to put you on a fast track, who knows where. But don't spoil it. We need you in an important place. For once we need one of our people to rise up through this fucked-up system. You'll be contacted one day. Someone will mention my name and you will understand. Help us, Lydia. Now and in the future. Don't forget. Please do as I say – for our people. For Israel.'

She tried to hold him, embrace him, but he was already running away. In a moment, he was out of sight. And she couldn't help sinking to her knees, couldn't help the tears that began flooding onto the summer grass beside her, the nausea that rose in her throat. She didn't know how to stop crying. Even when she returned to her parents' flat, the tears kept coming. But she wouldn't tell them what had happened. It was far too dangerous for them to know.

And yet they sat for several hours on the floor outside her room, knowing instinctively what it was. Two old people, holding hands in the darkness, listening to their daughter's anguish. It had been many years since fear had walked into their home and spread its shadow across their lives.

They knew all too well what lay in store.

Lydia sat in her car outside the Residence and wondered why the memories had hit her now. Thirty years had passed. Thirty years since she had denounced Sam, as he had wanted. Thirty years since she had made her peace with the Communist system, already in its dying years.

She had never seen or heard of him again. He was erased from Soviet society as he had known he would be on that far-off summer day in Moscow's Park Dubki.

But people had come to her over the years and mentioned his name and asked for the occasional service – and she had willingly provided it.

For Sam. She told herself. Always and only for Sam.

Even when she looked inside her husband's briefcase and photographed the occasional document – as she would do again today – it was not to do harm to him. She loved him and respected him. But she felt she owed a service to Sam, who had sacrificed so much and to the little community that he had built for her.

Sam, who had promised that one day he'd buy her a glass of tea in Jerusalem.

MOSCOW

'First floor, Dom Knigi – House of Books. Ten a.m.'

Arkady shut off the mobile he'd been given and removed the battery. When he got outside, he'd break it up and throw away the pieces.

The conversation with the Englishman had taken no more than twenty seconds.

Arkady arrived ten minutes early, mingling with the Saturday shoppers. Outside, the temperature had been a generous minus fifteen, but the heat in the store felt instantly oppressive. He took off his shapka, brushed down his thick grey hair and picked his way to the Antiquarian section. It was crowded.

Muscovites had always read voraciously even during Soviet times. They still did, scared perhaps that the new books might disappear one night and the drab curtain of state censorship would descend again.

Of course anything was possible here. Russia, he thought, had forever been on the brink of something, mostly terrible, occasionally less so. But it was better not to hope. That was how most people got through it. Hardship wasn't what destroyed you, it was hope – hope that gnawed away inside you, pretending you could be someone else and that a better future lay in sight.

The way I'm hoping now, he thought.

As he turned around, looking for the contact, he felt a sudden rush of fear. But he didn't know why. His eyes toured the sales floor, the stairs, a crowd of children, a mum and dad, two army veterans. And then he knew what had triggered it. The face three metres away, flabby, nondescript, nothing to get a handle on – the grey sharp eyes, constantly moving.

What had they always said? Look for the eyes and the hands. If they're out of sync you have a watcher. Yes, there was a book in his hand, but his eyes had gone for a walk somewhere else. A real amateur.

Is that all I rate these days?

In that moment Arkady could feel the crush of people behind him. A new crowd must have surged inside from the cold. At first the voice was so low that he didn't even think it was speaking to him. The words barely uttered.

'Don't turn round . . . go on reading . . . They're on board – you'll get an invite to a party at the UN. Old colleague's retirement ceremony – nice and jolly – just like old times. When it comes, apply for your exit papers. Party's in two weeks.'

'I need to hurry. Need to go sooner.'

'Serious?'

'Yes.'

'Understood.'

Arkady waited a full minute before turning round. The flabby face had gone. Had he imagined it?

It wasn't till he got outside and felt for his gloves that he realized a new mobile had been pushed into his pocket.

And he couldn't help the shocking burst of hope that gripped him full force, deep down inside – the first time in so many years.

'I may be leaving soon.' He stood just inside the doorway.

'You left a long time ago.'

'I came to see if you wanted anything.'

Yelena snorted. 'I want to re-run my life, without a creep like you playing a part in it.'

She was sitting at the old kitchen table, the one they had always eaten off and fought at and once, just once, a thousand years ago, had used for making love. The kitchen was strewn with boxes and books.

A pile of newspapers lay in front of her. The light was streaming in from the window behind her but he knew she wasn't well. Years of arthritis had slanted her head permanently to the left, her back was bent, the voice rough and wheezy.

'You still smoking?' he asked.

She took off the thick, black-rimmed glasses, rubbed her eyes and made for the stove.

'You'll get tea, nothing else. Understand? Then you can fuck off.'

He nodded and sat down where he'd always sat, at the head of the table. Same foul-mouthed ex-wife. Same threadbare cushion, same tatty lino on the floor. Probably the same cockroaches, he thought.

'So your fat friends in the KGB are letting you out of the cage,' she grinned and raised an eyebrow.

'I'm going to a ceremony at the UN. They invited me. Old colleague retiring. It's going to be a big event . . .'

'So why should I care? I haven't seen you in months.' She looked down at her skirt, discovered a white mark and began trying to rub it off with a handkerchief.

Arkady studied her for a moment. She had never cared about her appearance. The black skirt, threadbare and misshapen was probably as old as she was. And the once dancing, pushy, rebellious eyes that had been so hard to leave behind were watery and tired. 'I don't know what will happen afterwards. I may travel a little . . .'

'You may travel,' she mimicked. 'Oh no . . . no, no, no.' She began to laugh. 'Travel? You? That's funny. No, no. You're not travelling. You're going to make a run for it, aren't you? You're going to run and run till your stupid little legs can't run any further.' The smile died suddenly. 'What the fuck do I care anyway? Go and become Pope . . . who gives a shit?'

She replaced her glasses and began leafing through the newspapers on the table.

'I wanted to ask you something.' She didn't reply. 'I want to know if you'd look after Vasya, my dog. I'll leave money for his food, bills and things. He means . . .' He didn't finish the sentence.

'Fuck you *and* the dog.' She put down the newspaper and turned to face him full on for the first time. 'You have to be clinically insane, coming here and asking favours from me. Arrogant shit!'

Arkady got to his feet. 'There was a time when you cared for me, wasn't there?'

'Don't go there, Arkady – that time ended long ago. It ended when you weaseled your way up the Party ladder, stuffed yourself full of Party caviar and screwed all the Party whores. Don't bring me "there-was-a-time-when" stories. You made your choice and I'm glad I don't know half the things you did.'

'I was young . . .'

'So? We were both young and I had the bad luck to fall for a piss-head who fancied himself as a big shot in the Party and told me he'd change it from within. Just a little patience, Yelena. Just a little patience as they invaded Czechoslovakia and Afghanistan, just a little patience as they murdered their way through the ranks of dissidents and Chechens and anyone who stood up to them. Just a little patience as they lied their stupid heads off to everybody, got rich and chucked anyone with a brain into jail. You know what? I got through my rations of patience and now there isn't any left. And certainly not for you, so just get out of here and don't come back. I don't want to see you again.'

He pulled on his coat, turned towards the narrow corridor and then stopped.

'I need to tell you something else.'

'What?'

'They might come asking questions after I've gone . . .'

For a moment, she didn't answer. The eyelids seemed to have closed but he couldn't be sure. Yelena could always switch off the outward signs of life, make you believe that no one was home. But it was just an illusion. Her mind remained as formidable as ever, even if the body had slackened and slipped around her.

Mathematics had been her life, teaching it – her passion. That was why they had kicked her out of Moscow State University when she was at the height of her powers, winning international prizes, beating the American computers at their own game. All of it, because she wouldn't play along, wouldn't join the other KGB wives, wouldn't mouth the slogans. And worse, didn't care if they trusted her or not.

She would have worked out by herself that they would be coming to 'talk' to her, once he had gone. You don't live through the Soviet Union without knowing what it means when the KGB calls round for a chat.

'Goodbye Yelena.' He spoke to her back.

There was silence for a moment.

'Bring me the dog,' she said quietly, 'then you can say goodbye.'

Arkady smiled.

She turned to face him. 'Don't look like that – I'm a fool. Always have been. Who else would have married you in the first place?' She pushed him towards the door. 'And when they come here, your old friends, I'll do what I always did – I'll laugh in their fucking faces.'

LONDON

The church was almost empty when she slipped inside. An hour before Evensong.

Margo sat in one of the pews near the back. She knew it well. They'd always taken the same one at the Christmas Eve carol services when she'd been a child . . . Mum, Dad – her brother Anthony, always late.

The memories lay thick around her.

In the choir stalls a sextant began fiddling with prayer books. Far away she could hear hard heels on ancient flagstones, the slamming of a gate and then the silence returned.

She bent forward and shut her eyes.

Every day I lie to everyone in my life. I lied to Jimmy, my fiancé. I lie to my neighbours and friends. Only here do I whisper the truth. I sit in a public place and I tell God what I'm about to do or what I've done. I open up all the files – the secret, the top secret, even the handwritten stuff that never gets filed. I show it all to him and he never replies.

If I believe in God, how can I go on doing what I do?

Margo opened her eyes, scanning the long, silent aisle all the way to the altar.

She thought of the times she had almost said no to the Service. She thought of a life in the Middle East that she had helped extinguish, a reputation she had ruined, a rumour she had set rolling that had sparked a dozen killings in different countries. She thought of Mikhail.

Why had she crossed her own red lines? Sense of duty? Weakness?

Each time, of course, the Service had prompted her with 'compelling reasons'. National security, safety of the realm, the public interest – they never hesitated to use the really grand phrases when they thought you might waver.

And when you were in the office, out there by Vauxhall Cross with the view of Parliament and the Palace of Westminster – London's money-shot, Britain in all its glory – you could see the logic, understand the imperatives.

Not here, though.

Not with Christ up there on the Cross, the bearded God of Love looking down from the clouds and all the scriptures screaming at you to forgive your neighbour. Not quite so compelling anymore.

She sat up, looked around the pews, but nothing was moving.

He'd be a bad man, she told herself. Arkady Mazurin would have plenty of blood on his hands.

But it wasn't her task to judge him.

You have a job to do, so do it.

Abruptly, she stood up and made for the door. She was angry with herself for coming to the church. God wasn't the bloody man from Occupational Health. He wasn't interested in her state of mind. He'd written the rules a long time ago, sent them down the mountain and told the human race to get on with it.

And in his own way, Manson had done the same. The job he'd given her seemed straightforward, almost routine. And yet for the first time in many years Margo was frightened – and she knew damn well why.

WASHINGTON DC

Harry Jones looked round the Oval Office and wondered about the liars who had sat there before him.

Nobody came here to lie about small things. Lies in this room were always grand affairs with the power to derail history, to start wars, ruin careers, wreck lives around the globe.

And now he would tell one himself – the first of many, he reckoned. Because there's no such thing as a single lie. And with each one that followed the price would rise.

He looked down at his notes and waited for the president to finish his phone call. It was a scheduled conversation with the British prime minister. The two would be meeting at a Nato conference in Brussels before the end of the month and it was time to set the goals and the methods to achieve them.

'We don't seem to be on the same page yet,' the president was saying. 'We'll need to get our guys to start working on some of the differences. This has to be sewn up in a few days, if we're to make any headway in Brussels.'

He put down the receiver and stared across the desk at Harry. 'Fucking Brits.' He sighed, shuffled his notes and came across to his armchair opposite Harry.

'You don't look in good shape, my friend.'

Harry sat up and cleared his throat. 'There's no nice way to say this. Our mission into Syria – it's gone badly wrong. They made the crossing from Turkey a week ago, met the guide, as arranged, from one of the rebel groups and then went silent. The satellite tracked them to within twelve miles of their first rendezvous – which was on schedule – and then the trackers went dead. So did three out of four of the security guards.'

'Jesus, Harry.' The president slammed his fist on the arm of the chair. 'What happened?'

'We don't know. All we do know is that the bodies turned up in the hands of a different group. We even had to buy them to get them back. Doesn't get much worse.'

The president was shaking his head. 'I seem to remember months of planning went into this – we even brought in outside contractors, some of those characters outside the beltway. Security was paramount. That's why we did it this way for Chrissake. What are these guys telling you now?'

'They don't know, sir. They're checking. We're pulling in every asset we can find, asking the allies for help.'

The tone of the conversation had changed. Harry could sense it. Death always changed the mood in the Oval Office. It overrode friendship and camaraderie; rank and status. It humbled everyone – from the commander-in-chief down.

'Dammit Harry.' The president got up and went back to his desk. 'If we'd gone through the Agency . . .'

'The result would have been the same. Agency networks have been inoperable almost from day one – they've lost all their key Syrian assets, bar two or three. It's been a massacre . . .'

'And what would you call this?' he picked up the phone, then replaced the receiver. 'We have two survivors, right?'

'We don't know. We have two people who are unaccounted for. That means—'

'I know what it means, Harry. I know what that means.'

Jones removed two pictures from his file. On top was a boyish figure in uniform – the file said he was twenty-three – but he looked much younger. He couldn't bring himself to turn the other picture.

The president took the papers from him. 'This woman is the group leader?'

'Yes. Mai Haddad. Syrian American.'

'What's she like?'

'How d'you mean?'

'I mean, how resourceful is she, how professional, did she go rogue on us, was she bought, could someone have used her family as a lever?'

Harry shook his head. 'That's not possible.'

'Why not?'

'Because we know her inside out. Ten years in the intelligence community, one of the best minds . . .'

'*You* know her?' The president was staring straight at him.

'I met her briefly. She's pretty impressive.'

'Of course.' The president opened his mouth – but seemed to change his mind.

'You were going to say something?'

'It'll keep.' The president took off his glasses and waved them at Harry – his signal to be left in peace. 'Let me know when you get something on this.'

Back in his office, he tried looking at the intelligence digests, the crises in progress, the crises to come, but the words didn't make sense.

Only once had he met her here in the White House. By then, they had been together a dozen times and Harry saw nothing but the black curling hair, always rebelling, always untidy. The chipped front tooth. The eyes that had seen far more than they should have.

They had both lied about what they did, meeting as they had in a bookstore café. A chance look, a neutral smile. He said he was a teacher. She was into computers. Same the next day. Only by then the smiles weren't so neutral. And then a coffee. And dinner. And Harry was careering down the slope.

'I know who you are,' she had told him at their second encounter. 'I've seen your picture.'

'But I don't know who *you* are.'

'Find out,' she smiled gently. 'All those resources. Have me followed. Tap my phone. Do what you do . . .'

But he hadn't. She was separate from all his other lives. A gift way beyond his imagination or experience.

'Mai, I love you.' Fourth meeting.

'Don't be ridiculous,' she told him.

He had said it again at the next meeting, wanting it, willing it to be true.

'Harry, you're twenty years older than me.'

'Does it matter?'

'Yes, no . . . I don't know.'

'Please Mai, let's find out what it is we have . . . I'll resign, we'll get away from here . . . we need time.'

'No Harry.' She tried to push him away. 'No . . . I have a job to do. You know this better than anyone . . . you sanctioned this, you ordered it . . .'

'I sanctioned what?'

'You don't get it, Harry. You don't read all the documents, do you? The details. The names. The guys who're going to travel thousands of miles round the world and do what you sent them to do. You have no idea who we are, do you?'

'We?'

She reached up and ran her fingers through the thin, grey hair.

'I'm the one who's going to do it, Harry. I'm your team leader. Syria. There's nobody else . . .'

Hours later and they had both cried.

'I didn't know.'

'You're supposed to know everything.'

His face drooped. She remembered the steely, pedantic national security adviser, who spat blunt warnings on the TV talkshows to America's enemies – a velvet hammer, the same label that they'd attached to the former Secretary of State, James Baker. But this wasn't the same man.

She had sat opposite him on the bed, clasping his face in her hands. 'You're too important to fall apart, Harry. You need to get me out of your system.'

'I don't know how to do that,' he told her.

LONDON

Margo could hear the loud voices as she entered the flat. Jimmy and his friends, tinny music from the seventies, plenty of giggling.

She pushed open the living-room door – there were three of them slouched across the sofa, and another on the floor; pizza in boxes, beer in bottles. A couple of them shouted hallos, Jimmy waved and suddenly she was glad of the music, the distraction, the prospect of nothing more threatening than booze and calories.

She went into the bedroom to change, Jimmy right behind her. 'Sorry about this . . . We were all working late, needed to chill a little . . .'

'It's fine.' She managed a watery smile. 'It's your home too. Really. I'm glad they're here and I'm starving, so don't eat everything . . . go on, I'll be out in a minute.'

She shut the door behind him and sat on the bed. Perhaps, after all, he'd be a little more realistic about the way things were; realize he'd been selfish and immature. With luck they'd simply draw a line in the sand and do what everyone else did with the difficult stuff – shelve it and move on.

She didn't think it was a deal-breaker. Didn't believe he'd make it into one.

It was only three minutes before her mobile rang. She was still on the first slice of pizza; Jimmy's assistant Lisa was talking about her mum's leukaemia; someone was going out for more beer.

But she couldn't leave it unanswered. Even when Jimmy shouted after her 'tell 'em you're busy,' she knew she couldn't say no. Not if someone was dangling at the end of a rope – not if she was holding it.

There was no number on the screen, just Manson's late, tired voice in her ear. 'You need to come in. Car'll be with you in five.' Nothing else.

As she left, Jimmy was moaning, 'Oh for God's sake, can't they ever leave you alone?' He came out onto the landing, crestfallen, the smile and the warmth had drained away. 'What's the point of talking? None of this is going to change, is it?'

She got into the lift. 'Please understand, Jimmy. I'm trying to hold it all together. It's important.'

'Why? What's so important? Can't tell me, can you? Of course you can't.'

She looked away as the doors closed; she didn't need these scenes. Maybe she didn't need Jimmy either.

*   *   *

'We're bringing it forward. Our man's getting nervous.'

Margo sat down uninvited in front of the desk. A single desk lamp burned. Half of Manson's face was in darkness. Behind him, she could see restless London with the stream of headlights along the Embankment.

'Why's he nervous?'

'I don't know. Moscow station says he's different from the last meeting. Jumpy. Looking over his shoulder. Says he can't wait two weeks.'

'Could be just an attack of nerves. He's been out of this for a while. You lose your edge and then suddenly the fear jumps out at you from nowhere.'

Manson looked up from his papers. 'Know this, do you? Personal experience?'

She ignored him. 'I'm going in and I'm going to get him.'

'Impossible.'

'Listen to me. He's panicky and if he's left to his own devices, there's a risk he won't make it. I'll babysit him. Just in case.'

'What about the Americans?'

She shrugged. 'We don't have a choice. I'll have to tell them his name. All I can do is leave it till the last minute.'

By the time she reached the flat, Jimmy had gone to bed and his guests had left. The sitting room stank of pizza and beer; she opened the windows wide, letting the cold night air do its work.

Moscow was three hours ahead, and she wondered if Mazurin was asleep, if there was ice on his window panes, if his nerve was holding.

She tried to picture the little apartment that he lived in – it would be the usual Russian disaster zone. Not the kind of chaos that happens, but the kind you have to work at. Papers and pictures strewn wherever there was a surface – floor or ledge or sofa, it made no difference. Where Brits might keep the important things safe and tidy, a Russian's priority would be to lose them, to prevent them at all costs from falling into the wrong hands. Somewhere under a floorboard or screwed into a light switch or behind a picture, Mazurin would have hidden something of enormous value. And the chaos of the room would be designed to mask it.

As she stared out of the window Margo could feel the sense of loneliness and isolation that would be tightening around him, squeezing, until sometime soon, he would find it hard to breathe.

She knew it, because she felt it herself.

WASHINGTON DC

Harry Jones was home by nine in the white clapboard house near Chevy Chase, with the basketball ring in the yard, and the tidy lawns and the tidy snow-covered flowerbeds, because even if you were national security adviser, the neighbours got antsy if your house didn't look nice. Or if your curtains were the wrong colour, or your kid said bad words at school.

Good neighbours, all of them, he thought, but they only cared about the little things.

He could have sat them all down, he thought, and told them just what America was doing in their name and with their tax dollars. About the special interrogation units that hadn't closed, even after the president had promised they would; about the history of supporting death squads in Central America – those nice guys who murdered nuns and priests; about targeted assassinations and cyber wars and they'd probably tell him that it all sounded very important and they hoped they'd see him at Bible class on Sunday.

They had their beliefs and their certainties. The rest didn't matter.

As he came in the nurse was waiting for him in the hallway.

'She hasn't had a good day, her cough's been really bad. She wouldn't take any food.'

'Nothing at all?'

The nurse nodded.

'I'll go up and see her in a moment.'

'She's asleep for now. Best not to wake her.'

He wandered into the den and turned on the reading light by the desk. He couldn't help the tears when they came. Tears for his wife Rosalind and her failing health, tears for the way he had betrayed her while she was ill, tears for being powerless to stop himself falling in love with a woman twenty years his junior, now lost in Syria.

He wiped his eyes and climbed the stairs, pushing open the door of her bedroom, lit only by a nightlight in the corner.

As he bent down to look at her face, he was struck by its fragility. The skin seemed like paper that might tear at any moment. There were tiny rifts and fissures that he hadn't seen before. And yet they all told a story that he had known for some time; that while she lay there, the disease had begun sensing victory and would pursue her relentlessly to the end.

Only sleep brought her some peace. So different from the times when she was awake, battling the terrible coughing and the pain that seemed to come from everywhere at once.

He was in awe of Rosalind's strength. He couldn't imagine what it took her to smile and joke, to ask him about his day and his work, to make sure the housekeeper bought his favourite fruit and put his beer in the fridge.

She still remembered birthdays and friends. On the good days she would call her family, even sit out on the porch, wave to the neighbours. And on the bad days, she groaned and cried and wheezed her way through the hours and he would hold her tight and wonder if she would live till nightfall, and sometimes, yes sometimes, overcome by his powerlessness to help her, even hope that she wouldn't.

Two years of this, two years when his heart was broken and broken again with each new day.

He knew why he'd done it. He knew why a woman who could penetrate the darkness around him, had lifted his heart and helped him to carry the pain.

It didn't excuse it, could never excuse it.

Harry Jones had nothing to say in his own defence. Not even to himself.

'You gonna stand there like some teenage wimp or you gonna give me a kiss.'

He was startled for a moment, hadn't seen her eyes open, could hardly hear the words, slurred and cracked from the dryness in her throat.

He bent down and kissed her forehead, stroking her cheek.

'Wanna dance?' Her eyes looked up at him.

'Sure,' he whispered. 'You've always been a great dancer.'

She tried to smile. 'You were better. But I had a few other things to teach you.'

He grinned and she managed to wink. The memory of a far-off summer day in a field in Maine and the glorious, unabashed experiments of youth seemed to float between them. And then, just as suddenly, it was gone.

'I remember,' he said.

'Me too.'

It was after ten p.m. when Harry heard the car draw up outside. He knew it was the evening intelligence digest, brought by armed courier from the White House – a brief summary of what had changed in the key issues of the day, a collection of signposts, red flags – whatever the paranoid late shift in the National Security Council thought Harry should see, before he dared shut his eyes.

At the door, he thanked the military aide and took the locked briefcase into the den. Upstairs he could hear the nurse moving around, clearing and tidying. Outside in the neighbourhood, lights began to go out, dogs got a final walk, front doors were bolted.

A Washington day, dying down.

But the briefcase contained no bedtime story. A corruption scandal, about to engulf an Arab head of state, unusual military movements in East Africa. A key informant in the Pakistani government telling his intelligence handlers that Islamists had now penetrated the country's nuclear rocket command. And a former British agent in Moscow, due to defect on his way through the US. Priority signal from CIA London and with it, a request, by them to question the man, against the express wishes of the British.

Tiresome, thought Harry. Extremely tiresome. Allies were often more trouble than the enemy.

He took off his glasses and yawned. The rest of the file was the usual arse-covering exercise, packed with trivia to make it seem more substantial.

And then it hit him. He sat up quickly, extracted the single sheet from his folder and read it again.

I must have been so tired not to realize what this is.

A former British agent, getting out of Russia. Snap transmission from London. Heading to New York and then to the UK.

Jesus.

The name was missing in the file – but the man was said to have been active, high-level Intelligence for long periods of the

Cold War. A traitor to his own country, who would surely drink himself to death wherever he landed up. No one in the West owed him anything.

Harry read and re-read the few lines with mounting excitement.

He knew very well what it meant. More importantly, he knew how to use it.

He got up from his chair and stared through the window. An unfriendly moon in a frozen sky stared back.

Harry Jones had been presented with a way out for the woman he loved, who was lost in the killing zones of Syria.

It didn't occur to him for one second not to take it.

LONDON

'I've got to go abroad for a few days.' Margo stood in the doorway, still wearing her coat and holding her briefcase.

Jimmy took in the adversarial stance. She was expecting trouble, ready to go out again if it all went badly.

'OK.'

'I thought we might visit Mum and Dad before I go.'

'Have you told *them* what you do?' He read the look before she opened her mouth. 'Yes, of course you have. Silly of me. I was the only one who was kept in the dark.' He stood up. 'Cup of tea?'

She followed him into the kitchen.

'How long are you going to go on feeding this grievance?'

He turned back from the tap and switched on the kettle. Tall, curly-haired, scruffy – he was a million miles from the complicated young men at Vauxhall Cross. The reason she had chosen him.

'It's not a grievance. I'd feel the same, if you'd just got the job and you were telling me straight away. I understand why you didn't tell me until now. I'm just not sure I understand *you* anymore. Why you'd do a job like this . . .'

'A job like what?' She couldn't help the edge in her voice, the niggle deep down.

He put a teabag into her cup and poured the hot water. 'Why don't we sit down and do this?'

They went into the living room and sat at opposite ends. She kept her coat on, just as she had on that first day at school. The coffee table stretched like a border between them.

'What do you mean by a job like that?' She shot him an unpleasant look.

'I meant a job where you keep secrets, where I'm excluded, where I have no knowledge and nothing to contribute.'

'So you want every part of my life, laid out according to your terms.'

He shook his head. 'I want to marry you . . . I want to be the closest person in the world to you. With this job, I'll know less about you than the people you work with. How can that be right?'

'It isn't just about you, Jimmy . . .'

'I didn't say it was.'

'Some things involve commitment outside of a marriage. You need to understand that. Only someone who is close *can* understand that. I can't tell you everything, because they're not my secrets to tell. I'm a vehicle, Jimmy. You think a postman's wife expects him to steam open all the letters and tell her what's inside. They don't belong to him – just as the cases I handle don't belong to me. They're not mine to give out. If I did, I'd go to jail . . .'

'So there's no middle ground here, you won't even try to let me in . . .'

'Let you in where?' She could feel her face getting flushed, feel the irritation rising. 'Jimmy, for God's sake, you talk about this as if it's a playpen where anyone can come in and have a go . . .'

'So this is how it's going to be from now until—'

'Until I'm fifty-five. That's when they throw us out. Twelve years to go – unless' – she tried to smile – 'unless they fire me first.'

He didn't smile back, sat there tight-lipped, eyes fixed on the coffee table, right foot tapping the rug. Irritated, hurt, out of his comfort zone. She took in all the signs. He'd closed up the shop for now. Wouldn't come out until much later, till he'd sorted through all the things she'd said and found a new line.

'Listen to me.' She went and sat beside him but he wouldn't look at her. 'Do I have doubts about what I do? Of course I do. Like everyone. Don't you? Very serious doubts and fears, because if I make a mistake someone might lose their life, and if I make a very big mistake then thousands of people might die. So you see, the stakes are very high indeed.'

'You don't have to talk down to me . . . I can work that out for myself.'

'I need you to understand that Jimmy.'

'I don't know where I fit in your life – or even if I fit at all.' He shrugged.

'But I'm still the same person.' She tried to smile. 'Still like pasta and holidays in Italy, long jumpers, red Minis. What's changed, Jimmy?'

He got up and stood over her. 'I'm going for a walk. I'll call you.'

She could see the lights going out, the door closing.

'Please yourself.'

MOSCOW

F ive years since he was last inside the KGB's headquarters at the Lubyanka and Arkady hadn't recognized a single soul. Where were the old receptionists, the scowling doormen, the drivers, the *dvorniki* who hung around the courtyards, weasel-eyed, watching and reporting? The secretaries – *sekretutki* – they'd been called, halfway between typist and prostitute, and frequently required to be both.

Five years and they had changed them all.

He stamped the snow from his boots and took a seat in the drab vestibule. There was a time when such changes could have been easily explained. Plenty of the disappeared would have been jailed or transferred to the wastelands for seeing something they shouldn't have seen, for taking bribes from the wrong officials, for a loose word or a bad joke, or being too close to someone whose star had crashed.

Nobody ever fell on their own in the KGB. Once the primary victim had been located, they would delight in going after his associates. Business before pleasure, they used to say. The wider the net, the more fun they'd have. Like the waiter who'd once served the guilty in a restaurant, the hairdresser who'd cut their treacherous curls, the Aeroflot clerk who'd dared to issue them a ticket, the taxi driver . . . God alone knew where that lust for blood had led them.

But these days things were different. The old staff would simply have been re-assigned or died of natural causes. Russians had the lowest life expectancy of any major industrialized state. You went to hospital with one disease, you died a few days later of something else. Drugs, deemed essential by international health experts, simply didn't exist in the ordinary hospitals – only for the elite.

He breathed deeply and tried to stop his mind wandering through the catalogue of Russia's ills.

He was leaving and he wasn't coming back – and it didn't matter a fuck what happened to the country. All he needed was to be pleasant to the bureaucrat he would meet, convince him that the invitation to New York was genuine and get out as fast as possible.

If he could hide the hatred in his heart and stop his face betraying him, all would be well.

They showed him in after a forty-five-minute wait. Plenty of apologies – but they had made the point just as he knew they would. When you're out, you're nobody.

New Moscow man received him. A forehead, flat and sharp, like an escarpment, cut off a few centimetres above the eyes.

Arkady noted the poor grammar, the brisk, exaggerated movements. There were more cultured members of the Service – those who could, when they chose, exude charm and sophistication. Plenty who had studied in the West and knew how to hold a knife and fork. But not this one.

'You have the official invitation?'

Arkady removed it from his inside pocket. He had, of course, sent a copy the day before.

'How long do you wish to stay in New York?'

'Three days.'

'Why three?' The eyes focussed on him, but without interest. Arkady could hear a clock ticking in an anteroom.

'A day to rest after the journey, then the day of the reception and then my respects to our ambassador, an old colleague of mine and of course the secretary general.'

'You have checked with the Foreign Ministry on what you will be required to say?' The eyes looked down at the paper Arkady had brought with him.

'I assumed I would wait for official approval before . . .'

'Quite . . .' The paper was hurriedly put into a file. The man got up from the chair, smoothed his jacket, sniffed loudly. 'That is all,' he said. 'You will be notified.'

But it wasn't all. As they reached the reception area, the man stopped and turned to face him.

'You don't remember me, do you?'

The words seemed like a sudden blow to the head. He stared hard at the figure, the bloodshot grey eyes, the smallish nose that stuck out at a strange angle, as if it had once belonged to someone else.

'I don't seem . . .'

'We met some years ago under unpleasant circumstances.'

'Excuse me but you need to refresh my memory . . .?'

But the man had already turned and begun walking away, footsteps echoing along the stone hallway.

'Wait a minute . . .' Arkady started to follow, but out of nowhere, the receptionist barred his way.

'Your business is done,' he said.

'But I have a question. The man said something . . .'

'Come with me.' The receptionist pointed to the main door. 'There are no more questions.'

A few moments later, Arkady found himself back on the Garden Ring. Snow had begun falling again – a thick grey curtain, suspended above the city, the temperature dropping fast.

The security man had unnerved him – just as he had doubtless intended. But the knowledge didn't make any difference. Arkady could feel his pulse had quickened, the sweat now cold against his forehead.

What had the man meant? Unpleasant circumstances. Over the years there had been so many of them. Who in God's name was he? They all looked the same with their short haircuts and blue suits. How could he be expected to remember?

Arkady tripped and nearly lost his footing. But he carried on. The metro station was nearby. Inside it would be warm and he could calm down and collect his thoughts.

He passed huge snow clearers, lined up at the roadside, ready to be ordered into action. In Communist times they had been known as 'Kapitalisty' – because of their large, grabbing arms.

It struck him that these were probably some of his last glimpses of the Russian capital – and yet the security man's words upset him.

Such things never happened by chance. Perhaps the idea was to make him careless, so that if he had a guilty secret he'd give himself away.

Arkady didn't know – but he'd know soon enough.

He reached the metro where the warmth and the crowds seemed to settle his fears. If things went well, he would be in New York in a week's time. For the first time, yes, the very first time, he had a real chance.

As for the security man, he was just playing with him. Couldn't resist shaking his tree.

He didn't know a thing.

WASHINGTON DC

'I've given some thought to the "gift" that you mentioned at our last meeting.' Harry Jones stared expressionless across the table. 'I have such a gift.'

Yanayev sat back in his chair and said nothing. It was clear to him that Harry was about to step way beyond his normal boundaries. And yet, maybe he no longer had any. If Harry Jones even possessed a conscience, chances were he hadn't seen it in years and most likely had forgotten where he'd left it.

You didn't hold down the job of national security adviser by waving around ideals and fine words, or by doing the right thing. You did what you had to do – and left it at that.

In any case, consciences were for later life, when the really bad memories refused to stay in their box and began drifting back home.

'I have a name and an intention.' Harry looked up and sniffed loudly. 'The name I'll keep for now.'

Yanayev got up and walked to the window. The sky was bleak and cold. Powdery, new snow lay across sloping country. In the distance he could see the lights of a train heading south. He couldn't resist a shiver of excitement.

It seemed like a year since he had met Harry in the Georgetown restaurant. Today they were in a safehouse in the middle of Maryland with no waiters and no food.

Nothing would be written down, no memos or recordings taken, because no one had ever been here.

But this was The Game at its best. Information to be traded that would change lives and relations. States and individuals. Yanayev at the centre of it all.

He turned back to Harry. 'Just tell me what you have and I'll get it through to Moscow. They want to help.'

'Sure they do.' Harry made a face and folded his arms. 'This is how it goes, Vitaly. In a few days' time a Russian will leave Moscow on a flight to the West. He doesn't intend to return. He was once a highly placed State official and will be carrying in his head a large quantity of classified information – most of which is known to us, some of which may not be . . .'

'I see. The man is a former officer in the KGB?'

'He's a former official. That's all I can tell you for now. He's also a former agent of a Western power.'

Yanayev swallowed. 'Which one?'

Harry raised both arms. 'Wait a minute, Vitaly. This is a deal that works both ways, OK? I start giving you names and details, without anything from your side, and you can just walk out of here – what do I have?'

'My word.'

The American smiled for the first time. 'Don't take this the wrong way, my friend, but I think my government will require somewhat more than that.'

They went into the kitchen and Harry made coffee. Biscuits emerged from a cupboard. Milk and sugar on a tray. Someone had thought ahead.

So had Harry. He led Yanayev back to the living room, white, overheated, neutral like a hospital waiting room, and passed him a sheet of paper. It was unheaded and unsigned.

'I take it this is the name of your "package"?'

'Name and last known location.'

Yanayev scanned the note and blew out his cheeks. 'God, Harry – she's in IS territory. It doesn't get much worse than that . . . Right now this town flies a black flag. It's Sharia law, forced conversions, random executions. No one gets out of there . . .'

'Why do you think I came to you?'

Yanayev put down the coffee. He stared hard at the American. 'What's so important about this woman?'

'She knows a lot about us. Just like your own guy.'

'Is this personal?'

'Aren't they all?'

'Worth betraying one of your own best assets to get her back?' He saw Harry shiver but it was from anger not cold.

'I don't always have the luxury of principled decisions, Vitaly. Maybe you do . . .'

Yanayev shook his head and felt his pulse quicken. So many angles to this one. So many levers that could be used. But the risks were huge.

He looked down at the American, but was taken aback instantly by the sadness in his demeanour. Jones's head lolled forward, lifeless, arms straight, almost touching the floor. In that moment Yanayev had the impression of a man, sitting alone at a roulette table, gambling everything he possessed on a single number.

Harry turned and caught his glance. 'Just do it, Vitaly. I don't have a choice.'

In the early hours of the morning, Lydia slipped out of bed, tiptoed down to the study and found the report that her husband had sent to Moscow.

When it mattered, really mattered, he always kept copies for himself in his briefcase, to mull them over, check that he had said the right thing. And she would photograph them whenever she could.

She respected him both as a diplomat and a human being. Instead of dropping everything in Moscow's lap, he filtered his information with the emphasis on practical application. What did it all mean and what could they do with it?

She hoped he would go far and was determined to help him do so.

His report recommended helping the Americans. It was a good trade – Moscow would stop a traitor defecting and the US would get back its 'coordinator' from Syria.

Vitaly had also suggested activating an operative, called simply 'Ahmed'.

Ahmed, he wrote, had trained for such operations and could navigate better than anyone between the groups of murderous extremists that now controlled Syria. He was the last, best chance of finding the American agent.

Outside the study window the sky had begun to lighten. In the Middle East the day would already be half over. Lydia couldn't help wondering what kind of woman Washington had sent in to Syria and whether she would stay alive until nightfall.

LONDON

She hadn't heard Jimmy come in – but she found him in the morning with a cushion on the living room floor, still wearing his coat and scarf.

She sat staring at him for some minutes before she spoke.

'Have I become so repulsive that you can't bear to sleep in the same bed?'

His eyes opened slowly, but she knew he had heard her.

'Repulsive? No.' There was the beginning of a smile but it died almost instantly. 'But I need to know who I'm sleeping with, who I'm going to spend the rest of my life with . . .'

'Where did you go last night?'

'That's just great, isn't it? You with all the secrets and you suddenly want to know where *I* went. Why don't you have me followed, put a collar and lead on me . . . isn't that what you people do?'

In that moment, she could feel the snap, as if a muscle had torn or a cable had broken. One of those moments that you go on playing back inside your head, years after they've passed. Because it invariably means that a chapter has closed, even if you didn't know it at the time and hadn't intended it to happen.

She stood up. 'Enough, Jimmy. You want to go on day after day, making a fuss about this, then you do it by yourself. I've explained the situation. That's it. Wherever you went last night, go back there. This nonsense is over.'

She couldn't read his expression, didn't know if he'd expected it or wanted it. Didn't know why the revelation that she worked for the Service had drained him of his reason. But whatever cloud hung over him, she knew it was not about to lift.

Jimmy got up and went into the bedroom. She could hear him opening drawers and cupboards before slamming the bathroom door.

She had met him soon after Mikhail had died. A time when she had consciously folded her emotions and put them away in a strong drawer. Investing mental energy in other people seemed altogether too uncertain. You did your work, you came home, slept and did it again. If you were good, you made it to the end of the month. Everyone else had to look after themselves.

So she didn't plan a future with Jimmy. Or any other kind. And yet, all of its own accord, the 'thing', whatever it was, had started with a conversation at a bus stop and graduated to coffee in the market on a Saturday afternoon.

She had thought him funny and uninhibited. A teacher, badly in need of a haircut, but rampant with ideas and surprises, and hopes for what he wanted for the kids he taught.

He had sneaked her one afternoon into the back of his history class, where he had brought the Roman Empire to life in conversations between generals and senators, emperors and beggars, traitors and executioners. He had acted parts, sung songs, even played at a sword fight. And she had watched the rapture on the faces of the children, as if they were hearing today's news from a reporter on the scene.

'You inspired them,' Margo told him afterwards.

'Wrong,' he told her. 'That dreamy expression you saw was because I promised them chocolate on Thursday. It's my birthday. They know there's something in it for them.'

She had laughed and run a hand involuntarily through his scruffy hair.

'Maybe,' she said, 'if you can put on a shirt that isn't creased, you can take me to dinner on your birthday.'

So gradually the laughter lines came back.

Showing affection became OK too. Even, as it turned out, love. As long as it came in an email or a note and was written 'luv' or 'lurve'. No need, she told herself, to go over the top with declarations.

And when, six months later Jimmy's 'proposal' had come from behind a glass of red wine in a pub near Hampstead Heath, Margo had been curiously unable to say 'no'.

Instead she had offered him a 'maybe', like a voucher waiting to be cashed-in at a later date. And he had assumed it meant yes and got on with planning their life.

Why didn't I just tell him?

It was, she reflected, a history of things half-said, plans half-made, a barge that had drifted downstream, with each of its two passengers believing they were headed somewhere else.

No wonder they had sunk.

Margo went into the hall, put on her coat and stepped out into the city. She was certain Jimmy would be gone by the time she returned.

MOSCOW

As he pushed open the door, Arkady could see the envelope on the floor. No name or address. No markings of any kind. And he knew they had been there.

He bent down and picked up the envelope. Vasya was barking in the kitchen – but Arkady paid no attention. Didn't even notice the cockroaches, scattering as he turned on the lights; he tore open the envelope.

'Mazurin, Arkady, Semyonovich' – always the formality first – 'we inform you' etc etc – he could hardly bear to read to the end . . . but there it was, hand-typed, the way they always did, on an ancient office machine . . . 'Permission has been granted . . .'

He slumped down in a chair, still in his coat and shapka. The heat in the little flat was unbearable, but he didn't notice. He put his head in his hands and the tears began cascading down his cheeks; he hadn't cried for years; didn't know whether he was happy or sad, nervous or relieved. Silent tears, always silent, because you never knew if they were listening and what they would conclude if they heard them.

So there were two days left, he told himself. Just two days before he could leave, with a small bag and a thousand ghastly memories packed tightly inside it: all the shabby little kitchens that he'd sat in, the vodka-soaked evenings, the random easy violence and the false cameraderie. Russia was and always had been about betrayal.

The reasons didn't matter. It was a sickness locked deep inside each of them – immune to treatment.

He thought about the security man who had interviewed him. Polite and formal. The two of them had appeared to sit there in their fine, smart suits chatting normally – but in reality they had circled each other like snarling dogs.

Maybe it was always that way. To encounter a stranger in Russia is a cold and unfriendly process. There is very little neutral ground to meet on and no desire or time for pleasantries. The stakes are too high and the potential danger too great.

Kto kovo? – Who will screw whom? You have only seconds to answer that question.

Arkady pulled himself to his feet and looked out at the winter city. Scores of tiny, dark figures were stumbling their way home through the snow – but there was little comfort waiting for them. Centuries of brutality and repression had built a country where you sold out your friends and family and acquaintances before they turned around – out of choice or necessity – and did it to you.

Your fate was in constant flux.

And then Vasya barked again from the kitchen and he realized what he was missing. Vasya was never shut in; he could always roam the flat as he wished; but not tonight.

As Arkady entered the room, the animal was cowering in a corner. Normally he'd have shuffled towards him, with a slipper in his mouth. But he didn't get up, wouldn't look at Arkady; his tail wagged briefly; he licked his lips nervously and all the time his eyes were fixed on the ground. Someone had frightened him. That much was clear. Arkady could see it in his expression. He went over to the dog, knelt down and stroked his head.

'It's OK,' he whispered. 'It's over.'

But he knew it wasn't.

They could have left the letter in the mailbox downstairs – only that would have been too easy, too conventional.

The fact was that they had a point to make: we, the Russian Federal Security Service, precocious, overfed child of the KGB, young, brash and with limitless resources, we'll come into your life and shatter your privacy whenever we want.

So two messages had been delivered for the price of one.

Arkady could feel the anger rising in his throat, but he stopped it. Anger was what they wanted. Provocation: the tried and tested tactic. Poke a target and see what he does. Poke him again until he's afraid. Poke him again and again till he makes a mistake.

You play your games, he thought. But in two days' time I'll leave this asylum, and you and the rest of the lunatics can plot your stupidities without me.

Just two days.

The words seemed like a lantern that could light his path all the way to New York.

JORDAN/SYRIA BORDER

On the brow of a hill, ten kilometres from Ramtha, Ahmed stopped the car and got out to survey the damage.

The village had been obliterated just before daylight. Government jets had raged overhead, four of them from a clear, unsullied sky, shattering the peace of dawn. The innocent would have been sleeping; the faithful, praying; everyone else, good or evil, stopped dead before the day had begun.

As far as he could see, dust and smoke enveloped the ruins. And yet even after the killer blow, he knew that villages didn't die quickly or quietly. They sputter and burn and collapse, slowly and in terrible pain. Sometimes it can take days.

If you're close by you'll hear the cries and shouts of the injured, not many, trapped under the fallen buildings. And as the hours go by, they grow fainter and then disappear on the wind. Papers and filth and clothing gust through the ruins and the embers of the fire eat away at whatever is left of the dead and their possessions.

And then there's the smell of it. You can always taste death, right at the back of your throat – the bitter, nauseating stench of those who depart the world in violence.

Ahmed wondered how many had escaped – but the human cost didn't interest him. Simply the realization from years gone by that, however great the carnage, there is always someone who gets away; maybe an old man outside the village who had been smoking or chatting with a friend, an insomniac muttering nonsense to himself under a bush, even a dog, drinking from the stream.

Someone, something, would have survived.

Eight hours had passed since Ahmed had received the coded message from Moscow. Seven since he had set up the meeting at the village. He had thought the place would be peaceful and silent, that the contact would wait till the Jordanian border patrols changed shift and then crawl across the cold, hard fields till he found the barn where they had met before.

It lay among a sprawl of outbuildings, a little community of farmers that straddled a frontier that wasn't marked and didn't much matter in days gone by. A dot on a few local maps where business came from the land, where they dabbled in random smuggling, where no one minded as long as the men in uniforms with big, shiny buttons got paid off.

The sky was clouding over and Ahmed thought snow would come by the evening. From his coat, he took a small pair of field glasses and focussed them on the village.

The barn had been incinerated where it stood. Around it, not a single structure remained upright. And yet he was sure the contact would come.

The contact would know that Ahmed had pull. *Wasta*, they called it in the Middle East. He would know that Ahmed was a man of exceptional influence and considerable resources. But above all he would fear Ahmed and all that he was capable of doing.

If the contact still had a beating heart and blood in his body, he would be there before the day was out.

LONDON

She walked to Victoria and took the bus to the Finchley Road. It was the only journey that ever felt like going home.

Margo remembered the first time she had moved away from her parents, couldn't wait to leave, carted her three suitcases to a studio flat in Bayswater, with a full-width mirror along one wall and a shagpile carpet and all the signs that it had been rented by the hour. What did it matter? It was the day she pronounced herself lucky and happy and free.

But it was never home.

There had followed a succession of other flats. Longest stay: just over two years. Explanation to self: they felt temporary – places to transit rather than live.

For someone who could plan other people's lives in such meticulous detail, she was curiously disinterested in charting her own. She abhorred 'navel gazing' and 'wallowing' and 'bum chat' – pointless mental meanderings that led nowhere. Real life, she had felt sure, would collide with her when the time was right – and the two of them would sort it out as best they could. There was no need to talk it to death before it happened.

Two decades spent thinking that way and now she knew different.

'My fault,' she had once told Dad. 'If I'd really wanted the kids and the four-wheel drive, I'd have done it. But there's still something in me that prefers a park bench with the foxes.'

'They'll be lucky to have you,' he had replied.

He opened the door to her in the little house in Platts Lane and ushered her into the hall.

'You look well,' she said, shocked for a moment, because he didn't.

As he led the way, he seemed oddly fragile in his movements, each footstep deliberate and measured, as if he were frightened of falling. And yet the boyish, trademark smile was still the same, just as it had been in all the family pictures from the sixties and seventies – the smile that had been so useful to a young foreign correspondent, intent on opening and rattling all the doors he could find.

'Your mother's not here. If you'd said you were coming . . .'

'It's OK. Really Dad. I just came for a quick chat.'

He made tea and they sat on two unmatched armchairs and stared at the sad little garden with the half-dead grass.

'Jimmy's gone,' she said suddenly, knowing that Dad wasn't going to ask.

He knew her better than anyone, knew that you had to wait until she was ready to speak and that questions were pointless.

'You told him.' Statement not question.

'Yes.'

'And he couldn't handle it?'

'Went all selfish on me – suddenly it was all about him . . . when would he see me, where would I be . . .? What if I didn't come home?'

He put out a hand and touched her shoulder. 'Will he get over it?'

'I don't know . . . not sure I even want him to.' She shrugged. 'I could have handled it differently, put it in a shiny package, tied it up with a red ribbon – but what the hell? It is what it is.'

Dad stared straight ahead at the garden. She knew what he was thinking – that there wasn't any point going over things, fannying around, wondering if there'd been another way. He had told her so many times over the years that there was only one thing that mattered: the way forward. Not the best way, not the ideal way. Not even the right way. Just the one you could live with.

He had also told her that whatever happened in her life, there was a place she could come to, where she wouldn't be judged or blamed. A haven in a mean and chaotic world. A narrow terraced house, with floorboards that creaked absurdly and a neurotic, old boiler that had struggled far too long to survive.

Dad got up to fetch more tea.

'There's something else . . .'

He caught the change in her expression and sat down again.

'I'm trying to get someone out of Russia . . . he's pretty experienced but I need to hold his hand till he's out of the country. And then we have to get him through New York – the Americans aren't exactly cooperating . . .'

'They want a piece of him as well?'

'That's the problem . . . you know what happened the last time I had one of our assets on their soil.'

'Yes.'

'So I'm worried . . .' She finished her tea and poured another cup. 'Issues of trust . . .'

'What does Manson say?'

'What he always says. Get on with it. It's not about trust – we're stuck with the Americans and we have to make the best of it. They're the ones with all the sweets and we have to go and play nice, hoping they'll open the jar and give us some. Problem is they're just as likely to try and snatch the ones we already have.'

There was silence for a moment. Far away upstairs she could hear the telephone ringing, some traffic outside.

Dad shifted in his chair. 'You'll do the best you can for this fellow. I know you will. If anyone can get him out . . .'

'Yes Dad, thank you' – she couldn't help the sudden flash of anger – 'but my track record isn't exactly great, is it? Not after New York . . .'

'Wasn't your fault.'

'Doesn't matter whether it was or not. Fault, blame, responsibility – just words, Dad. A man died on my watch. I can dress it up anyway I like, but that bit doesn't go away.'

'I'm sorry I snapped.'

He hugged her tightly. 'Your mum'll be sad to have missed you.'

'Me too.'

She turned and walked away along the lane and back to the bus stop.

She remembered the days when she had hurried through her homework just to go and meet Dad at the bus stop.

She remembered how his face had shone with happiness when he caught sight of her; how she had wanted to carry his papers up the street; how hungry he had been when he'd sat down for his supper.

She could still remember what a normal life looked and felt like.

She could remember everything.

'You think too much,' Mikhail had told her.

That too, she remembered.

Dad watched her from the dining-room window till she was out of sight. Margo – daughter or not – was the most capable, most resourceful person he had ever known.

But she worked in a snakepit, dominated by conflicting loyalties and priorities and ever-changing expedients. And she couldn't win all the battles.

He knew that three years ago she had lost heavily. Mikhail's death remained fresh in her mind and unresolved. And the half-smile was painted on fresh each day and worn to keep the world and its questions at bay. Was she up – or down? No one would ever know.

Jimmy, he thought, was finished business. Margo never spoke about her feelings but, known only to a few, the ones she had were deep-rooted. She was loyal in a basic and uncomplicated way – but she didn't do forgiveness. Cross her and you would find yourself removed overnight from her phone book. You wouldn't see it coming. She gave no warnings or ultimatums.

You just knew that her door had closed.

JORDAN/SYRIA BORDER

Before the war, the contact had been a police officer in a suburb of Aleppo. Proud of it too. Had the gun in a shiny, black holster at his hip – a Russian-made Vostok – trousers a size too tight and a raft of little ventures on the side that made it all worthwhile.

One of them had been to play the local drug gangs, selling each one information about the other and betraying them selectively when it became clear who was going down.

He had good instincts, didn't back losers, clung to the winning side and made them love him. Until someone stronger came along.

And the winning side was always glad to have a guy in uniform. Made them feel protected.

But the war had changed the game – the gangs did fewer drugs and more guns and politics – and all the players changed sides or went away and died with remarkable frequency.

All the same, the most prized commodity was still information and the people still needed a postman. Taking messages, telling stories, delivering the news that everyone wanted. Who was still alive and who wasn't, where the guilty or the innocent were hiding . . . Where the bodies were buried?

No one paid more for such things than Ahmed, but Ahmed was the most frightening person he had ever met. It wasn't the voice – sometimes so quiet that you had to strain to hear it – nor the confidence that stood out from all the panic and terror and shouting around him.

But the knowledge of what he had done and what he could do – things that the contact could no longer bring himself to contemplate.

'Why are you so afraid of this man?' his wife had once asked him.

'Who says I'm afraid?'

'When you talk about him you piss in your pants like it was your first day at school.'

'Watch your mouth,' he had snapped. But he knew it was true. Ahmed was way outside his league, came from a different world that he would never see and could never imagine. Played a different game, wrote different rules. Which meant no rules at all.

Sure, as a policeman, the contact hadn't been averse to some gratuitous violence. A beating or two in the cells could lead to all sorts of happy outcomes: confessions, offers of bribes, even a car, if you picked the right person.

But Ahmed came from a different planet.

With Ahmed you said a prayer and took the money, and muttered your grateful thanks and a dozen exaggerated salutations. But you didn't look back. You didn't ask questions and you would swear on the life of your mother and sixteen of her blood relatives that your meeting had never taken place.

Because Ahmed was a ghost. And death was all around him.

For half an hour, he had watched the contact as he lay low in a dip between the fields. The temperature had dropped and the man would be freezing, but he wouldn't come across until dark.

Although lines kept shifting, the Free Syrian Army currently controlled the eastern side along this stretch of border. There would be no problem with them. But sometimes the Jordanian patrols were more active. Jordan was creaking under the weight of refugees and not averse to throwing some of them back into Syria.

He could see the grey shape begin to move, head down, dark jacket, hoodie underneath.

In the darkness, the man almost missed him. Ahmed snatched his arm and pulled him down into a ditch beside him.

'You're late.'

The contact began to whine. 'Sincere apologies sir, but it's not—'

'Shut up.' Ahmed put his hand over the man's mouth. 'I don't have long and I need information. Someone in or around this area is holding an American woman – she's of Syrian origin – speaks Syrian Arabic. I need you to find her.'

'If Daesh has her I will not come out alive. Everyone is watched. They cut off your head and skewer it onto railings . . .'

'I know all about their methods. I also know that they pay for information – just as I do. I want this woman found and I want to get her out – alive. Do you understand me?'

'I understand but it's impossible . . .'

'Use your old police contacts. Some of them must still be alive. A few have gone over to the Islamists . . . Bribe them, blackmail them. Do what you have to . . .'

'Everyone I know is dead.'

'Then you will find the last useful creature left alive in the city and you will bring me what I need.' The voice had gone quiet. Ahmed removed an envelope from his pocket. 'This is what you will use to purchase the information. But be careful. If it's known you have cash, everyone will try to steal it. Be selective. Be clever. You know how this works . . .'

The contact took the envelope and shoved it into his jacket.

'You have twenty-four hours. That's it . . .'

The contact raised himself on his knees, a cloud lifted and the moonlight hit his contorted face.

Ahmed read his expression: the tight, dry lips, the darting eyes – the contact would not have expected the money. Now he was torn between fear and opportunity. Between fear and greed. Which would he choose?

Ahmed's left hand fastened on the tight curly hair of the contact's skull, pulling it towards him, his mouth right up against the man's ear.

'You would be unwise to come back here without the information I need. You would be unwise to tell me stories about how the package has been lost or stolen. You would be unwise to deviate in any way from my instructions. Do I make myself plain?'

The man nodded, pulled himself to his feet and, crouching low, slithered back into the darkness that marked the border.

Ahmed waited a few seconds until the clouds had pulled across the moon and ran back to his car. The cold had eaten into him, his hands were frozen, nose a block of ice. It took a few minutes for the inside to warm up as he pulled through the dark, half-built streets of Ramtha, heading south to Amman.

He thought the contact would find a way to keep some of the money for himself and use the rest to buy safe passage in and out.

Perhaps, after all, there was nothing to be found or the information would be out of date. Or maybe the contact would be stupid enough to betray him to the Islamists and hope that he would simply fall into their trap.

He drove on and focussed on what lay ahead. Moscow was adamant. The American woman had to be found and extricated. He didn't know why and had no interest either.

As for the contact, he was of no importance. Whatever happened, Ahmed would kill him.

LONDON

'Let's make this official, Dean.'

'All the same to me.'

Margo had called the meeting. A café on Duke Street, three minutes from the US embassy. No chit-chat, she had told herself. Get it over with and get out.

'Our man's coming out day after tomorrow. Aeroflot direct from Moscow to New York JFK, due in around 2200. I'll be with him.'

'OK.' Anderson produced a lukewarm smile. 'Listen, there's no reason why any of this has to get unpleasant. We'll take him off to a nice hotel, feed him a good meal and then spend a couple of days chatting about old times.'

'I need him on a plane back to London Thursday night. If there'd been any other way of doing this . . .'

'I'll let them know.'

'It's a fixed deadline, Dean. We agreed on—'

'And I'm sure if he cooperates he'll be out of there well before that deadline . . .'

Margo leaned forward. Her blue eyes locked and immovable on Anderson. 'I want to make myself perfectly clear, Dean. Our man is on a flight to London by Thursday night. And I'll be with him in New York every step of the way.'

Anderson raised his hands in mock surrender. 'I got it, Margo, OK? Be nice to us and we'll be nice back. Isn't that how allies are supposed to behave?'

She got up to leave.

'Aren't you forgetting something?'

'I didn't forget. I'll send you his name, once he's on the flight.'

'That's no good.' Anderson rose abruptly, his smile lost in the movement. 'I need it now. We have to assemble the right team in New York, the right files, the right experts – otherwise there's no point. You know that as well as I do.'

'His name's Arkady Mazurin.' She spoke so quietly, almost whispered, watching him strain to catch the words in the crowded café, wondering, in that moment, if she would look back and regret for years to come and in ways she couldn't even imagine, what she had just said.

WASHINGTON DC

He had left the White House early that day. Traffic had been horrible. But he stopped at a flower shop in Georgetown and bought Rosalind the yellow daffodils she loved.

'They're flowers that look forward,' she had said once. 'Yellow means someone's coming back home. Put out a red flower and it's like they're already dead and buried.'

So yellow it was.

And I, Harry Jones, the hypocrite, am buying.

Options. Harry's mind always turned to options. But he knew he'd already taken the decisions that counted. The major ones that mark you, define you as you really are. Sometime back in early September, with summer well on the wane and autumn inbound, he had, in his own mind, left his sick wife and his vows by the side of the road and driven off in full knowledge of what he was doing. There was no undoing what he had done . . .

As he headed back to the house, he could hear Mai's voice, calling out just a month before from the tiny kitchen in Adams Morgan; Gershwin, cracked but triumphant on the ancient turntable. They had sat at the blue kitchen table looking out over the yard.

'Why are you staring at me?' she had asked him over coffee.

'I want to remember this.'

She laughed. 'You're just looking at my chipped tooth.'

'It's endearing.'

'You say that but you're wondering why I haven't got it fixed.'

His turn to laugh.

'You Americans – unless you all look the same, same noses, same teeth, same button-down shirts, you feel insecure.'

He wasn't smiling anymore.

'You're so inventive, creative – and yet you all want to belong to a herd. It's a big contradiction, Harry. I leave my car in an empty parking lot and when I come back someone's parked right next to me. When there's a thousand other spaces! How do you explain that, mister?'

'Do I have to?'

'Harry Jones . . .' She slurred the words intentionally. 'Don't look so down. We can talk about other things if you want.'

'Us?'

'Aren't we real enough already?'

'Yes, but . . .'

'You want me to tell you things . . .' She looked up as if searching for a word. 'Endearments. Is that it?'

'Maybe.'

She had leaned across the table and taken his hand. 'They're just words, Harry. We both know that. They don't mean anything.'

He forced himself to concentrate on the road but the memories were discomforting. Each of the days before she had left seemed shorter and faster and darker.

They had taken the wine to the sofa and lain side by side, every-thing said, his love declared, hers unstated, the sky hovering between orange and blue, thin lines of charcoal cloud.

Harry parked the car and cleared his mind. Inside his home was a woman who needed him now, tonight, fully committed, as she fought her way in terrible pain towards the end of her life.

He couldn't let her down again.

She hadn't woken at all that evening. The doctor had called after midnight. His verdict: it hadn't been a good day for her. And, yes, the good days were surely diminishing. There wouldn't be many of them in the time she had left.

'You need to know that, Harry.'

He must have dozed for a while. The banging had started in his dream but was now very real at the kitchen window. He could see the uniform, took in the red nose of one of the president's military aides.

Harry wide awake now, realizing his shirt was open to the waist, trousers loosened.

At the door, the marine handed him a package and asked him to sign electronically on a tablet.

'Sorry to disturb you, sir, but they said this was urgent. Should I wait to see if there's a reply?'

'That won't be necessary.'

Harry muttered his thanks and opened the sealed plastic envelope. It was from the CIA – the source was Dean Anderson in London.

He couldn't help the whistle, the sharp intake of breath. A day of surprises was ending with one he had least expected.

The identity of the former British double agent, now about to leave Moscow for good.

He didn't know the name and didn't much care. Arkady Mazurin was nothing more than the means to an end.

Harry took a mobile phone from his pocket and sent a text to a number with a Geneva prefix. The phone had come to him a year ago from a friend in Lagos who had bought the device in a slum, hacked and unlocked, so that nobody else in the world would have a clue into whose exalted hand it had now passed.

The Geneva number offered its owner a remarkably similar level of protection.

Across Washington, Vitaly Yanayev read the message twice in his official car and nodded to himself. In the darkness on Key Bridge, he wound down his window and threw the mobile into the Potomac.

MOSCOW

V asya looked at him with suspicion as Arkady rolled up his blanket, a favoured old shoe, a water bowl and a tin dish from which he ate his food. The entire inventory of the dog's possessions.

He had indeed travelled light through life, asking little from it, but giving his loyalty and his companionship without question.

'I'm sorry to do this to you.' Arkady looked up, Vasya inclined his head.

He seemed to be waiting for an excuse or an explanation, but Arkady had none to offer.

He finished tying the bundle of Vasya's things and sat down at the kitchen table. The two of them eyed each other in silence.

You can lie to humans so easily but you can't fool a dog because he can read your mind. Whatever you say, he seems to know the truth. Vasya is my conscience. No wonder he looks disappointed.

They took a taxi to Yelena's flat. He had to bang on the door for at least five minutes before she came.

'Why the fucking noise?' she asked by way of a greeting and then dropped to the ground hugging Vasya, who was snorting and snuffling and wagging his tail and licking her face, all at the same time.

They hadn't seen each other for five years, but neither had forgotten the other.

Perhaps dogs were better to live with than humans, thought Arkady. No permanent sense of injustice. No requirement to talk when all you wanted was silence.

'I've brought his things,' he said lamely.

She stood up. 'I can see. He'll have a good supper and I'll let him out before I go to bed.'

Sounded so normal, the way she said it. Yelena and Vasya beginning a life they would live happily ever after.

And yet they both knew that wouldn't happen. They would snatch a day or so and then there would be a knock on the door and life would never be the same again.

Arkady's thoughts began to race. 'I don't think this is a good idea. I need to sit down.'

She fetched him a chair and he sat in his winter coat in the middle of the tiny hall, with the dark, dirt-stained walls, unpainted for decades and the book shelves stuffed to overflowing. A baby began howling in the next-door flat.

'What is it, Arkady?'

'You and Vasya. Once I'm gone there could be trouble for you. You know what they're like.'

She looked at him and sighed. 'You made your decision. You should go. One of us should leave this chamber of horrors and I don't want to. Never did. I hate it, but it's mine. I hate these people – brutal, arrogant and so incredibly stupid, but they're my

people. You never felt that way. You had your career . . .' She raised
her hands as if to halt her own train of thought.

'Listen to me, Yelena—'

'No, you listen. Just this once. I'm prepared for anything, however
bad. That's what this country did to me. Turned me into the kind
of person who's always waiting for disaster. And not just me.
Tens of millions of us. This is what they did. Whenever something
good happened, we always waited for the bash on the head or
the punch in the face. We're Russians. Our life is hard. But we
make it like that. We're stupid people who create our own problems and then battle with them unsuccessfully all our life. How
much more idiotic can you get?'

'Maybe if I stay . . .'

'If you stay, you'll just piss me off even more. I stopped you
when you came here last time with your sob story, but we had
something once. Better than most people. And nothing lasts forever.
Why should we try for something more and then just end up hating
each other all over again?' A thin smile appeared on her lips and
he couldn't remember the last time he'd seen it. 'So fuck off and
leave us in peace.' Even that was said kindly. 'Send me a postcard
from somewhere and sign it "Vasya" – and then we'll know that
you've got to where you're going.'

He stood up, leaned forward and kissed her on the forehead.

Yelena turned away and went into the kitchen. Vasya limped
after her. Residence and loyalty had been transferred. The animal
understood that.

Arkady blew his nose and shut the front door quietly behind
him.

So a new life had begun – as it always did – with a farewell.

SYRIA/JORDAN BORDER

The contact was pleased with himself. A few miles inside the
border, at a rat-hole called Tell Shihab, he had stopped at
the house of a former colleague in the Syrian police to see
if the man might know something.

It wasn't an easy encounter. The man, in underpants and stinking T-shirt, had been drinking and hadn't wanted to let him in. But when the subject of money for information was raised, he had become increasingly hospitable.

Muttering nonsense to himself, he had led the contact to the kitchen and seated him by the warm stove. 'You're hungry, aren't you? Course you are – look at the state of you . . .' He produced some bread and another glass, filling it from the wine bottle he had hurriedly concealed beneath the table.

'Drink, my friend. In a while, we talk business. But you are my guest and at least we can celebrate the fact we're still alive!'

The contact sipped the wine and put down his glass. 'So which side are you on these days, brother? Uh? Or maybe you're on everyone's side?' He grinned broadly, trying to put the man at his ease.

'Perhaps I should ask you same question. Brother.' The smile wasn't returned. 'You come here, middle of the night . . . and you ask which side I'm on. The question has no meaning. All of us are on the side that lets us live a little longer. One day this one, tomorrow the other.' He sneered. 'Let me tell you something. There's no difference between any of them. They all kill, they all torture. They would all do the same terrible things if they came to power.' He stopped for a moment, listening. 'Dangerous times, my friend . . . talking to you could get me a bullet in the head.'

In the pocket of his tracksuit, the contact felt the butt of his revolver.

'I'm looking for someone and I need your help.'

'Listen carefully to me. I have many sources of information. People are searching these days for friends, for loved ones. Our country is a slaughterhouse. You know this just as I do. Every day we drown in blood, every day there is more.'

He pushed the wine bottle across the table towards the contact. 'You need to be very careful, my friend. People here will kill for nothing. For a suspicion, for a word they didn't expect; because they don't like your face; because they sense danger everywhere and fear you are part of it. Information is the most dangerous thing you can buy . . . more than bombs, I tell you, even guns and bullets . . .'

'Can you help me or not?'

The policeman stared straight ahead. Seconds passed before he spoke.

'If there's radio traffic about your friend, or phone calls, we can try. There's a man who has the technology. It belonged to the Americans, but was stolen at the start of the war. It can monitor transmissions over a long distance. I tell you, my friend, it can pull words from the sky . . .'

'Where is it?'

'I'll take you there, but it's expensive. A very big risk. To me. You understand? There must be compensation.'

'I said I'd pay.'

'You have to pay first . . .'

For a few seconds the two men stared unkindly at each other. The contact had divided the money in advance into $500 bundles. He pulled one from his pocket and laid it in front of the policeman.

The officer didn't look at it. 'We leave in the morning, my friend. It's late, get some sleep.'

'I need to leave now. The morning's too late.'

The policeman raised his hand, as if signalling a car to stop at a junction.

'I won't go in darkness. It's impossible. Life is dangerous enough.' He picked up the pile of dollars on the table and threw it back down. 'Besides, this will cost you much more than you've given me.' He raised his eyebrows and smiled. 'Relax my friend. Drink. Be calm. The sun will rise in a few hours.'

For just a moment the contact shut his eyes. All his life he'd been a gambler, come close to the edge a few times, but he'd been lucky till now. He had a good instinct for danger.

He reckoned the odds were about even that the policeman would try to kill him before dawn.

LONDON

There had been no sign of Jimmy at home. Not that she had time for him. Mazurin's exit from Moscow had pushed her own life to the sidelines. It was always that way. You negotiated a path between the extraordinary and the mundane – and everyone with a normal life had to get out of your way.

A selfish life?

Of course not. Wasn't about her. Wasn't as if she were chasing a career or a fat salary or a bigger car. It was simply about getting the job done, saving a life or even many lives.

Was it really so difficult to understand, if she had to work odd hours or nights or weekends – or couldn't tell someone every moment of her life where she was and what she was doing?

No wonder the Service personnel got together, slept together, cried together.

Sure, they shared secrets – but when she looked at some of her colleagues, they didn't seem to share much else.

Two offices down the corridor she had known a Charley, a Brenda and a Philippa and they had all seemed to pass each other around when needed. Like a bottle of pills, you took a Charley when you felt low and then Brenda might take Philippa for a bit of a high, and Charley might take one of each, even at the same time if life was a pisser that week.

So they got each other through the weekends or an odd evening here or there. But the general view was that office relationships were crap. Convenient but you wished you didn't have to. Like holding onto a handrail.

She zipped up her bag, locked the front door and shook herself like a dog. The flat had felt unbelievably cold, the pizza and the laughter long gone.

Could they piece something back together, 'work on it' in earnest, late-night encounters in the local Café Rouge, when she'd be tired and he'd be brittle? And the same old stuff dredged up and dissected; his weeping wounds, her 'unfeeling, hurtful' responses; respect draining away.

Probably wouldn't go well.

She called Manson from the secure mobile.

'I'm on my way to Heathrow.'

'I know. You want a medal?'

'Listen to me. I want to be sure that if the Americans try to screw us, my government will make a bloody great fuss and resist.'

'I can't promise you that.'

'Of course you can't. You know what? I sometimes wonder whether you bloody exist at all.'

MOSCOW

I t felt lonely without the dog. He hadn't realized how the animal had substituted for human contact. Decent human contact. A creature that didn't have an angle, didn't want to use you or trade you, wasn't looking to climb over your body to get promoted.

In the flat overlooking Leninsky Prospekt, Arkady allowed himself a small whisky and then another.

Tomorrow, he thought, is almost here. My plane ticket is in my pocket, my passport in my jacket. My permission to leave Moscow and fly to New York – all typed and stamped and folded in an official envelope. Wrapped like a Christmas present – the best he could ever have imagined.

'New York.' He mouthed the name silently, stifling an urge to fling open his filthy, frozen windows and yell it out across the rooftops to anyone who could hear.

For the first time in so many years he let his mind return to the city. Three years he had spent there – a trophy posting for the KGB – only the rising stars went there, the brightest, the most trusted. The ones who could recruit and handle their own agents, who understood the duality of the American psyche: the need to be loved and admired coupled with that brutal, extreme focus on the job in hand.

Their arrogance often made them myopic, gullible: believing only in what they wanted, not what they saw.

So it had been easy to hide there in the open. People accepted you at face value. You said you were a nice guy, they believed you. As long as you had a sad story and a smile and a generous wallet. Americans were suckers for warmth, suckers for a hard luck tale. Suckers full stop.

He had done well in New York, studied the people at work and play, looked hard into their faces, watched how the gangs and the cliques got things done; how they broke rules and re-made them as they wanted.

He watched how patronage and power were traded, how money was seemlessly converted into influence.

Felt familiar, so very familiar because it was just like home. The only difference was that the Americans had a soft surface. Pat them on the head and they'd lie on their back with their legs in the air. But inside they were the same duplicitous snakes as the Russians.

And they all loved a thug. As long he was their thug, killing, torturing, humbling their enemies, betraying their friends. Didn't matter, in either country, as long as he got the job done.

But Britain would be different. Altogether more complex.

He could see ahead of him the months and years of constant probing. The British no longer believed in anything. Still less in anything they were told. Perhaps it was how small countries survived. Big countries could afford big hearts and naïve assumptions – the little ones needed to watch their back.

He knew the Brits would be wary of him. You never trust an agent who suddenly appears on your doorstep. To be frank, you never trust them at all. But the film from Leningrad would be the clincher. He'd be lauded and feted all the way to Buckingham Palace. They'd be dancing in the corridors at Vauxhall Cross.

Or maybe they wouldn't care. Maybe an ancient grainy piece of film was too big for them to handle. Too hot . . . too complex.

Maybe all he'd get would be a thank-you at the local pizza place and then they'd stick him in a little, red-brick house on the bad side of a big town, with a view of a railway line, or a motorway, where nobody cared who came or went.

Perhaps they'd assign him some retired ex-cop for a while to watch the neighbours and then he'd be on his own. New name, new haircut, some regular money – not that much – and a life to spend on the cheap in scabby cafés and public libraries and the crowded waiting rooms of immigrant doctors.

Arkady shut his eyes.

Is that what freedom would look like?

Just before dawn he got up from the chair and lay down in the bedroom. What had happened to his spirit, his ambition?

To make it in the KGB, as he had done, you didn't do negative. You were confident and unflinching, utterly ruthless in the execution of your duties.

He wasn't going to the West as a broken victim. He was a prize catch and he would prove his worth. He'd meet the prime minister; there'd be high tea and sherry; they'd pay him handsomely for the risks he'd taken and the gift he had brought.

Brits still had a sense of what was right. A sense of justice, fair play. Didn't they?

Christ only knew.

Arkady breathed deeply, trying to slow the engine in his chest.

Today he would leave Moscow for good, his head held high. After a lifetime of Russia, like a ball and chain around his leg, his fate was *his* affair – and his alone.

He smiled at the darkness around him. Freedom was a state of mind.

He was already free.

SYRIA

The contact couldn't remember if he'd slept. Perhaps a few minutes. No more. His right hand had rested all night on the pistol in his pocket – the shiny, black Glock that had always got him what he wanted and disposed of what he didn't.

He had imagined the policeman would come for him just before dawn. A single bullet in the head and they'd chuck him into one of the many graves that were dug daily across the country, with any old name spray-painted on a stone.

But the man never came. At five the contact tiptoed into the kitchen. He could hear the snoring from there. The drunken shit was dead to the world.

At six he woke him.

'You want more money. Get the fuck up and earn it. I need some information.'

The policeman had coughed for ten minutes, thrown up and then made tea. The place was freezing. They stood over the single gas ring, rubbing their hands.

Outside, the sky was still dark, but the birds knew it was dawn. The contact couldn't remember when he'd last heard their song. Besides, who cared? A new day was shuffling in, bringing its usual quota of hatred and violence, just as it had done for as long as he could remember. And one day, like everything else, the birdsong would cease.

He pulled on his jacket and got into the policeman's car.

The man's greed had woken up with him. 'I want the money before we start.'

'How much?'

'Ten thousand dollars.'

The contact laughed. 'I'll give you two thousand now – if I get the information I want, you'll get another two. It's all I have.'

The man snorted, but he turned the ignition and after two tries, the engine fired.

They drove for a while without speaking. In the half-light of dawn, the contact could make out no more than a few black shapes along the streets, burkas that billowed in the wind, a dog with only half a tail that ran across the road in front of them. Many of the doorways were covered with blankets as wood was in short supply.

'I'm hungry,' he told the policeman.

'Where do you think you are? New York? We don't have hamburgers here. You take what you find.'

Down a side street they stopped at a bakery and bought warm white bread – but there was nothing to drink.

The contact looked at his watch. In a little over five hours Ahmed would be waiting for him in the same place by the border. If he had nothing to tell him, it would be a seriously unpleasant encounter. Ahmed was unpredictable in almost every way – but not when it came to violence. Those who displeased him were killed or badly beaten. The thought struck the contact that he might make a run for it – but Ahmed's reach was everywhere. There was nowhere that was safe from him. He'd have to deliver.

They left the sprawl of the town and headed out into open country. No sign of war or destruction there, but the contact knew plenty of people were suffering. Only the odd food shop remained open. No one bought luxuries except those who killed and stole, like the fat businessmen who overcharged everyone, profiting from the shortages and the national misfortune; or the mercenaries who went off to do a day's killing and then returned home for dinner, with the rings and watches they'd snatched from their victims, rattling in their pockets.

It was a country where the evil strutted the streets and the inno-cent cowered in basements. And they had called this the Arab Spring!

The contact reckoned he had known all along how it would

end; had seen the brutality that had lain below the surface of every Arab society; been a part of it himself.

For all his faults, the dictator had kept a lid on the worst of it. Yes, people got tortured, even killed when they went too far. But millions of others had still gone about their business, studied at university, fallen in love, started families, made a bit of money.

Not anymore. Now everyone was losing: the people they loved and the things they'd worked for.

This was where all the stupid talk of freedom and democracy had brought them.

To the graveyard.

The policeman pulled off the road beside a line of shops. All were shuttered. He banged on a metal door but there was no response.

'Where's your man?' The contact was shivering in the grey light.

'Shut up and I'll find him.'

He disappeared round the side of the buildings; the contact followed. Together they forced the main door open, heard the cheap lock snap and climbed the stone staircase, quietly, on the balls of their feet.

It was clear the policeman had been there before. At the second floor he branched off down the corridor, surprisingly nimble on his aging feet. He stopped at the last entrance on the left.

In the cold darkness, he whispered to the contact, 'I'll break down the door. You go in first, show him the gun and then he'll cooperate.'

'And if he doesn't?'

'We'll persuade him. You remember how to do that?'

At the first heave the door gave up and buckled noisily inwards. From close by, they heard a shout of surprise, then fright and as the two of them stumbled into a bedroom, a bearded man was sitting up in bed in striped pyjamas, waving his fist and cursing their ancestors.

'Shut your mouth,' the policeman grunted. 'You know who we are?'

'A pair of thieves, too stupid to enter and leave without waking me up.'

'Get up.' The policeman picked up some clothes from the floor and threw them at the bearded figure. 'We want some information and you can make some money. If you prefer to do this the hard way, my friend and I can shoot your balls off – and then you'll have to help us without them. All clear?'

'I've seen you before,' the man nodded. 'I know your ways.'

He threw off his blanket and struggled into his clothes. The contact thought he was probably about thirty-five. It was clear he had once cut a fat, portly figure but now the skin hung in folds and creases from his belly and the fat had gone. His arms and legs were spindly and discoloured. Much of the skin had a yellow, almost jaundiced tint. But the contact couldn't have cared less about the man's state of health. The only question was whether he still had a brain.

In the kitchen, they sat at a small, round table while the policeman told the beard what he wanted.

'Friend here says a woman is on the run, probably been labelled a spy, might even be American. Chances are everyone's after her. We need to know if there's been any mobile traffic about her. She could be hiding up somewhere, or trying to head for the Turkish border or maybe a route into Jordan.'

The beard looked interested.

With the lights on, the contact examined his face. The man had probably been a teacher, one of the clever kind. Most likely at a university or technical college. Read a lot of books, didn't go out. Only interested in his work, or the tight jeans of the female students. He recognized the type: quick movements, nose twitching like a rat. A man who would live in twilight and sleep through the day, dreaming algorithms, while the world was being blown up around him. Perhaps he wouldn't even notice.

The contact leaned forward. 'You still have your equipment?'

The beard said he did.

'Does it work?'

Again the reply was affirmative.

'Show me.'

He took them into the corridor and opened a walk-in cupboard. There was barely space for a single person in the windowless alcove, but shelves had been built on both sides of the wall and a desktop crammed with communications equipment, consoles, green and red lights.

The contact whistled in awe. 'Where in the name of God Almighty did you get all this?'

'Who cares where he got it?' The policeman had pushed in behind them. 'Don't waste his time. He has it, it works . . . that's all that matters. Now let him do his fucking job and we can get out of here and I don't have to see either of your ugly faces again.'

The beard sat at his console and threw switches. Flashing lights appeared and tinny, short-range radio transmissions could be heard on a small loudspeaker. Beside him, the contact was watching the scanner screens intently.

'How do you know who these voices are?' he asked.

'Got used to them. Been doing this for two years now. I also keep records.' He hesitated. 'Not here of course. But somewhere safe. An insurance policy.'

'Meaning what?'

'Meaning I've heard a lot of things, sitting here. Some of them pretty dangerous. Could get a lot of people into trouble. Evidence that could be used against important people. Orders given. Orders carried out. You know what I mean?'

The contact knew perfectly well what he meant. If he'd had the time he might have tried to plunder the beard's archive, wherever it was, extract some compromising material and make some money out of it himself. But time was running out fast and he needed results.

Ahmed had no reputation at all for rewarding failure.

An hour had passed without result. The beard had swung his dials and the contact had listened with mounting impatience to the cacophony of hateful voices: crying, shouting and talking nonsense.

At times the airwaves were alive with trivia. Mobile phone talk about who might be where. What had they eaten? Orders for taxis. A doctor who could find no medicine.

And then there were the found and the lost, the hopeless and the lonely, the distraught and the dying.

Soundbite Syria at war.

Once or twice the beard pulled in a police or military report. Someone had been shot, ammunition was needed.

A soldier could be heard shouting at a unit that was under fire from rebel forces. 'Hold the street. At all costs you have to hold the street.' But after twenty minutes the voices had died away. So he assumed the street had been lost.

He put his hand on the beard's arm. 'I need to hear about an American woman. Find a mention of her, a name, even a curse. But find her for me.'

'You ask too much . . .'

'And you give too little,' the contact hit back. 'Get yourself together, my friend, and think fast. If this doesn't work, you'll see a very angry man . . .'

The beard picked up his mobile.

'Wait a minute . . .' The contact snatched it from his hand. 'No calls. You talk to no one until you find—'

'But I've got friends who might help. They scan the frequencies like me. Maybe they're closer . . .' he began to whimper.

'Then do it.' The contact slapped him twice hard across the face with the flat of his hand. The beard yelped in surprise. Time was running out. The contact hit him again, just to make sure he understood.

WASHINGTON DC

Lydia Yanayeva could tell that her husband was nervous. She knew all his moods. The silent and the more silent. The anger that could flare quickly inside him, but almost never got out of control.

If she'd been asked about his character, she would have described him as unfailingly amiable. Not a trait much in evidence with Russian government officials, who she knew to be a little too amiable when they drank, and a little too surly when they didn't.

Yanayev had returned unexpectedly from his office shortly after breakfast and found his wife getting ready to go out.

She kissed him on the cheek. 'I thought you'd gone for the day.'

'So did I.' He sprawled in an armchair. She thought he looked frustrated, uncertain what to do next.

She sat beside him on the arm of the chair and put her hand through his hair.

'I was about to go to the Russian school – they asked whether I would give away some of the prizes.'

Yanayev nodded.

'But I don't have to go,' she added. 'I'll make you some coffee instead.'

He joined her in the kitchen. He wanted to tell her something, wanted to share a confidence. She knew that. But she wouldn't ask him. Let him circle and think and decide all by himself – and then he would give away his secret.

The moment came as they sipped the coffee in the atrium, over-looking the gardens.

'I'm in a difficult position, Lydia.'

'Talk to me. Maybe I can help.'

'I wish . . .' He raised his hands. 'I don't know, maybe. Perhaps no one can help.'

He looked out into the garden. An embassy cleaner was sweeping snow from the paths. Lydia said nothing.

'I have a deal with the Americans that's reached a very critical stage. If it works, it will bring me much credit in Moscow. If it fails' – he shrugged – 'if it fails, they will blame me for the whole thing . . .'

'But it's not your fault.'

'Since when did that worry them? There are plenty of people back home who want my job. "Yanayev is too old, too stupid, too fat. Way past his best days. Time he was brought back to Moscow where we can keep an eye on him. Maybe he can run the traffic police".' He sighed. 'This is the kind of thing they say about me. I have friends – not many, but a few. And they tell me these things. Any failure from my side and I can rely on the Ministry – some of the highest officials there – to use it against me.'

She took his hand. 'But why would it fail? You always plan meticulously. You've never failed in the past.'

'Too many things to go wrong. Too many people involved. And there's danger as well.'

'But . . .'

Yanayev finished his coffee and put down the cup. 'Perhaps it's best that you know nothing about it, my dear. They might ask questions. Even of you. They're quite ruthless when things go wrong.'

She looked hurt. 'And you think I'm so stupid that I can't share my husband's troubles with him and that I'm afraid of some cheap, state thugs who ask questions?'

He smiled and put his arm around her. 'I know . . . I know.' He got up and stood in front of her, his decision made. 'Put your coat on and we'll go for a walk.'

He led the way into the garden. The wind had come up, blowing snow from the trees, scattering it over her thick, dark hair.

'Listen to me.' He held her hand tightly. 'The Americans have lost an agent in Syria – a woman. We're using a contact there to help locate her and get her out?'

'Why do we care who the Americans lose or don't lose . . .?'

'We care because of the price that Washington is ready to pay to get her back. If we find the woman, they will betray a Western agent – one of our own citizens – who is preparing to leave the country. It's a straight swap. We extricate their agent – they give us a traitor.'

'Only you don't know if you can find the woman?'

'We're searching. Every minute that passes is of concern. I'm doing nothing else, only waiting for the call from our agent in Syria.'

'But how good is he, Vitaly?'

'Good?' Yanayev shrugged. 'Not an adjective I would use to describe Ahmed. Let's just say the man is effective. Enormously and utterly effective. Cruel, brutal in the extreme and totally devoid of conscience.'

Lydia shivered. 'I would not wish to meet such a man.'

Yanayev kept his eyes on the path and said nothing. Moscow had plenty of Ahmeds, deployed around the world. Men who were trained in what they called 'exhibition violence'. Violence, designed as much to shock and intimidate, as to wound and kill. Violence that carried a message way beyond the act itself.

It was better that Lydia remained ignorant of such things.

MOSCOW

A rkady sat very still in the apartment, but his thoughts wouldn't leave him alone.

How do I spend my last hours here, who are the friends I should like to hug, where are the places I love that I will never see again . . .?

He stared through the window onto Leninsky Prospekt. Hours earlier, a thick grey daylight had flooded in over Moscow, sealing in the cold. At this time of year the Russian capital would be dark by mid-afternoon, just as he'd be travelling to the airport at Domodedovo – his final journey across the city where he'd been born.

In the bottom of his suitcase, he had hidden the only picture that would travel with him: a small black and white photo of his parents, taken when he was six, on a beach by the Black Sea. He had found it days earlier, wedged between the pages of an old schoolbook, and for a second or two had even wondered who the figures were – his father in baggy trousers and an ill-fitting shirt, mother in the usual, awful, striped shift and the little boy that he'd been, wearing nothing more than swimming trunks and a silly smile.

The sun had been so bright that they had all squinted into the camera, leaving the impression of excruciating pain.

It was the only holiday Arkady could remember. His parents had been killed just before his seventh birthday, by a drunken truck driver who had veered out of control on an icy hill in Moscow and slammed them against a stone wall.

There had been no more pictures after that. And certainly none of him at State Orphanage No.63 in Yugo-Zapadnaya, where every object that he had ever touched belonged to someone else.

Strange never to have owned anything at all – not even a toothbrush – until the day he had left the building, aged eighteen, with a cheap, tenth-hand jacket, far too small for him, and a pair of trousers with an eclectic collection of immovable stains down the left leg.

He let the memories wash through him. Today it would, perhaps, have been appropriate to visit his parents' grave – but no one had ever told him where it was and, truth to tell, he had never asked.

He tried hard to think about the few years of family life that he'd experienced before the State had taken him over. But the pictures in his mind were faded or missing entirely. Fifty years had slunk past him, without so many of the emotional milestones that mattered to other people.

When he thought of his mother it was in disjointed fragments: the rubber band in her hair, the striped skirt, a laugh that had embarrassed him once on the crowded metro, a chocolate bar that she had passed him, like an exotic jewel, for his birthday.

Not her warmth or her kisses. Because he no longer knew if they were real or if he had imagined them.

So I'm taking just a few scraps of my history, and I leave behind a woman who was married to me and didn't love me – and a dog who did.

Pack your bag, said a voice inside his head.

I've done it, he replied. I'm ready to go.

WASHINGTON DC

Harry Jones sat waiting for his phone to ring. If the Russians located Mai, it would ring twice and he would get in his car and go direct to Nathan's Bar in Georgetown. And hand Yanayev the name and itinerary of Arkady Mazurin.

Seemed so simple.

And yet if there was no news in the next four hours it would all be too late. Mazurin would have left Russia and the bargaining chip would be worthless. Mai would be irretrievably lost.

He couldn't let that happen.

He wondered how many other national security advisers had sat in the same White House office, planning and executing operations that were morally questionable or downright illegal?

But that wasn't the right question. You took the position, you did the job.

No point moaning about betraying people – betrayal was Washington's currency. Look no further than the political quicksand on Capitol Hill or the snakepit out at Langley. Betrayal was business.

He got up, paced the pannelled room and sat back down again.

When he closed his eyes, he could see Mai's face in painful detail, feel the energy she had lent him, see the lightness of her movements.

Passive faces held no depth, told no stories, offered no glimpses of life lived or life to come – but hers did. The perpetual motion of the eyes, the mouth that opened so slowly to give – or shut tight like a trap.

And wherever she'd been and wherever she was going, Harry wanted to be there.

Sometimes her hard edge would appear without warning, like a knife drawn from its sheath – and maybe hours later the softness would return. No little girl stuff, nothing mannered or contrived but a gentleness that men would always wage wars to win.

Each time she went away, she would put something small into his pocket; a coin, a bookmark, a button or a badge. 'Keepsakes,' she said.

'So you do care about me?' he'd asked her once and instantly regretted the question.

'Why do you want to know?'

'Curiosity.'

'Harry . . .' Her voice had hardened. He could see the trap closing.

'Let's leave it,' he'd said.

She shook her head. 'I don't want to leave it. Fact is I care about lots of things. What's happening in Syria, the country I grew up in, the death and destruction. I care about my friends and the people I'm close with – and yes, you're on the list too. But don't ask me to tell you where. It's a long list and' – she pointed an index finger at him – 'you have a pretty long list too.'

'Which means what, exactly?'

She had smiled and taken his hand. 'You're a clever man, Harry Jones. You work it out.'

The White House was quiet as a church. Last to leave the building had been the interns – or 'slaves' as the staffers called them – hurrying out into the snow to grab their Saturday night and swing it by the tail.

But he wouldn't have changed places with them. He didn't want their 'fun' or their bar chat. He had wanted to be important – to play big games with big stakes – Harry Jones in his tweed suits and bow ties and wispy grey hair. They had no idea of the ambitions that he harboured or the random and exceptional stupidity with which he had thrown them away.

Harry wasn't the first official in this building to have fallen in love with a woman outside his marriage. Nor was he the first to misuse his power and his office.

And as he knew, far better than most, he wasn't by a long chalk the first to betray an ally.

But he realized with pin-sharp clarity that if the big game went wrong this time and Mai didn't make it home, life, as he had come to understand and value it over the last weeks and months, life, written in big, bright letters, would simply be over.

MOSCOW

Moscow was in darkness when she reached the hotel. From her window she could see pockets of the new bling: garish neon lights, hoardings that shouted western brand names, fast cars. But the rest of the city lay grumpy and dismal, as it always did, beneath the freezing snow.

You could never fall in love with Moscow, she thought. But there was a magnetic pull that was hard to ignore.

Unlike the West, Russia seemed unfettered by procedures and committees and legal restraints. Its power was raw and available for immediate use. Its options unlimited.

In the distance she could see the staggering beauty of the Kremlin against the rolling night-time clouds. Inside it, the silent, secretive heart of a gigantic beast.

And wherever you went in the city you could hear it beating.

Arkady Mazurin was a brave man to betray it.

She didn't unpack her suitcase, just lay down on the bed and closed her eyes. Two or three miles across the city Arkady would be waiting to make his move.

In a few hours, she too would head for the airport and make hers.

WESTERN SYRIA

The contact awoke startled.

'Come outside – quickly. Don't wake your friend.' The beard pointed to where the policeman lay inert and snoring in the corridor.

They stumbled outside onto the rough tarmac.

'What is it? What's happened?' The contact could hear the desperation in his own voice.

The man looked up and down the street and spoke in a rapid whisper. 'I talked to a colleague. There's been some unusual traffic on the mobile phone networks.'

'What, for God's sake? I need facts, details.'

'Talk of a foreigner. I think it's a woman. Nothing specific yet.'

'Where? Where is this talk coming from?'

'Radius of thirty kilometres. Thirty-five maximum.'

'I need more. Go back.'

Inside the doorway, the contact lit a cigarette and sent Ahmed a message.

'First sign of life,' he wrote. 'More soon.'

WASHINGTON DC

For a moment Vitaly Yanayev stared at the phone in disbelief, as if unable to accept that it was buzzing in his hand.

His secretary was on the line. Same bored voice as ever. Same Foreign Ministry robot. 'You have a cable, Ambassador. It's very urgent.'

'Send it round immediately to my residence.' He cut the call. Could she not have thought to despatch it by herself?

Within five minutes, he had it in his hand. Moscow had not bothered with details. They would follow later. The American woman appeared to be alive after all in Syria. They were trying to pinpoint her position. When they did, extraction would follow.

He read the last sentence twice because his hand was shaking and he wanted to be a thousand per cent sure, and because this was the biggest thing he had ever undertaken in the whole of his long and often spectacularly tedious career: 'Imperative you complete transaction immediately.' There was no room for misunderstanding.

He sent Harry Jones a text from his unlisted phone and ordered his car sent round.

Outside, the temperature had dropped but Vitaly Yanayev was sweating heavily as he lowered himself into the passenger seat.

MOSCOW

At dawn Margo left the hotel and took a taxi to the British Embassy.

Her cover story had been a meeting with consular staff to agree new procedures.

But instead she had been taken straight to the Station Chief Robert Evans.

A camp bed beside his desk told its own story.

She had met him a year earlier at a gathering of section chiefs in Vauxhall Cross. They were all so different. At one of the sessions they had all confessed their out-of-hours pursuits and discovered, to general amusement, that they had nothing whatsoever in common.

One sang in an amateur jazz group, another drove souped-up hatchbacks in local rallies.

Evans, by contrast, was a committed Christian, ordained as a Church of England vicar in his early twenties, and recruited into the Service after deciding the devil should be fought on the streets, not in the pulpit. At weekends he still played the organ.

And yet, none of that, she reflected, had prevented him from becoming the most ruthless and determined of agents.

Shortly before midday he left to keep watch outside Arkady's flat.

'I need you there till he gets on that plane,' she had told him. 'No last-minute surprises.'

Evans nodded. 'You think he's up to this?'

'You know him better than I do.'

'He's rusty but let's not forget who he was. Top-rank KGB. They weren't made of sugar, were they?'

Margo looked at her watch and wondered if Arkady was also counting the hours and minutes. Evans was right. The Russian had been one of Moscow's prized possessions, spying his head off in America for years and never getting caught.

He'd have known all the risks, been trained in the ways to mitigate them. And yet there was always another dimension. She knew that herself. Always something that you hadn't heard, didn't know, failed to factor into your perfect plan.

She thought back to the great pile of approvals and signatures for the dozens of operations she had conducted over the previous twenty years.

They had all been magnificent – each one of them – utterly magnificent. Right up until the day when they weren't.

She arrived early at the airport. Plenty of time to get noticed by the security cameras and then ignored. They'd be concentrating, as always, on the people who hurried, the last-minute travellers, the young and the agitated. A businesswoman in black business suit, with papers in hand and an easy smile would be no one's idea of a threat.

She took a seat in the coffee shop, chatted to the woman behind the counter, even dropped a few papers on the floor. A business prospectus, some spreadsheets, printed and designed for the purpose at Vauxhall Cross. She laughed at her clumsiness, a man got up to help her.

Don't overact, she thought. Be friendly and open – and if you can remember what it feels like, be normal. You've had a business trip. Major deal in the pocket. You're happy to be going home. That's all anyone will see.

They wouldn't know that she had left a black VW Passat on the diplomatic concourse outside the terminal, with its key in the ignition. Or that a miniature earpiece connected her directly to Robert Evans.

She swallowed a double espresso and clasped her hands together under the tiny coffee table. No one had ever seen her nervous. She was determined to keep it that way.

Evans had seen the taxi pull in outside Arkady's block, but his eyes scanned backwards and forwards along the rest of the road. The snow had been piled several feet high along the pavement.

Five minutes passed. Ten. Had the Russian overslept? Had he taken a phone call?

'He's late,' he told Margo. He could hear the sounds of people milling around her. 'No wait, I see him, coming out now. It's him.'

'Let him leave, keep watching his building.'

Evans didn't move. He saw the figure ease himself onto the back seat of the saloon and watched it nose slowly into the traffic. He couldn't see the point of waiting around, but his job wasn't to argue.

On the seat beside Arkady was a single case. Inside it: a suit, three shirts and some underwear. Everything else he had left behind and was glad of it.

After all, mementos meant nothing. Especially if you wanted to forget. They cluttered your life and impaired your judgement. You spent years buying and minutes disposing. What was this human fascination with collecting? It had all been so pointless.

And lastly there was a pair of old leather gloves – one in each coat pocket. They were worn and scuffed and would attract no attention. Inside each of them were tiny strips of film, cut into little bundles and sewn into the linings. Their hiding place for more than thirty years.

The film from Leningrad that would buy him his freedom and his retirement in London.

The night before, Arkady had checked the flat a final time, trying to picture how the security men would force their way in. Would they pick the lock and creep around, sifting and sorting? Or would they smash down the door and destroy as much as they could? Rumour had it that the younger officers enjoyed that best, armed themselves with baseball bats, clubbing and shattering any object they could find. Perhaps they'd also pocket a few things for themselves when no one was looking.

But it didn't matter. Things didn't matter. Nothing belonged to him now except the future.

I should have gone years ago.

The mantra he kept repeating as the taxi headed south from the city centre.

As always the ring road was crowded with late shoppers and people heading for their weekend *dachas*.

What a quaint image, he thought, but so unlike the real Russia! Oh yes, they drove out in their hundreds of thousands to their retreats – anything from shacks to country estates – but they all did the same when they got there: drank themselves senseless, only to return with dead eyes and blotchy skin from a weekend they could barely remember.

No wonder so many died early.

The driver was from one of the new taxi companies – smart, but thankfully disinterested in conversation.

They inched in silence through the outer suburbs. Arkady paid no attention.

From now on, Moscow would be mentioned only as history – all memories of it grey and faded. Perhaps one day, he could shut them in a box and throw it away.

He remembered that he still had his mobile phone in his pocket. Now that too could go. He opened the window next to him, as if to get fresh air, and threw it out into the street.

Ahead of them, he glimpsed the first, bright blue signs for the airport.

Just a few kilometres to go.

He felt a surge of energy.

WASHINGTON DC

As soon as he entered, Yanayev could see Harry at the end of the crowded bar. Not the kind of Harry he had met before. This one was in jeans and pullover, face unshaven.

'You want to go outside?' Harry raised a hand in greeting. The noise was deafening.

'No time, Harry. I've got news and I need a quick answer from you.'

Yanayev sat on the stool beside him and leaned in close to his ear. 'Your package is alive. We have an approximate location. As soon as it's confirmed, we'll get her.'

Harry didn't move.

'You heard what I said?'

'Yes. I just couldn't . . .' He seemed to pull himself together. 'Where is she? Can you get to her?'

'I'll give you all the details. Right now, I need you to fulfil your side of the bargain. We're running out of time. May already be too late. You need to tell me who it is that's defecting from Russia? Now, Harry. This minute, flight details, everything you know. Otherwise, there's no deal.'

'What if you don't get her out? I get nothing from this.'

'We're down to the wire, Harry. No guarantees. If you don't give me the name, we pull out and you'll never find her. That'll be the end of it. I promise we'll do our best. I can do nothing else.'

Harry stared straight ahead of him. Row upon row of bottles from all over the world were piled up behind the bar, but he didn't see any of them. He hadn't planned for the way he'd feel when the moment came.

Yanayev began speaking again but he couldn't hear him. People were singing and shouting, waves of laughter rose and fell and it seemed to Harry that the world didn't give a damn what he was about to do.

In a moment, surrounded by raucous revellers in a Georgetown bar, he would reach into his pocket and sign a death warrant for a man, thousands of miles away, heading for an airport and dreaming of a new life. A man he had never met.

Too bizarre, almost, to comprehend.

Sure, he had done terrible things in the past – but always for the country. Never for himself. This time it was personal.

My own hand on the gun.

Harry reached inside his jacket and took out an envelope.

'I don't do this with any pleasure, Vitaly.'

Yanayev stood up and stared angrily into the American's eyes. 'Since when has any of this been about pleasure, Harry? You want your package, you pay for it.'

Inside his car, Yanayev tore open the envelope and swore involuntarily.

'*Yob' tvayu Mat'.*' The most brutal, commonplace obscenity in the Russian language.

Mazurin's name meant nothing to him – but the paper made clear his flight was leaving Russia in just over ninety minutes.

There was no time for security. Against all protocol, he dialled a Moscow number and dictated the name and the flight number that Harry had given him.

He was asked to repeat it.

'For fuck's sake I just told you . . . you want it broadcast on every TV network? Mazurin, Arkady. Flight 640 from Domodedovo.'

The connection was cut and Yanayev sank back into his seat. He was breathing heavily.

Had it worked? Had he sent it in time? Would Moscow get its act together and detain the man – or fuck about for two hours and then blame the disaster on him?

He didn't know, but he'd hear soon enough.

DOMODEDOVO AIRPORT, MOSCOW

Much, much later Margo Lane was to recall the sequence of events that followed in excruciating detail – as if it had transpired in slow motion.

She had become part of the airport furniture. Around her the travellers, coated and scarved, hurried to their flights. To all of them she appeared relaxed and good-humoured. Until Evans's voice broke into her ear.

'What is it?'

'Visitors.'

'How many?'

'Six in two cars.'

'Blue lights?'

'No. But they're in a hurry.'

'You sure you know where they're headed?'

'I am now. Light just came on in the fourth-floor apartment.'

'Keep watching.'

Less than thirty seconds later, Evans came back to her.

'They're leaving in a hurry – both cars. They've just put the blue lights on the roof. FSB, I'm guessing. Looks like he's blown.'

Almost in slow motion, Margo finished her third coffee, picked up her mobile and dialled Arkady's number but the call diverted immediately. She tried a second time.

'He's not picking up.'

'I don't have another number. Can you head him off?' Evans's voice seemed to have risen an octave. She didn't reply.

Beyond the coffee shop and the check-in desks she was already scanning the main doors for any sign of him. Crowds were streaming into the terminal. Harder to make out the faces, raw from the cold, shrouded in caps and fur hats.

She tried Arkady's mobile a final time but still there was no reply. Where the fuck was he? If she couldn't find him, the man would be dead within minutes.

'How long is this going to take?'

Arkady leaned forward to the driver. Traffic was blocked solid on the main approach road to the airport.

'I don't know.' The driver was surprisingly breezy. 'Always like this around six. Especially in the snow. Last week I sat here for almost an hour – just to go the last 300 metres.'

Arkady breathed deeply. It was to be expected. There was no cause for concern. He sat back and shut his eyes.

He remembered the first time he'd travelled in a taxi – that was in the early days when the KGB had posted him to Kharkov in Ukraine. He and the other trainees were just a bunch of kids, looking for something different, some fun; didn't really believe all the crap about building Socialism – it was just a way in . . . You had to buy a ticket to see the show.

And the show was all about joining the Party and going to discos and special shops, and Beatles records and caviar, when you really made it. And girls, only too happy to sleep with your Party card.

What's more there had been travel – you acquired the magic label 'Viyezdnoi' – literally 'eligible for travel abroad' – and that had been gold dust. It meant you could pass through the borders, not just to the other miserable East Bloc states, but all the way to the spanking, brand new West, with cafés that sold food and coffee on clean tables, reached along clean streets with glossy shops, with assistants who smiled and asked if they could help you – and even a little money in the pocket to spend. So that when you came home, you had a gift or two for the ladies and you could lord it over everyone, how you'd seen London or Paris, drunk champagne even if you hadn't – and pissed yourself at midnight along the Champs-Élysées. Which of course you had.

It meant you were someone in a land where most people counted for nothing at all.

Arkady opened his eyes and studied the faces in the cars alongside. Everyone fraught, impatient. In the distance, he could hear sirens. Probably an accident. Russians were lousy drivers.

For the tenth time he felt for the passport and ticket in his inside coat pocket.

They were all that mattered. A passport out of Russia and a ticket to the West.

And they'd be there at the airport to watch him through. He knew they would. Brits were solid, reliable. It was good to have them on his side.

A question occurred to him. How would he celebrate when he reached New York?

He smiled.

Probably with a hot dog from one of the cheap mobile stands on Fifth Avenue. Plenty of onions and mustard on top, and the steam rising from it into the clear, cold, city air. Arkady could taste it.

Behind him, the sirens sounded much closer.

Margo could hear them too. Where the hell was Arkady?

Casually, she moved to the side of the main door, found a set of stairs and climbed two or three to get a vantage point. Mazurin was blown. The only question now was whether she could save him. She checked that the black VW was in position on the concourse. As she watched, the traffic began to flow again.

Someone would have told the airport police to clear the lanes because the big boys from Moscow were on their way. They weren't going to leave this one for the locals.

The usual Russian pissing match – with everyone trying to scramble up the ladder on someone else's back. Stand aside for the pros. A very big someone wanted to make his name and wanted it today.

And then she saw him – the long, black coat, silver hair, the single suitcase. Quite unmistakable.

In the same moment, a hundred metres away, she glimpsed the first of the blue lights. Police were shouting at drivers, waving wildly at them to get out the way, cars began skidding on the rutted, icy tarmac . . .

Margo knew there were only seconds left. She dropped her bag, jumped the stairs and pushed her way to the door.

Mazurin looked up – but the eyes registered nothing.

Time for a quick pass, a single hopeless chance, nothing more.

She knocked into the Russian, held his arm briefly and apologized loudly. A quick hand on the shoulder let her lean in towards his ear.

'You're blown . . . Get out of here . . . you'll never make the plane.' Just a whisper. 'Black VW opposite, keys inside. Find a safe place. We'll get to you.'

And Margo had already passed, lost among the dark winter shapes and the cold, white faces, pushing in all directions through the airport.

Arkady stood still for a moment and looked around. His face registered no expression – he simply turned abruptly and headed towards the outer doors.

It must have been the first whistle that made him run.

And the fear that they'd seen him. He was still ten yards from the main door but he took in the grey uniforms in the distance. He barged into an elderly couple, saw others scatter in front of him, scared at the sight of a wild figure, too old to be running, too dangerous to be near.

Even before he's through the doors, he can see the black car in the distance. They didn't let him down. Didn't throw him to the wolves.

Traffic everywhere. The jam cleared. Cars picking up speed outside the concourse.

And he's through the glass doors now, shoving anyone in his way, his eyes seeing only the black car across three lanes, keys in the ignition, the one chance to get away, to save the dream.

He crosses one lane, skidding crazily on the ice and snow. And somehow a thought begins to arrive, half-formed, half-imagined, the start of a realization that he isn't going to make it.

There's too much in the way, too many uniforms around him, too many guns out.

He can see the sneer on the sharp rock-like faces. They would shoot him without a qualm, but they know they can save the bullets. He's unarmed and cornered. An old man in a hurry, going nowhere.

But he isn't going to stop. Won't go quietly. The thought of the days and months of beatings and interrogations won't let him give up.

And there's a way out. But not the black car. A blessed way out. Past one more set of railings and he's seen it way over to his left. A freight truck with a driver in a freezing blue cabin, the police shouting at him, gesticulating with their sticks and guns to get him out of the way. And he's scared, scared like a rat. His right foot flat on the floor and the wheels spinning insanely in the ice.

Arkady catches sight of him and his heart jolts.

The driver stares straight ahead seeing nothing but the road.

Three feet away and Arkady launches himself into the truck's path.

There is nothing the driver can do to stop. His brakes shudder, but the wheels race on regardless. Impact is so fast that he's barely aware it's happened. And the vodka that he drank, to keep from dying of cold in the heater-less cabin, has slowed his reactions.

The truck jacknifes, hits a bollard and lurches violently onto its side.

Somewhere, under the massive superstructure, Arkady Mazurin felt a flash of relief. His heart stopped thumping and he could feel the new calm flooding into his bloodstream. His run from the airport, his refusal to give in – these were life-affirming gestures. He was indeed free. He had exercised that freedom and made his choices. And in the moment before darkness, it occurred to him that now, after all, he might reach the new life he had wanted for so long.

Margo walked away and didn't turn back. She spoke into the two-way microphone for no more than fifteen seconds, then caught a taxi outside the arrivals hall.

Another few minutes and they would surround the airport, close the whole area. No one would get out for hours.

All the way back, the images kept repeating, Arkady's face, the cold, wide eyes, his clumsy dash through the concourse, the shocked faces, an old man in a long, black coat, tearing headlong across the blackened ice towards his death.

Dozens, scores of people had turned to watch his final seconds on earth, the police with their guns drawn, the rest with open mouths, the ending of this desperate, last bid never in doubt. Not for a second.

It had been the worst of all sights, seeing the dogs surround their victim, ready for the kill. The point, visible to all, where hope finally trickles away and the dying begins.

At least Arkady had cheated them of the torture and misery they would have enjoyed inflicting.

Small comfort on a lonely airport road, way outside Moscow, frozen in by the Russian winter.

Two hours later she found the British Embassy all but deserted. Only Evans was waiting for her. He retrieved his key from the main desk, let her into his office and watched in silence as she wrote the coded cable to London.

The facts, the impressions, the context. Ministers always wanted context – a working hypothesis – something to indicate they knew what they were talking about. Especially when they didn't.

She couldn't know what had gone wrong, but it was clear that Arkady had almost got away.

Even before he left his flat, she was certain Moscow had known nothing about him or his intention to defect.

And yet a snap tip-off, a gift from a clear blue sky, had reached them just in time.

Margo got up and looked out across the city.

She'd seen other women cry when bad news had hit the Service. Men too. There was no longer the same pressure to 'button it' and 'hold it together' as there had been. The fact was that these days you could cry your bloody eyes out and no one took any notice.

But Margo felt not the slightest inclination to cry. Besides, she decided, Arkady would have had no use for tears. Not with his childhood in an orphanage, nor later at the KGB where they had worked on decoupling his emotions, marrying him to an ideology, buttressed by fear. No, he would have found a more useful way to show his feelings. And he'd have been right.

She thought she'd grown up since Mikhail's abduction, but there was a coldness inside her that she hadn't felt before.

Manson called on the secure line. No greeting. No enquiry about her or the Moscow team. 'What's the working hypothesis?'

Pompous arse, she thought. 'He was blown for God's sake . . .'

'Or he fucked up himself . . .' Manson seemed out of breath, as if he'd just climbed the stairs.

She was going to answer but didn't want them to squabble like two children in a playground. Seemed undignified, disrespectful after a man had died.

'Anyway,' he said, 'this conversation can wait. Get yourself to London in the morning. Meeting at midday. By then we might know a little more.'

'I'll be there.'

'You'd better be.'

Margo caught the blame in his intonation.

She cut the connection and looked across at Evans. So there was to be a witch hunt in London and Manson was already leading the charge. Hadn't taken long. Mazurin's body would have barely reached the mortuary. By the time she arrived in London the venom would be flowing everywhere, especially in her direction.

But she wasn't finished yet in Russia.

'Thank you for what you did . . .' she told Evans.

'I was just a bystander. He wasn't going anywhere.'

'I'm worried about his family – ex-wife, really. You know what they'll do.'

'Maybe not. They've been divorced a long time. But I'd be surprised if they didn't bring her in for questioning at some point, especially since he's not around anymore.'

'We need to look in on her pretty quickly and move her if possible. We owe her something for what happened.'

Evans put on his coat and held the door for Margo. He could have kicked himself for not having the same idea.

MOSCOW

Somehow she knew. The same way people often do. Knew that Arkady had gone. The dog had felt it first. Ever since early evening Vasya had lain in his basket and refused to get up or to eat. His bowl of water lay untouched beside him.

Yelena had tried reading her papers, a new scientific journal, some mathematical research, but her eyes kept sticking on the lines, absorbing nothing.

As a scientist, she had little faith in telepathy but she also had a keen sense of the limits of her knowledge, reminding her students that a little humility in science went a long way. 'You should always allow for the universe of the unknown,' she would say. 'And that's pretty much everything around us. A hundred years from now and people will be wondering why we were so stupid, why we didn't see what was staring us in the face.'

She looked down at Vasya, his eyes open, fixed on the wall ahead of him. Whatever had happened, he had felt it and his mood had darkened visibly. Something of that unknown universe, had come into the little kitchen and sat down beside them.

Poor Arkady, she thought. His mistake had been to want the

wrong things. Like a different life. Dream if you have to but you're always stuck with the life you were born with. The one that shapes and conditions you. The one that never lets you go.

Escape – real escape – was nothing more than a dangerous fantasy.

She pulled an ancient scrap of linen from her skirt pocket, blew her nose and wept a little for the man she had once loved.

At midnight she turned on the radio news, heard of an accident at the airport at Domodedovo. A man had been killed by a truck. There'd been a huge police presence, so far unexplained. A cordon remained around the airport. It looked as though flights might be delayed well into the morning.

So that was it. There would be no sleep tonight. And by the time the sun came up over Moscow, her life would be changed forever.

'Someone might come and ask questions.' That's what Arkady had said.

Damn right, someone would come. Maybe five or six someones, breaking down her door in the hours to come and inquiring about what her 'traitor husband' had been intending to do.

They'd beat her first. That was the way such 'inquiries' began. And then the interrogation, on and on, hour after hour.

When did you see him last? What did he say? Who put him up to it? Who was he working for? You're lying, lying, lying.

She remembered it all so well – the time when they'd caught her in the sixties with some underground literature, a few flimsy sheets of nonsense that she had found in the street, and had banged her up in a cell, before finding out her husband was KGB.

That had really made them shit their pants. One by one they had lined up to offer their abject apologies – their 'didn't knows', 'hadn't thoughts', 'would never have done its', 'please forgive us'. Like little boys with fear dripping from their noses, scared stiff that the bullies from the Lubyanka would go after them and rearrange their testicles.

She had almost laughed at the thought of one bunch of Soviet thugs, humbled by another – until she remembered how much she hated them all.

Tonight, there was no point going to bed. She fetched a blanket and wrapped it around her. Outside, the temperatures had sunk again and the heating was struggling. She switched off all the lights except for the one in the hall and left the door to the kitchen ajar. That way she would see them, before they saw her. It was the last advantage she would enjoy.

Finally, she took the largest of the kitchen knives from its drawer, tested the blade with her thumb and hid it in the folds of the blanket.

She had a pretty good idea what to do – as long as her courage held.

From the British embassy, they took the metro to Taganskaya, then walked a mile to a set of small garages where two unmarked Zhiguli cars, blessed with Russian plates, were kept for occasional use.

On payment of a sizable bribe, the registrations had been falsified at the State Auto Inspectorate and if the vehicles were stopped, they would survive all but the most detailed checks.

Evans chose the dirtiest of the cars and drove fast and in silence through the Moscow night. Snow had been forecast earlier in the day, but the winds had blown it inexorably eastwards and it looked as though the city would be spared fresh falls. Ahead of them, to the south-east, he glimpsed a strong moon in a clear sky.

He stopped three blocks from her apartment building and Margo pulled a plastic bag from the back seat. Inside it were some old potatoes and apples. She gripped it and took his arm with her other hand. Another Moscow couple, heading home after a late night and some shopping.

After a few minutes they dropped down an underpass and crossed under a four-lane highway. In the distance, a local train, the *elektrichka* clattered out into the suburbs. A vast street hoarding shouted about a lottery and the millions of rubles that could be won. Beside it an elderly woman tried in vain to lift a drunk, lying inert in the snow, and then gave up.

Margo hesitated for a second but Evans steered her on.

'Almost there,' he whispered. 'Sorry about the nightlife.'

They passed more red-brick blocks, grimy shop windows. The darkness and the cold unremitting.

And then she knew they'd arrived. Fifty yards away two black BMWs had parked at crazy angles half on, half off the pavements, blocking the entrance to a six-storey building. One of the cars had its front wheels yanked at right angles to the chassis, as if to break a skid. Someone had arrived in a hurry.

'Keep going,' she told him. 'Don't stop now.'

They were too late. Margo could see that. Her professional instinct, her good sense told her to get out immediately, as far away as they could. But the voice inside wouldn't let her. They turned again into a dim-lit courtyard. A few lights burned in the other blocks but almost all the flats were in darkness.

Most cities just sleep at night, she thought. This one dies.

She pulled up her collar and the two of them stepped further into the shadows. There was a chance the security men would simply frighten the old woman and leave. After all, she couldn't get away on her own. They could arrest her anytime they wanted.

But she knew it wouldn't go that way. Violence was the default setting in Russia. The instrument of first resort. The FSB would be charged with handling a monumental screw-up. Not an occasion for gentleness or mercy.

She realized she was still holding Evans's arm but she didn't let it go. They would wait until the cars drove away and pick up whatever pieces were left. She doubted it would take very long.

Yelena was calm and at peace.

Twenty minutes earlier, she had knelt down on the floor and stroked the dog's head. He was still refusing to eat. Perhaps he was sick. In any case there was nothing more she could do for him.

In the darkness they looked at each other and drew comfort from each other's presence.

She had caught a single footstep on the landing outside the apartment, so it wasn't a shock when the door smashed open. Three huge bodies, armed with pistols and flak jackets forcing their way in – somehow everywhere at once. Within a second, a powerful flashlight shone into her eyes – and then the kitchen light was on and the three of them stood in front of her. Creatures of the night, she thought. Killers who worked silently and in darkness. Untamed. Unstoppable.

'Federal Security.' The lead man was thin and wiry, close-cropped hair, moustache. He put his gun in his pocket. 'You know why we're here?'

She smiled. 'Someone hasn't paid their phone bill, I suppose.'

He crossed the room in two strides and slapped her hard across the face.

'I don't like jokes.' He hit her again and stood over her. She winced a little, but he couldn't wipe away the smile.

'You are Mazurina, Yelena Fydorovna?'

She nodded and spat a tooth onto the floor. 'You people don't change, do you? Every new breed, just as violent as the last.'

'Then you know what to expect. Get your coat, you're coming with us.'

'I can't leave my dog . . .'

The man next to the moustache lifted his gun, calmly attached a silencer and smiled at Yelena. 'You don't have to worry . . .' Carefully and with evident enjoyment, he shot Vasya twice in the head. 'You see, now you don't have to worry at all. Not a care in the world. The dog has been well looked after.'

She turned away and threw up over the floor. She had expected everything except that. Even after all these years, they could still surprise her with the most staggering displays of cruelty. There were no limits to it. Perhaps there never had been.

In any case, it was enough. Arkady and Vasya were both gone. It was time to end it.

She got up shakily and turned towards the sink, as if to throw up again. One last bit of strength. That's all it would take. Inside the blanket, she turned the knife towards her and with all her force, sank it into her chest, just below the ribcage.

She couldn't stop the cry of agony from her lips, but as they seized her and spun her round, she managed to laugh out loud. She didn't hear their shouts and obscenities, didn't feel them trying to drag the knife from her hand, the cries of disgust as her blood spurted over them.

Yelena sank to the floor and tried to speak. She tried to say she wouldn't be going with them, after all – and they could fuck themselves to hell and back again, for all she cared – but she didn't know if she'd said it out loud or just thought it.

In that moment the room seemed so cold and dark and yet the light was still burning. And the men . . . With her left hand she tried to wrap the blanket tighter around her, staunching the flow of blood, a survival instinct that even at the end was impossible to fight. Within seconds, though, she was unconscious.

They heard the two BMWs leave. Not in a hurry, but quietly, slowly, their tyres scratching at the packed ice by the roadside.

Evans led the way quickly to the main entrance. Like most Moscow apartment buildings you needed a code to gain entry – but he kicked the door hard and it opened easily, as if it was used to it.

The hallway, in old, Soviet, light blue, was daubed with graffiti and stank of cigarette smoke. They took the stairs.

At the apartment door, Margo signalled Evans to wait and listened for a moment. The door had been left ajar, lights still burned inside. She took off her shoes and tiptoed into the kitchen but she couldn't prevent the involuntary gasp at what she saw.

Yelena was on the floor, leaning at an angle against the cupboard beneath the sink, a blanket drenched with blood lay around her, a knife handle protruding from its folds. Beside her, Margo registered the body of a dog with two clear bullet holes between the eyes.

She crouched down and felt for a pulse on the woman's temple. It was barely there. She was dying in front of her eyes.

'Can you hear me?' She spoke quietly into her ear. 'I'm from the British embassy. Can you understand what I'm saying?'

The eyes didn't open, but she saw a finger move and reached down to hold her hand.

Yelena seemed to mouth the word 'Arkady'.

'I'm afraid he didn't make it.' Margo gripped her hand more tightly. 'I'm so sorry. There was nothing any of us could do.'

She realized then that Yelena had gone. There was no need to search again for a pulse. She placed the woman's hand back on the blood-stained blanket and stood up in the tiny kitchen.

Everywhere she looked there was blood. On the walls, in the sink, spattered across the body of the dog.

Even worse that it was in the kitchen – the room where life was always lived in Russia, where vodka was drunk, songs sung, guests seated, jokes told and retold.

Not a room for dying. Not this way.

Back in the car, she sat still for a few moments, inhaled deeply and closed her eyes. In more than twenty years in the Service, she had never experienced a day of such irretrievable darkness.

There was no way to finesse the carnage. You stand in a cockroach-infested kitchen and an elderly woman sits on the floor with a knife in her chest, accompanied only by a dog with two bullet holes between the eyes – and fine words don't help you.

Perhaps they never can.

* * *

Right up close, she had seen two elderly people die in fear and extreme pain. So close that she had touched them both in their final seconds of life. And been of no help to either.

Her job had been to babysit Arkady out of Moscow and all the way to a new life in Britain. But the old one wouldn't let him go. The moment the security police had arrived at his flat, he was finished.

Evans started the car and drove out slowly onto the highway. She couldn't look at the city, couldn't look at people who lived and died in cruelty and violence and thought it was normal. Accepted it, *made* it normal; told lies to themselves, pretended everything was fine and taught their children, generation after generation, to close their eyes and do the same.

Kneeling in that kitchen, Margo had told Yelena the truth about her ex-husband, that he hadn't made it, that his life was over. And she was glad she'd done it. You don't send people to their grave under false pretences.

The car stopped at a traffic light and she watched a crowd assembling beside a bus stop, the morning light pale and uncertain. The shadows of winter never far away.

She was tired of lying. Tired of the damage it left behind.

Every lie, she thought, destroys something, however small, for someone.

When you lie and go on lying, nothing is real.

WASHINGTON DC

I t was long past midnight. Yanayev stood still in the hall of the residence. He didn't remove his coat or hat. Didn't answer his wife's greeting from the bedroom.

Lydia hurried down the stairs. 'What is it, Vitaly? What happened?'

He shrugged as if to indicate he didn't want to talk about it.

'Is it all fine – did they get the man in Moscow?'

'Yes, yes, yes. Everything happened as it was supposed to. No doubt I'm a hero of the State and I'm told the Foreign Minister himself will call me. He hasn't, of course. Probably can't find the number . . .' He tried to smile.

She put a hand on his. 'You didn't like this, did you? Didn't like the way it was done . . .'

He nodded. His head suddenly seemed heavy, like pig-iron, bolted to the body. She took his coat and hat and led him into the living room. No lights, just the two of them, the grey, snowy garden, at peace and silent beyond the windows.

'A man died today because of what I did . . .'

'But—'

'Wait, hear me out, Lydia. This man who I had never met, never even heard of. He made a run for it at the airport, was chased of course by our goons, and got run over by a truck.' He sighed. 'So they won't need to bother with a trial and won't need to rig it either – which of course they would have done, just to be on the safe side. You can't be too careful . . .'

'Vitaly . . .' It came as a warning this time.

'I know, I know – microphones everywhere, but I'm with *you* – here – now – and I'm damned if I won't say what I feel.'

She moved closer and put her arms round him.

'All these years . . . first the lunacy of Communism, then the drunkenness and corruption of Yeltsin, and now this lot, with their prisons full to bursting and the law torn into shreds. Even Gorbachev says so. Whatever happens, we can't seem to live in a normal country . . . I, I'm a diplomat, I should have stuck to that, left all the secret nonsense to Dmitrov and his clowns on the second floor. But Harry Jones came to me – I was flattered, I admit it, and I wanted to do something. Something for once that wouldn't end in blood and death.'

'The man who died was a traitor, Vitaly.'

'Maybe he was. In other countries that would have been decided by a court with judges who think for themselves, instead of lapdogs waiting for a call from the Kremlin before they can open their snouts.'

'That's Russia, my dear . . .'

'That's what we always say.' His voice lowered to a whisper. 'And that's why it never changes.'

WESTERN SYRIA

Just before you die, you will make a discovery. She forgot who had told her that – but she now knew it was true.

They had forced Mai to stand, bound her hands behind her back with cord, kicked her down the broken, wooden staircase.

A gust of air caught her face. She saw a wall half-standing, blackened plaster, a lightbulb swinging gently in the breeze. More steps into the basement. Three, maybe four of the men were there – or were there more? Light dropped down intermittently through holes in the ceiling. There was no talking, no hysteria. She couldn't see their faces, but she could hear the breathing.

What do you think about, when your time is up? She had often wondered.

Her mind groped for the faces she had loved, the hands, the warm smiles, but it was moving too quickly . . .

And then the bag over the head. And that's where your life hits the wall at the end of the road. But there was no terror. *That* was the discovery. Terror is not about what *will* happen to you. It's about what *might*.

Certainty of any kind is comfort. Even now, she thought, as the final seconds of life rolled away.

So she draws herself up to full height, legs slightly apart, and she can feel that her pulse is normal.

I can play your game and beat you at it . . .

A gun is cocked beside her head, just an inch away, and then just as the words of a childhood prayer start to form in her mind, the trigger is pulled.

And there is only the dull metallic click of metal on metal.

She loses her footing, stumbles, but doesn't fall – her hand collides with cold, rough concrete. The building half-destroyed or half-finished – that was the choice in the Arab world, nothing ever completed. Not even a farce like this.

She now knows today was sport not business.

Today was to remind her that it isn't God who'll decide when she's to die. It's a stinking little rat from a Syrian village she's never heard of, who can't even read a book or multiply two numbers. But he has a gun and an unbelievably inflated sense of his own importance and he will finish the job when he feels like it. Tomorrow or the day after, or in a week's time, when the excitement and lust for blood will be too much for him to contain.

Someone whipped the bag off her head. And she can see them against the bare brick walls. Kids, no more than twenty. All grinning stupidly as if they were playing tricks at school.

And she can't stop the rush of blood to her head, the ragged breathing, her legs threatening to buckle. But it's only a few moments. Nobody moved.

She held up her head, looked at them and spat on the floor in contempt.

Only then did they hit her.

She slipped in and out of consciousness. Time shaken, then stopped, then shaken again.

Each time her eyes opened she would grasp for the image, try to hold it in both hands. And each time someone dragged it from her, forcing her back into darkness.

Once, she remembered being a little girl. She sat on a swing and shrieked with laughter – but she didn't know why. A crowd of people looked on and laughed with her. Even her dog was laughing. She reached out to touch his head, but he turned away.

And then there were tears that fell through the laughter. Cold tears, like winter rain. She wondered where they came from, wondered if she still had a home, wondered if anyone would ever come to take her back to it.

It was after five in the evening when Mai awoke. She shivered from the draft along the bare floorboards, and felt the stabbing, seething pain return.

She remembered the two young Arabs standing over her in the half-light between day and darkness, the close-cropped hair, their studied, immovable expressions; remembered them backing away from her, washing their bloody hands in a bowl of water, drying them on clean, stripy towels they had brought with them, as if they had simply finished their shift and were going home after a good day's work.

Remembered the avalanche of pain.

To a torturer, she recalled, the interval is just as important as the violence. It gives the victim sufficient time to replay the deep and abiding pain that has been inflicted and to build maximum fear before it all begins again. Time was on their side, not hers.

She could hear traffic in the distance but it was the smells that reminded her where she was: cordite and cigarette smoke, the sweat of unwashed bodies, unwashed for days – and old blood, spattered on the streets and in the skewed, punched-in houses, like this one.

Darkness had drifted in across the jagged rooftops and satellite dishes, a blue light flashed in an alley on the other side of the square. There were voices shouting, always shouting. No one talked anymore in the Arab world. All they did was scream and cry and wail against the madness that had closed in around them.

She didn't sit up. You learn very quickly that movements are a dangerous luxury. Only move if you have to, when you know where you're going, when you have a plan.

Her eyes toured the dismal room, empty except for the chunks of crumbling plaster, blown away from the ceiling, smashed china in the corner, paper and boxes everywhere. A single men's shoe stood alone on a window ledge like a prized artefact.

They had asked her only two questions in Syrian Arabic – the language of her family, her childhood and the innocence she had left behind.

What are you doing in Syria? Who sent you?

And each time she repeated the answers they'd given her in Washington and each time they beat her.

She turned painfully onto her back and wondered about the time. Three hours, she reckoned, since she'd arrived. Two days since she had understood with absolute certainty that she was going to die.

'My name's Mai.'

The American security guard had shaken her hand and smiled in disbelief.

'No really,' she said, 'it's my real name. There's no reason why you shouldn't know it. Especially since we're going to be spending some time together.'

For a moment they had both stood there in silence on the tarmac at Incirlik airbase in southern Turkey.

She thought he looked about fifteen. Too young to be doing this.

Two other guards had joined them – they looked ill at ease, sharing names – Matt, Charlie and Owen . . . all in jeans and T-shirts. She could almost have been their mother.

They gave a little whoop of excitement as the helicopter spun its rotor and lifted them into a cloudless, blue sky. She could see on their faces – they all believed they'd be going home when it was done.

Hours later they had landed in darkness outside Antakya, close to the Syrian border, and been taken to a small house on a hillside.

The smell of apricots and olives made her smile. For a moment, she thought she remembered a summer evening in Damascus, happy voices, singing, long before the war and the treachery that had taken her to America.

Someone had left food in the house, kebabs and flatbread – she had warmed the meat on the stove, before clearing the table and getting out the maps.

It was always the same with plans – too many or not enough. But this one seemed better than most – devised outside the federal agencies by people paid from so-called 'black budgets' – un-announced in public and unapproved by Congress. This was the money that let the president of the United States do what he wanted, when he wanted.

And he had wanted a little team to go into Syria and do some serious damage to the leadership.

He had wanted it to join forces with any of the moderate rebel groups that could be bought or rented, to cut through the terrible confusion and mayhem, and in an operation way off the books and never to be acknowledged, to take out Syria's presidential palace.

An operation with no footprints and no attribution.

Which was why they had turned to Mai.

The daughter of a Syrian émigré doctor and an American mother, she had done her time in Washington's spy community. Native Arabic had helped – so had mental agility. But there was something else as well. The guts to tell the men with the red power ties and the button-down white shirts the real story, instead of the one they wanted to hear. They could have put it about that she was a lousy team player – but somehow the charge never stuck. And the guts did. Besides, her teams went out to the violent and volatile places around the world and came home again. One or two without legs or teeth. But there weren't many who achieved even that. And when she spoke in the tiny, classified gatherings, mostly in rooms many storeys underground, Mai had a quiet authority that made even the young officers lean forward so as not to miss her words.

For all that, there could have been a desk waiting for her high in the CIA hierarchy – but the White House talent spotters had seen her first.

Job one had been to get her outside the Beltway – spirit away the woman, with the big dark eyes and the jet black hair and put her with the grandees of US Intelligence who rarely, if ever, showed their faces to anyone.

A few of them had surfaced briefly over the years. Not in pretty pictures but in scandals such as Iran Contra or the allegations that the CIA had helped drug smuggling into the US, or the killings in Guatemala and El Salvador.

She had asked around in Washington and the view had been pretty much unanimous: these were formidable players on the outer edges of the establishment and the law.

But there was a choice that had been spelled out as well: if you want to spend all your time answering stupid questions in congressional committee hearings then you go to the CIA – if you want to get things done, there's another place.

And when she had watched in silent fury, month after month, the endless killings and the destruction of the country she had loved, Mai had gone looking for that other place and had knocked on the door.

Outside the room, she could hear them climbing the stairs, two maybe three of them. More shouting, more anger. She knew what to expect – and she realized in a moment of sudden clarity that the blood she had smelt when she woke up had been her own.

AMMAN/JORDAN

By early morning Ahmed could read between the lines. The Russians were unhappy. The information he'd sent had been useful – but too late to be of maximum benefit.

'What do you need now?' he had asked.

But Moscow had gone silent.

He knew better than to ask again. Russians weren't touchy-feely employers. Even when things went well there was no jumping up to lick his face, no lavish praise, no cake.

There was, however, an occasional, curt 'thank you' and an extra 2,000 dollars in an envelope – and that passed for gratitude. The kind you could take to the bank.

Ahmed preferred it that way. He didn't do pleasantries either. Moscow would tell him soon enough what it wanted.

WESTERN SYRIA

They hadn't come after all, the two torturers, with their clipped moustaches and plastic briefcases.

Perhaps there had been someone else to visit. Perhaps she had simply imagined the footsteps in the wounded, battered house.

Mai lay on her back and tried to remember what had gone wrong.

She could still see the friendly, open faces of her security guards: Matt from the limitless plains of Montana, Charlie from New York, Owen from all sorts of places, none of which had earned the coveted title *home*.

They were good and solid – stuck to the script, followed the map – didn't deserve what happened to them.

There is always fear. You allow for it, use it to keep you sharp, just as she had on the night-time dash across the Turkish border and the awful ride in the back of the pickup. The roads were moonscape – craters and rocks, untouched, it seemed, by human engineering. But they'd known that all along. You took bad roads to avoid bad people. Golden rule of the covert op. No one expected a joyride.

At the edge of a village, they took on a guide. A young fighter from the Free Syrian army, no more than twenty. He was exactly where he should have been at the time he was supposed to be there.

Only that never happened in the Arab world. Too damn easy to be true. Should have set off all the red lights from there to Cincinnati. But they had wanted to believe it – wanted an early success. Weren't in the mood to turn down good fortune. Her fault.

She opened her eyes, staring at the cracked ceiling, counting the holes. She should have known better. Did know better. But she hadn't wanted to dampen the boys' morale, knew how quickly it could drain away. Maybe it would work out.

So very stupid to think that way.

In the back, the young Syrian fighter stank of sweat and pressed his leg against her thigh. He couldn't resist, could he? The boy might die that night so he wanted a grope before he went. 'Animal,' she whispered to him. But she didn't push him away. So maybe she'd wanted it as well.

They got out after two hours, pissed and changed places. Owen drove, Matt riding shotgun, she in the middle. Fifty miles down, another seventy before they would meet the local team. The route meticulously planned.

The boys had their coordinates, GPS systems, best of the secret stuff, with a dedicated satellite all for them, they said. They'd done this before, they said. Plenty of times, said Matt. Just a few, whispered Owen, who didn't do hype or bravado.

They didn't talk after that.

They had looked so fresh, all three of them, heading into darkness.

And then the guide started shouting – Arabic first, then mutilated English – seemed they had missed a turning, were way off track.

'Jesus, fucking unbelievable.' The first volley of expletives, the first sign that nerves were on edge.

'Get a grip guys, keep steady . . .' She was between Charlie and Matt. Owen said nothing. He'd be the strong one, she thought, if it all went to hell.

They stopped the truck. Changed the number plates. Buried the green tarpaulin that had covered the back, exchanged it for a new one: filthy grey, decades-old, covered in oil. Standard procedure in case they'd been clocked.

Owen was driving when they made the turn. The guide said they'd screwed it up. He was yelling into his mobile phone. 'We're on our way, we're on our way.'

'Cut the phone,' she told him in Arabic.

But he wouldn't do it. Went into local dialect, said he didn't like the way things were going, wasn't happy . . . She tore the phone out of his hands, slammed it on the dashboard, glass everywhere. She flipped the sim card and threw it out of the window. The Syrian put his head in his hands.

'You OK?' she said to Owen.

He didn't reply, maybe hadn't heard, his entire focus on the road ahead. No markings, no barriers, no lights. The van was heading for a ridge, the moon bright against the hilltop. The tyres weren't gripping, so the wheels skittered and slid and the gears jarred as he fought to change them. But the boy knew what he was doing, knew how to drive. The van kept moving.

She looked across at the others – big black, military tablets in their hands, data pumping out across the screens.

How many times had they rehearsed this in Washington, checked and re-checked with the local teams, checked their backgrounds, their parents and cousins and distant aunts? For fuck's sake, they had done the best with the crap choices on offer. Information was patchy, stories didn't always add up, facts were omitted, memories short and fallible. Not every question mark indicated a lie. Not every dubious explanation came from a fabricator. People don't always think or recall in logical, sequential bites. Especially in warzones.

Mai checked her watch, verified the coordinates. Her satellite phone registered a single codeword which meant the local teams were in place. For the first time she felt a jolt of excitement. The word was 'Gazelle'. It made her smile.

The locals were to meet them at the southern end of a hamlet, three hundred metres past the last house. They'd seen the satellite pictures, knew that the territory was open, that any lights would be visible from far away. But open was safer. That had been the expert judgement from Washington.

She thought back: so much wisdom imparted, so many earnest men and women, sharing their best calls and judgements, tracing you a path between fear and confidence, always reminding you that confidence was the final treat that had to wait until the journey home. You never unpacked it before then.

They had known that the ridge would be the hardest part – for at least a minute, they'd be lit up by the moon – a noisy, clumsy target that would be visible for miles around. Worse, they'd have to manoeuvre their way between giant rocks, where the road would be little more than a surface smear.

'You guys need to hang on from now' – Owen leaned forward and seemed to hug the oversize steering wheel – 'this is gonna be a bad part.'

They all reached for a handle or the back of a seat and the van had skidded wildly in the corners.

She could remember thinking that the moonlight was brighter than she had ever known. And then Owen was braking hard and swearing, and right in front of them, blocking the road was a dark truck.

Owen glanced over to her. 'I can't get through here . . . what do you want me to do? We're going to have to stop.'

Instinctively, she had drawn her pistol; she could hear the others cocking their machine guns.

And in that moment, she had known why the light was so bright, known that it hadn't come from the moon at all, that the danger was behind them, not in front.

But there was no one in sight. Not before the stun grenades and the first clatter of machine gun bullets, smashing into the van from all angles.

And then, just as rapidly, the firing stopped. She couldn't tell who was injured. Nobody was speaking, so maybe they were all dead already. A strange silence seemed to descend on the van.

She could see around her a grey mist, all the movements in slow motion.

A hand with a pistol attached to it came through the window, calmly and with no sense of urgency and she watched Matt's head jerking sideways with the blood and tissue exploding around him.

Turning, she saw Owen half out of the truck, caught twice in the back, catapulted forward and lost in the shadows beside the vehicle.

And then darkness seemed to stamp on her head, squeezing out the air, forcing her into a tunnel with nothing at the end of it.

In all probability, someone had swiped her with the butt of a rifle, pushed her out of the car and let her drop on the stone track. One of the highest-rated operatives in America's clandestine services, trained and trained again for emergencies like this one. Trained for the day when her lifelines would break, her communications went down, her presence betrayed and she was the last person on the team left alive.

But all they had needed to do, was pick her up like a broken puppet from the rough track, where she lay face down and inert, sling her in the back of a truck and take her wherever they wanted.

She didn't know why it had gone so badly wrong. But she knew they'd made mistakes. The mission had been fatally flawed. They'd ignored the glaring question marks and the inconsistencies and the biographies of their contacts that didn't quite add up. Why? Because nothing in the fucking Arab world ever added up. Nobody told the truth. Nobody. All they ever did was find out what you wanted to hear and tell it back to you.

And instead of walking away from this farce, you went in because these catastrophically, lousy odds of success were the best you were ever going to get. This year, next year or at any other point in this grotesque conflict.

Small wonder then that the whole thing had fallen apart before her eyes and taken her to hell in a dying land.

Look at it, she told herself, and cry your heart out.

But Mai was long past crying.

WASHINGTON DC

Soon after nine a.m. Lydia Yanayeva drove her car to the Safeway along MacArthur Boulevard and hurried inside with her shopping bag.

She was tired. Vitaly had fallen asleep the moment his head hit the pillow, but she had got up and stayed writing for more than two hours.

It shouldn't have taken so long, but she wanted to include as much relevant detail as possible and to make sure that her handwriting was neat and legible. After all, there were no copies and nothing had been written on the computer.

As she walked around the aisles, she searched for the things that Vitaly liked most. Kiwi fruit, yoghurt, French cheese. Really, the choice was excellent.

At the hardware shelves, she put down her bag, to reach up for some cleaning fluid, taking a few moments to choose the one she wanted.

She was aware of several other people in the same aisle but she paid no attention – simply located the item she sought, picked up the rest of her shopping and paid for it.

Once inside the car, a quick glance at the bag showed that the papers she had written were gone – and she smiled inwardly at the efficiency with which it had been handled. The way it was always handled, ever since the process had begun.

Lydia switched on the engine and drove back towards the residence. In about thirty minutes, she estimated, her report would be in Tel Aviv.

No one at the White House had asked why Harry Jones was absent. The people who needed to know, knew. Or thought they did. To the others, everything about Harry was a classified secret.

As is the custom, a military aide had brought the overnight intelligence briefing from Langley, with inputs from State and the Pentagon.

So he knew what had happened at Domodedovo airport. The outlines, at least. He knew events had transpired. From New York, came the signal that Mazurin would not be transiting the city for reasons that were already clear.

So far then, it seemed the US Intelligence machine was running in 'report' mode only. No one had begun asking the 'whys'.

Why had Mazurin died? Why had the security services gone after him? Why did it all have the feeling of a last-minute leak?

But it wouldn't be long before the agencies were tasked to answer those questions. And answer they would.

He might have made mistakes, but he had done so with his eyes open – and he wasn't naïve. The formidable array of listeners, roaming the digital galaxy, sucking out and filtering words by the billion, would track the communications footprints, one by one, right down to the earpiece radio on a Russian traffic cop at Moscow airport.

And eventually, they would tell you the origin of the orders that ended in the death of Arkady Mazurin.

Everything left a trace, the noise of the wind in the trees, seagulls beside the Verrazano Narrows; treachery in all its many incarnations.

If it moved, they could see it. If it emitted a sound, they heard it. Task the big machine, throw money at it, and it would go out and bring back whatever you wanted.

Harry had not the slightest doubt that one day soon an official car would draw up outside his house – with a police SUV parked a little way down the lane – and that a combination of local and federal officials, with their handcuffs and pistols on their belt and their practised little scripts, and a dozen different epaulettes and brightly-coloured shirt badges, would come up the path for *him*.

So let them come.

He closed the file on his desk and pushed his chair away from it. He felt nothing for Mazurin. His moment of doubt the night before had gone. You can shut out those feelings, he thought. You have to. The Russian had been the means to an end. Nothing more.

Besides, there had been no other way. A life for a life. Mai's for Mazurin's. Same old game since time had begun.

WESTERN SYRIA

This time they had brought her food. Some bread and cheese, flyblown and stale. A piece of watermelon, wrapped in newspaper. Mai didn't know if it was a prelude to execution and at that moment it didn't matter.

Dying well was all that mattered – which meant that whatever they did, you built a wall inside your head and put them on the other side; you didn't beg and you didn't cry. You held fast to the memories of those you had loved and carried them safe and intact into the next world.

She ate everything they had brought, licking the paper, tasting the sweetness of the juice. The two men watched her expressionless. She understood what they did, had seen the way they were trained, even read the makeshift manuals. They alternated cruelty and kindness because that was the quickest road to her mental destruction. Maximum uncertainty, and the crushing of hope each time it surfaced.

After the mock execution, Mai had had plenty of time to rehearse the real one – to play out the steps in her mind, to feel the sack dragged across her head, to smell the filth of it, to feel the blade against her throat.

If they couldn't induce terror in her, she knew they would settle for pain.

It was what the two men craved. Two men you would never look at on a street, or in a bus or train. Waiters or taxi drivers, perhaps. So ordinary that you might wonder if they had somehow stumbled into the wrong place. But not for long. Not when their hands began burning her skin or pounding the soles of her feet with a baseball bat, or forcing her head into a stinking bucket of water. Then you would wonder no more, at least until the work was done, when they combed their hair, washed their hands and headed home, God knew where.

She knew they wouldn't be satisfied if she simply faded away or died from bleeding or a heart attack. They had planned her death as a grand, meticulous performance which she, as lead actor, should experience to the full.

She was their enemy and they would insist that she die, screaming in defeat.

Long after they had left, Mai could hear the sound of cars and motorbikes snorting their way through distant traffic. Noises from another world. Close, but way beyond her grasp.

For a moment she imagined breaking down the door, fleeing into the damaged, night-time streets. But she knew that the Syria where she had grown up had long since been destroyed. The warm, funny, talented people, her friends from childhood, were out on the streets dying and killing, like everyone else.

And what you didn't see was worse. The rage inside a people, mad with grief, stripped piece by piece of their security, their certainty, their loved-ones – everything and everyone they had cherished, torn from their hands and blown apart. Each death to be mourned, each gravestone a call for vengeance, until no one would be left standing and no one could win.

Except Washington.

Harry's world. A world away from the broken, bloodied streets of Syria.

She was shocked that she hadn't thought of him till now. Dear Harry, who should have been a friend, not a lover. How had she let herself get close to him? Was it his power? His focus? She struggled to recall her feelings.

Back in America, it had seemed so clear. For the first time in so many years she had lain with a man who she knew with absolute certainty she could trust. Yes, a Washington animal. A spinner, a dealer, a power broker – a man who lied for his country and his president and pressed buttons that killed people around the world.

But the real Harry, the one inside the strange tweed suit, was someone who could manage all things and bear all burdens for the woman he said he loved.

And on the eve of a dangerous mission, back to her hate-infested country, she had needed some certainty.

He had told her he could make it all work. The mission. Their relationship. In her mind he became the sorcerer with unimaginable powers. And somehow, even with a wife so critically ill – he would arrange the pieces of their life – agonizing as they were, into an order they could accept. There would be process and result. They would eventually be together.

She shook her head in disbelief; all she could see was the madness they had created between them.

Even if she returned to America, there would be nothing left. She knew that now.

No way for them to sit at home in years to come, talking by the log fire about the people who had died, or the mistakes that were made or the downward spiral of her country into self-destruction.

Their relationship would always be the bastard child of a mission that had ended in catastrophic failure. It had no chance of surviving – didn't deserve to – probably never had.

Mai had never seen Harry's home – the clapboard house among the trimmed and pampered lawns of Maryland – how could she? But somehow she could picture a study full of books and a man with his fists clenched, sitting at his desk, out of his mind with worry about her. Harry, who would use every power and every lever he had to find her and get her out.

Harry who didn't know that it was all too late.

My poor Harry, she thought.

None of it was ever going to work.

WASHINGTON DC

Rosalind could hear him moving about downstairs, the opening and closing of the fridge, the drawer of a desk, his voice on the phone.

It seemed strange that in the midst of such a terrible illness, she could experience moments of incredible clarity. Sunlight seemed brighter, sounds more intense, the mind uncluttered by material and trivial concerns, now focussed on the single journey that remained.

She sat up in bed and looked out over the neat squares of garden and the white clapboard houses.

She had loved Harry Jones from the day she met him. The man who resembled a rural schoolteacher, but who had the intellect and the drive to make it to the White House and sit beside the president.

Such a surprising man, her father had once said.

She recalled her pride when they had been invited to the big gala events, the intimate dinners and barbecues and the tennis games with some of the biggest names in the world. How proud it had made her feel!

But not anymore. Not for a long time.

It had changed Harry. But then how could it not have? Gone were the lightness of spirit and the quick, easy smile. The ability and inclination to talk to anyone, whatever their rank or importance. In their place had arrived a new Harry who took himself so very seriously and had lost the joy of life. And the joy of her.

He was still attentive, did his duty. But the two of them, she realized, had gone from summer to winter – and there'd been no autumn in between. No companionship or affection, the way others seemed to enjoy it.

They kissed each other goodnight and good morning, but it was simply a part of the daily ritual, like brushing teeth or shoes, checking your tie in the mirror. No more than a habit.

She thought to herself that he might have had another woman in his life, but she dismissed the notion. Harry – strong, careful, conservative Harry – would never risk his job for something as mundane, as common, as that.

Not that she would have minded so much. She often told herself that she came from a time when women had so few expectations of their life, or even their husbands.

So what if he had a fling?

Besides, she wouldn't be around much longer and didn't want him to live on his own. Perhaps he would find a socialite with lots of big diamonds and a great white house on a hill. And Harry would be happy.

All the same she wanted to know, had even toyed with the idea of asking him outright. But then why spoil a pleasant atmosphere?

She didn't wish for any bad blood when she departed.

The only essential to pack was a little love. Asking for the truth as well would be a little excessive.

And so unnecessary.

When she got to the other end, she was certain they'd have everything she needed.

She listened for his voice but could no longer hear it.

Where are you, Harry? she wondered. Where did you go?

WESTERN SYRIA

Pain is what pain does.

She remembered the instructors writing it on a blackboard.

It can destroy logic and memory, sap your will to live, or resist. Even as you attach the last piece of mental armour you possess, pain can render it useless.

Mai had no idea how she had fallen asleep, nor whether the screaming was real or dreamed.

She opened her eyes, startled for a moment to see another pair, inches from her, staring calmly back.

As she focussed, she saw they belonged to a boy, no more than seven or eight years old.

Her first thought was that he might have wandered in off the street, or maybe he belonged to one of the torturers.

The creature was filthy, his once-grey T-shirt torn and faded, patchwork striped trousers with the legs caked in mud. Hair thick and dusty. A random witness, silent, his mind somewhere else. He brought nothing into the room, would take nothing away.

She sat up and coughed into her hand, seeing the dark red blood, spattered on her palm. Dark was worrying. But so what?

Her eyes met those of the child. He too looked down at the blood, but showed no reaction.

In that moment she thought she knew how his life would go; thought that when he grew up a little, reached the age of twelve or thirteen, he'd do some killing himself, because it wouldn't penetrate the brutal normality that had already shaped him.

Perhaps he had killed already.

In any case, Mai had a premonition that he would come back to this place to watch her die. Not out of interest or concern, but because on that day, whenever it came, there would be nothing better for him to do.

'Who are you?' she asked.

But the question brought no response.

She was about to speak again but the gunfire outside the building was sudden, shocking and intense. And the words never came. Heavy automatic weapons had opened up across the street and fire was being returned – but in single shots. Someone was heavily outnumbered.

Mai had barely moved in days, but when the fighting broke out she had flung herself on the boy, pulling him onto the hard stone floor, face down, breaking his fall with her arm.

There were shouts now. More firing in the distance. She wanted to catch a glimpse through the window on the other side of the room but couldn't leave the child. First instinct.

She looked around. One open door, leading somewhere, who knew where, in the broken building. Dust everywhere. More gunfire. A shout. 'Dead, dead.' And then there was silence.

She didn't move, couldn't know where the fighting was centred, who was shooting, who was dying.

Think. You need to think.

Beneath her, the boy was struggling. But she couldn't release him, couldn't let him run away. He was a threat to himself – and to her.

She kept her weight on top of him but lifted herself a few centimetres.

Outside was darkness. The street lamps had gone, shot out. Far away she could hear a siren, more shouting but the words were indistinct.

The single most difficult place to understand a battle is in the middle of it. They had always said that. No bullet carries a readable marking or label. Each is despatched with vicious, terminal intent towards a target that may or may not be you.

Even as a bystander to violence, you are overwhelmed by solid walls of heat and noise, way beyond any levels you have imagined or encountered.

You can do nothing except wait for a set of complex, random events – over which you cannot exercise the slightest control – to decide if you will live or die.

All this Mai knew.

A minute passed and the noise had gone somewhere else . . . a block away, maybe more, sporadic gunfire, car doors banging, a motor gunned and the sound of a car that sped away into the night.

She loosened her hold on the boy, didn't expect him to push upwards so fast and with such force, his head hammering against her jaw, slamming her backwards to the floor.

As she looks up he's already at the window, moving fast like a cat, climbing onto the sill, heading for the street outside if there is still a street. In that moment she wants to shout at him to stop, to come back into the shadows . . .

She sees him turn – it's just a tiny fraction of a second – but as he does so she can feel the force of a single bullet that punches straight through him, the tiny creature in his torn T-shirt and filthy striped trousers, lifting him clean off the sill and felling him to the bare stone floor, snatching away his life, even as it slams into the wall behind her.

She thought later that she had screamed but no sound came from her.

A few feet away, the boy's body lay face down, frozen against the floorboards. No need to check if he were dead. Mai could already feel the stillness, clinging to him like a shroud.

*   *   *

She shivered. A sharp, insistent wind had whipped into the damaged house, where once there might have been windows and life and light – and maybe even normal people.

Mai gathered what she could. A loose shirt, still in the rucksack she had carried when they took her. Socks, a pullover. The black leather jacket, though, had gone.

Glancing at the boy, she wondered in that moment if anyone would miss him and how they would get to know what had happened and who would bury him. Questions that had become mundane in a punished, violent land.

Into the corridor. The stone floor was strewn with rubble and broken glass. By the doorway, she found the upturned body of a young man. Even in the semi-darkness the bloodstained shirt was visible, evidence of a massive chest wound.

She knelt down and pulled off his jacket – heavy work, because the body didn't want to give it up, didn't want to be pushed around in death anymore than in life. In the struggle, she ripped one of the sleeves, but who would care? Even if the garment was stained in blood, it was dark and padded and would keep some of the wind at bay. As she got up, she caught a glint of light beside the body. It was the automatic pistol the man had used when they shot him. Maybe it was out of bullets. She ejected the magazine. Four left.

Rifling his pockets, she came across a spare magazine and felt a jolt of relief. For the first time in so many days, she had something. A single lucky chance in a lousy game.

Her eyes swept the street. On the other side was a burned-out shop, and a deserted villa, damaged, discoloured, deserted like all the buildings. Only the moon offered a meagre, unwelcoming light.

I need a plan.

In the distance there was more shooting. Heavy artillery. Perhaps it had gone on all the time and she had simply stopped listening.

I need shelter and I need food. And I don't know where I am.

She slipped out of the house and ran shakily across the rough gravel. There was no one in sight. An ancient car without wheels had been left on scrubland behind the shop. She knelt down beside it to catch her breath. Days had passed since she had even moved her legs.

In a little while, she would look for lights and families and people who – like her – were trying to survive.

If she could make those contacts and find shelter, she might somehow get through the night.

And yet it wouldn't be long before her torturers – if they were still alive – came looking for her, found her missing and shouted their heads off. And if they didn't talk, someone else would – like the kids who had pulled a bag over her head and played at executing her, or their masters, further up the ramshackle line of command.

Either way, whatever passed for an authority in this flea-pit town, would know soon enough that a captured American spy had escaped and was now on the run.

And at that point, the usual grotesque Middle Eastern collection of killers, bounty hunters and extremists of every political stripe and creed would crawl out from under their stone, sensing blood, and attempt to hunt her down.

She reckoned on an hour or two at most before the dogs were turned loose.

WASHINGTON DC

They met in a café on K Street. No time for pleasantries. Yanayev noted that Harry had dispensed with the tweeds. This was dark suit day. It was business. Harry was tight-lipped, impatient.

'I want to know where we are with our deal. I delivered on my side.'

'Yes, but you delivered late.'

Harry moved his chair closer. 'Listen carefully, Vitaly. I know what happened in Moscow. You identified your man and he died under a truck at the airport. If your guys were too late to hold one of your friendly question-and-answer sessions with him, that's your affair. I delivered. Now get me my package out of Syria.'

'We're working on it.'

'What does that mean?'

Yanayev looked at his watch. 'Ten hours ago we knew roughly where she was. But the situation is very fluid. There's been heavy fighting in the area. Information becomes out of date very quickly . . .'

'Just give me the last coordinates you had and I'll take it from there . . .'

'I don't have them, Harry. Moscow's handling this. The situation is very fluid, changing hour to hour. There are different militia groups fighting each other. Your people would never get in or out.'

'And yours can?'

'It's the best chance you have. You know how difficult the terrain is – and the lines between the factions keep shifting. Then there are the thousands of refugees on the move. Jordan has closed its border. Many people are desperate to cross. It's chaos, absolute chaos.'

'Then you can smuggle her out more easily . . .'

'Yes and no. The camps have their own hierarchy, their own watchers. The Jordanians are terrified of infiltrators. There's enough support in the country already for the black flag.'

'I don't want to hear about problems. Give me solutions.'

'And I'm not one of your junior staffers at the National Security Agency.

Remember that, Harry.'

They looked at each other in silence.

Jones leaned forward. 'I want you to remember something. I may have exceeded my brief here. I may have crossed the line in doing a deal with you. But unlike you, I can fight my case in a system that has laws and procedures. You don't have that luxury. Screw it up and you'll be enjoying the Vladivostok nightlife for the rest of your days.

Think about it. Don't fuck with me Vitaly.' Harry sat back. 'I want to know who your operative is in the field.'

'One of the most effective we have anywhere.'

'Has he been ordered to go in – is he preparing the op, getting his team in place?'

'And I told you, Moscow is handling it.'

'Christ almighty!'

Harry got up to go, but Yanayev reached out his arm to stop him.

'Listen, my friend. I need to ask you this . . .' He paused for a moment as if searching for words. 'If we can't get her out for any reason – whatever it is – is there anything else you want us to do? You said she has valuable information about you. It may come to this.'

'You mean kill her? Jesus, Vitaly . . . I'm going to try and forget you asked that. Don't ever speak that way to me again.'

Yanayev raised an eyebrow. There was a look in Harry's eyes that he hadn't seen before. It was, he reflected later, a rare glimpse of the man's other identity, the one so often obscured by the old-world charm, the good manners and tweed jackets. For all that, this was the president's enforcer-in-chief.

A man with some very jagged edges.

WESTERN SYRIA

Something had changed. Nothing you could see or hear – but it felt different. Normally when the guns went silent, people would come out into the streets – even late – just to see who was still alive, exchange a greeting, cuddle a child.

But not tonight.

The clouds were racing by, hounded by an easterly wind and only the rubbish and the sand danced in front of her.

Mai took a side street, pulling the dead man's jacket tight around her, searching for lights, a house with a car, a way out of the torturers' town, whose name she had no means of knowing.

As she looked back two pickup trucks were speeding fast through the deserted streets. Two was a bad sign. One driver could get lost, come home late, risk the streets at night. But two was something else. It signalled purpose and intention.

Mai was close to the outskirts of the town when she saw the light. Single light in a small window, half covered by a blind. It glowed for at least ten seconds so she hadn't imagined it. The one-storey villa was concrete and brick. To the front: a scarred, uneven drive-in, and an old Nissan Sunny, probably as old as her, shunted into the shadow of a tree.

She checked both directions. Behind her in the distance she could hear a dog barking angrily and then there was silence.

Perhaps the light had come from a bathroom window, but why had it flickered and gone out? Power cut? That was possible. No other lights burned in the vicinity.

Whatever the cause, she couldn't wait any longer. She checked the gun in her jacket and made for the door at the back of the villa.

What kind of people would live here? She didn't know, but it was certain they'd be armed. The country had more guns than people.

She drew the pistol and knocked hard on the wooden door. There would be no element of surprise. She would talk her way in with whoever was there and kill them if she had to.

I'm down to my last throw . . .

Two windows along from the door, Mai saw a blind move. For a second, she thought of opening fire, but it was too risky.

A moment later she heard a bolt being drawn back and the door opened slowly.

The first thing she saw was the darkness inside the house and it was only when her eyes lowered that she caught sight of a child, standing just beyond the threshold.

A girl, no more than thirteen or fourteen, with twisted, blonde hair and an enormous dark pullover, many sizes too big for her, that stretched almost to the floor. She looked up at Mai and the voice was calm. Her right hand clasped a kitchen knife with a serrated edge.

'What do you want?' she asked quietly.

Instinctively Mai knelt down on the concrete floor beside the girl and reached out a hand to her cheek. The skin was cold and damp. A ray of moonlight caught the sunken, bloodshot eyes. The child was weak and seriously undernourished. She stood at a strange angle, the feet rooted and immovable, eyes locked in the middle distance.

'I need help,' Mai whispered to her. 'Please let me in.'

The girl said nothing but beckoned Mai into the darkness and shut the main door behind her. Only then, with the kitchen knife still in her hand, did she switch on a single light.

The hall was in chaos, half-open boxes lay strewn across the flagstones. Clothes, dumped in a pile, a spare tyre . . .

Mai could feel the tiredness blurring her vision. Pain clawed at her stomach and abdomen.

Ahead of her, the girl pushed open a door to the kitchen. Instantly, there was the pungent smell of rotting food – but there was something else that drew Mai's attention.

The dead figure was lying on a sofabed in the corner, wrapped bizarrely in a yellow dressing gown, a check scarf across the face. Mai leaned forward but couldn't see if it was a man or woman.

'My father,' said the girl simply. She was watching from the doorway, her face expressionless. 'He died about three hours ago. I was sitting with him, holding his hand. He was very cold. I tried so hard not to let him go.'

Mai turned towards the kitchen table and sank down on a dark, wooden chair.

The girl stood awkwardly beside her. 'He'd been away for weeks. Came home yesterday.' She spoke in a low monotone, as if she had learned a script. 'There was blood everywhere. He'd been shot in the stomach. I don't know where it happened. He didn't say. I tried everything to get a doctor, but there are none here. Everyone's dead or gone. Dad kept asking, "Where's mother? Where is she?".'

Mai put her head in her hands. 'Did you find out?'

The girl lowered herself painfully to the floor. 'My mother disappeared. Left a week ago to look for him. She knew he'd been hurt. Said she'd be back soon, but I've heard nothing. When you banged on the door, I thought it might be her. It's the only reason I opened it.'

Outside Mai could hear a siren. She must have flinched because the girl seemed to notice a reaction.

'Are they after you too?'

'Maybe. I was kept in the town. Days and nights. I don't know how many. You don't want to know what happened.'

'I know what they do.' Said so simply.

Mai wanted to add something but the words wouldn't come.

Perhaps, she thought, this is how the world looks just before it ends – a place where even the kids have run out of tears; where their parents die in dark kitchens in front of them, where they wrap the still warm bodies in scarves and coats, where outside, day after day, civilization is rolled back and obliterated.

My last throw . . .

And then there's nothing left.

Many hours later, she remembered how quiet the room had become, how much she had wanted to lay her head on the rough, wooden table, with the long, deep scars and scratches – but she was unconscious way before it hit the surface.

WESTERN SYRIA

I n the fading light, the contact examined the man beside him. The beard was falling asleep. They were both exhausted.

'Tell me again how this machine works.'

'I told you a hundred times. You tell it to hunt for words from the mobile phone networks, and it does it. It's pretty new stuff. European companies brought it first, then the Americans. Then they gave it to the fucking Arab governments so they could spy on everyone and torture them.' He rubbed his eyes. 'But if you feed it the wrong words it won't deliver.' He turned to face the contact. 'Maybe you gave it the wrong words.'

'Then give it what it needs. You have forty-five minutes to get me what I want. After that I'll destroy your machine and cut off the little finger from each of your hands. Enjoy!'

He smacked the man hard across the head. The beard yelped like an animal but he bent again over the screens, his fingers stabbing wildly at the keyboard. From outside the room, they could hear the policeman, snoring on the floor.

WESTERN SYRIA

T he man had been weeping for hours, crying to God and his dead father, alone and helpless in his terrible misfortune. Gone were the swagger, the confidence and the fine, straight back. The finely pressed shirt was creased and dirty, and the smooth, shaven face, on which he so carefully removed each unwanted hair and treated each blemish, was tear-stained and swollen.

For days he had worked on the American woman, calibrated the pain he would inflict, stepped up the pressure to get a confession. Another day, another two at most, and she would have cracked.

He had been looking forward to it. The confession would be recorded on High Definition video. He would have stood next to her, masked of course, but proud and steadfast, having done his duty to his God and his people. And then in a final flourish, and on a signal from his commander, he would have produced the knife from behind his back and cut off her lying head.

He had practised with a cat he had captured the previous week. And when it came to it, he had been certain he would be capable of the task. There would have been back-slapping and congratulations. Already he had visualized the smiles on the face of his compatriots. Youssef, the hero, they would have called him. Youssef, who had humbled America and whose masked face and proud bearing, would strike terror into the heart of the 'kuffar' scum.

But life had cheated him. A small unit from the Free Syrian army had fought its way into the town and it had taken hours to push them back.

Pinned down by gunfire, Youssef had been unable to get back to the house where they had left the prisoner. He had assumed that the guard would have kept her locked up and secure. But the guard had been shot, apparently by a sniper. Youssef had seen a single wound in his chest. Another question mark; the dead boy in the woman's room. He had no idea how he had got there – or why he had died.

For ten minutes he had stood in the house and wailed against the injustice of it all. And then, with his heart exploding, he had run to the commander's house and confessed what had happened. Youssef, in his black trousers, streaked with dirt, apologies tumbling from his lips, overcome by the fear of what would happen to him next.

The commander had stared at him in disbelief. And then in fury he had lashed out at Youssef, first with his fists and then anything else he could find – a stick, a bottle. He had fully intended to kill the man where he stood but a thought had stopped him.

What if he too might have to explain to his superiors what had gone wrong? Better therefore to keep Youssef alive. A live scapegoat was worth a great deal more than a dead one. Let them all interrogate and harangue him, humiliate the worthless idiot, and when they were done, they could set on him and tear him to pieces. Perhaps that would sate their appetite for blood.

Abruptly, the commander stopped his assault and held out his hand to the frightened man.

'I'm sorry, brother. Forgive me. The heat of battle – enemies everywhere. What has happened is regrettable, but it's not your fault. I reacted badly. We will find the woman, search every house, every farmyard – whatever we have to do. She won't get far.'

He pulled Youssef to his feet, tried to dust him down, offered him water.

Youssef drank gratefully and mumbled his thanks.

'Go home now.' The commander patted him on the back. 'Go home, eat something. Tell no one and stay away from your phone. We'll call you when there's news. All will be well.'

Youssef had found himself alone on the street and had taken more than an hour to walk home. The commander's words had reassured him at first, but by the time he had eaten a small meal of bread and soup, he felt considerably less confident.

He remembered one of his friends objecting to the commander's treatment of a young girl. She was the daughter of a traitor and had been singled out to pay for her father's crime.

Without any warning, a group, led by the commander, had taken her from her schoolroom and raped her, one by one, in the yard outside in full view of everyone who passed.

Youssef's friend had tried to intervene, to reason with them. They had smiled at him, put their arms around him in a gesture of love and solidarity – and then strangled him where he stood.

If the woman was not found soon, Youssef knew he too would be dead.

He got up from the kitchen table and took his mobile phone from his jacket pocket. The commander had said he should call nobody, but he could wait no longer.

Only one person would understand what had happened – the colleague who had worked with him on the American woman. He was smart, lucid, a little older than Youssef and well in with the commander. He would know what to do.

Youssef couldn't help the tears as he dialled, couldn't help the feeling of utter hopelessness and the fear that was building inside him.

When his colleague answered the phone, he blurted out the news in hysterical shrieks, hoping, begging for mercy, calling on anyone and everyone to hunt the prisoner down.

*Almaraa mafqoudah . . . almaraa mafqoudah . . . Outhoruw
alayha wa ouqtulouha amama al jamee . . .*

'The woman is missing; the woman is missing. Find her and
kill her on sight.'

Youssef switched off the phone and sank to the floor. His
colleague had sought to comfort and placate him. The commander
was not a bad man. Not at all. He had a family himself. Moreover
he was steeped in prayer and piety and would look after his loyal
subordinates, just as God dictated he should.

Youssef felt relieved. After all, the escape had not been his fault.
How could he know that the town would be attacked and the woman's
guard shot dead? He had worked diligently for days, carrying out
all their instructions. His loyalty was surely beyond question.

He shut his eyes and tried to sleep.

They both heard it. The contact jumped to his feet and punched the
air. The Beard grinned stupidly, shook his head and wiped away a
tear. He hadn't enjoyed the previous few hours with the strangers,
pushing him around, threatening him, drinking his coffee. For a
while he had even feared for his life.

The policeman had woken at the noise and he too was grinning.

'Where's the voice coming from?' he asked.

'I'm trying to get a fix . . .' The beard played with his software.
'I can maybe get an approximation . . .'

'Be accurate, my friend. It's important.' The contact squeezed
the man's cheek, in an effort to ingratiate himself.

After ten minutes the Beard wrote down some figures on a piece
of paper and gave it to the contact. 'My best estimate. I have done
all I can for you. Now pay me and go.'

The contact threw a thousand dollars onto the table. It occurred to
him that perhaps he should destroy the man's equipment after all.
But he didn't know if he might need him again, or whether Ahmed
himself might want to pay him a visit. Besides, there was other business to transact.

The policeman drove in silence back to his house. When they got
there, he excused himself, but the contact had no intention of leaving
him alone. Quietly he followed the man into his dismal bedroom and
watched as he rifled his drawers, apparently looking for his weapon.

The man glanced back, saw the gun in the contact's hand and

shrugged in submission. 'I should have killed you last night when I had the chance.'

'You were too drunk.'

The policeman grinned. 'It's true. I meant to do it. The whisky . . . I thought, I'll sleep for ten minutes and then I'll finish you off and pinch the money. But I just went on sleeping . . .' He looked up at the contact. There was silence for a moment. 'Maybe you could just walk away. I won't tell anyone you were here . . .'

'Until someone else comes with a gun and makes you talk.'

The policeman nodded. There was no point denying it. He looked around the room, took in the rubbish, the old papers in piles, shelves that had fallen off the wall, smashed crockery, the remains of some bread. For years the place had been falling down. He remembered so many decisions he'd made to rebuild it, paint it, repair the roof, somehow get it all straight and put things in order. But it had never happened and never would. Life – and now death – had got in the way.

He turned back to the contact and wiped his mouth with the back of his hand. 'I'm tired of all this. Why don't you just get on with it? What the fuck do I have to live for anyway?'

THIRTY MILES FROM THE JORDAN/SYRIA BORDER

Mai slept on, her breathing so faint that the little girl had to press an ear against her chest to make sure she was still alive.

She was entirely unaware that the girl had wrapped her in a blanket and covered her face, that she had taken so much care to leave an airhole through which Mai could breathe.

She knew nothing of the girl's foresight and ingenuity.

She didn't hear the truck that flew a black flag, skidding to a halt on the rubble outside or the banging and shouting that followed.

She could not have known that, on opening the main door, the little girl had pointed to a single fighter and beckoned him to follow her down into the kitchen.

She remained oblivious as the man descended the steps and peered into the gloom, overcome almost immediately by the stench of death, and unable to control his nausea.

He had run outside and thrown up, cursing the girl and the country and been laughed at by his fellow fighters.

'It was disgusting,' he told them all. 'A corpse wrapped in a blanket, stinking to hell and back. Let's get out of here.'

But Mai knew nothing of this as she slept away the day, watched over by the little girl.

SYRIA/JORDAN BORDER

They met at the same place – a dip in the the rolling farmland that straddled the border area. The night had come suddenly. From daylight to darkness in less than an hour.

Ahmed sensed immediately that the contact's mood had changed. The hang-dog expression, the exaggerated politeness and fawning had gone. Something had clearly gone right for him. For once he had not come to beg.

He led him back to his car on the Jordanian side and turned on the engine. The night was freezing.

The contact rubbed his hands and held them against the heating vent.

'An old colleague of mine, we had worked together in the police force. I never trusted him, but . . .'

'Get to the point.' Ahmed slammed the steering wheel.

The contact smiled winningly. For the first time in a long time, there was a success to report. And he had done it with his own knowledge and ingenuity.

Where pressure had been needed, he had applied it.

Ahmed took the piece of paper with the Beard's scribblings and scanned the coordinates. Perhaps the contact was more useful than he had thought. Perhaps he had earned a reprieve – for now.

He leaned across the man and opened his door. 'Get out. Go home . . . I have messages to send.'

'I trust you're satisfied with my work.'

To Ahmed the contact sounded pathetic. 'You did your job. When I return you will account for the money I gave you, which you have omitted to mention.'

'But is this not the news that you wanted? The woman is alive!'

'It would appear so, from what you have said.' Ahmed fired up the engine. 'The question is how long she will stay that way.'

Five minutes later, he stopped the car and reached for a miniature computer, with direct satellite connection. From a tiny, matt-black keyboard, he sent a three-line snap message to Moscow, promising more when he reached Amman. He had no idea why the news about an American woman was so important to them; no idea if it would arrive in time to be of use.

THIRTY KILOMETRES FROM THE JORDAN/SYRIA BORDER

For hours on end the little girl had sat watching Mai – but she didn't wake up.

On the other side of her kitchen lay the body of her father, too heavy to move, too sad, too difficult.

One is asleep, the other is dead. The girl added the components of her life together but the equation had no result.

There was nowhere else to go and no help to be sought.

If the woman they had tortured didn't wake up, she had no idea what she would do.

She caught sight of the kitchen clock and noticed that it was close to midnight. Without choices, though, time was meaningless.

It would move forward when it felt like it and stop when it stopped.

She pulled herself onto the table and swung her legs backwards and forwards, wishing away her life, hoping the night would pass more quickly and that dawn would bring answers.

JORDAN/SYRIA BORDER

The contact had not been at all happy about the meeting with Ahmed. The man had not even acknowledged his skill or his loyalty. He'd been treated like a third rate office boy, caught robbing the boss's safe and promised a beating when the man returned.

For a moment, he considered how he might get even with him – but rejected the idea immediately. Ahmed was poison. Best left alone and kept as far away as possible.

He wasn't happy either about the policeman. It had been a messy affair. No sooner had the creature told him to 'get on with it', than he'd rushed him with all the speed he could muster. The contact had shot at the head but missed, hitting the shoulder instead and finding himself on the ground with the furious, groaning animal on top of him. He'd been forced to fire another three rounds, before the man fell off him. Winded and shocked, he had staggered gingerly to his feet only to discover the policeman was still twitching. So he had fired again into the neck. *W'allah'ee . . . My God, the man was unstoppable.*

The contact arrived home and sank down on a chair in the kitchen. Thankfully his wife had gone to bed, so there'd be no need for any stupid questions or explanations.

He swallowed two cans of beer and reflected some more on the policeman.

He hadn't disliked the man. In the past they had even shared a joke or two at work. Sure, he had stunk and been greedy. But that hadn't been enough to kill him. No, no. He had killed the man because of what he knew. And because the fellow, by his own admission, would have done the same to him.

Nonetheless, he couldn't help reflecting how casual, how mundane, killing had become. Hardly more than a brush-off; the removal of an irritant, the termination of an awkward encounter. Almost, the local pastime of choice.

The fact was that bodies were piling up right across the country – some days the dead seemed to outnumber the living. Whole families and neighbourhoods, the men he had known and smoked with at the shisha café – half at least were dead or missing.

To kill, he told himself, was no longer special. Now that everyone was doing it.

AMMAN/JORDAN

Ahmed took out the coordinates which the contact had given him and married them to his map of the region. Within about ten kilometres, he could gauge the spot from where that one hysterical call had been made.

'The woman is missing, the woman is missing – kill her on sight.'

Ahmed wondered what kind of jerk would scream out like that. He despised emotion and lack of self-control and considered it the worst of the Arabs' failings. They reminded him far too much of his Jordanian mother, sentimental and capricious as she'd been. He preferred to think only of his father, Russian to the core.

The man had been an unkempt giant, with his shirttails always hanging in the wind, sometimes funny and sweet, but more often brutal and drunk. 'A moody, fat, fucking bastard,' his mother had called him. But she had only said it once. And after she came out of hospital and the bruises and broken wrist had healed, she had never said it again.

Happy days.

From the sweet, silly mother and the tyrannical dad, he had learned how one animal gets to dominate another. The key was always violence.

Ahmed sifted through his computer records and began putting together a team.

If the American woman were still alive, he would need all his cunning – and a great deal of force – to get her out.

The hours passed and he worked on, honing the details.

TEL AVIV

S am was about to leave the office on Ben Yehuda when he saw the message from Washington.

It had been given the wrong coding and taken more than two hours to reach him through the system.

'What the fuck's the matter with you people?' he yelled out to no one in particular in the corridor outside. A few of the junior staff smirked, one or two pretended they hadn't heard. Sam was just being Sam, they thought. Even after thirty years in Israel, a Russian bear was still a Russian bear.

'Fucking people,' he muttered again, lower this time, as he read through the printed report, underlining words and phrases, circling, querying. It was his way. He scrawled on everything.

Decades earlier when he had first joined the Mossad, his supervisor had asked him, 'What's with the graffiti, Sam? You scribble and doodle and write on everything . . . didn't they have paper in Russia?'

Sam had thought of an obscene reply, but changed his mind. He was a junior. The supervisor was an idiot. Why bother to tell him that there'd been a shortage of everything in Russia – including brains? If he didn't know that by then, there was no point trying to enlighten him.

He finished reading the report and put his feet up on the table. Often, when he heard from Lydia, his mind went back to their last meeting – the hurried farewell in Moscow's Park Dubki, his request that she denounce him, the terrible fear that they had seen in each other's eyes.

What was it that had endured so many decades?

He had known her star would ascend in the Soviet establishment, but she had reached higher than he had ever thought possible. And she had surmounted all the contradictions and pressures that their 'relationship' had created.

To be able to love her husband, as she clearly did, and to rob his secrets at the same time, made her a very special asset.

On the face of it, her two lives lay in sharp contradiction but somehow she had made them complementary. In her own mind, there was no betrayal – she was simply satisfying two distinct and separate demands, instead of just one.

And yet there remained an essential, unanswered question.

To this day, he had no idea why she had proved such a faithful friend. They had never been lovers, not even the closest of friends. Perhaps he had simply provided her with a cause that she could believe in – not the Party thing where she had so excelled – but a proper cause, embraced by people like her, afraid of their true identity, trying to survive in a hostile land.

As he read the report again, one of the junior officers stuck his head around the door.

'Yes, Ari?'

'You've seen the signal from Washington?'

Sam lifted the piece of paper, waved it in the air and put it back on the table.

The young man was bright but often said stupid things. Perhaps if he spent more time reading and less in front of the mirror, he might learn something.

'What's on your mind?' He gestured to Ari to sit down on the other side of the desk.

'So the US is screwing the Brits once again. Nothing in it for us, I assume.'

Sam leaned back and put his hands behind his head. 'I don't agree.'

'Why not? Why should we care? We don't have a dog in this fight.'

Sam let his chair fall forward and leaned across the desk. 'Wrong, my little friend, we have dogs in all sorts of fights, but sometimes they just sit and watch for a while.'

Ari shook his head. 'As long as the Yanks aren't screwing us, they can screw anyone they like. That's my view anyway. And as for the Brits . . .' He raised his middle finger to finish the sentence.

Sam sighed and took off his glasses. They no longer seemed to teach the bigger picture at the intelligence schools. Instead they hired kids with their certainties pre-loaded and no requirement to question them.

Life, thought Sam, was all about questions. Only Ari didn't seem to know that. It was what had first attracted him to the Jewish faith into which he had been born in the city of Moscow.

He had been just thirteen when the rabbi had told him, 'Judaism is the start of a question. It's not an answer. Get that into your head before anything else. You go through life asking your questions and if you ask them in the right way and the right order, God may show you what you need to know.'

Or not.

He shook his head and fixed Ari with an unpleasant stare. 'Listen, my stupid friend. Try to open up your mind and put some new ideas into it. What makes you think we have the Americans where we want them?'

'Money.'

He nodded. 'Money is a big part of it, but not everything. When you look back at the last 100 years, why did America betray so many of its friends?'

'You tell me, Sam.'

'Because they got bored with them. To them new is better than old. New friends are better than old ones. Old ones become complacent, difficult, hard to manage, demanding. New ones are keener to please, easier to manipulate.' He raised his eyebrows. 'We are old friends, Ari, we and America. Which means that for them we have a sell-by date. Like everyone else. We don't know when it will be. But it will come.' He shrugged. 'Besides we have other areas we need to work on.'

'Such as?'

'We're short of friends in Europe – desperately short, I would say – and the Europeans are not all as stupid as our political masters would like to maintain.' He raised his eyebrows. 'Or as stupid as you are. So just as the Americans have bought themselves a very questionable favour from Moscow, we will buy a favour from the Brits – or at least they will owe us one. Got it?'

Ari looked puzzled. 'You mean you're going to tell the Brits what Washington has done to them. Pretty dangerous if they ever found out, no?'

Sam put his glasses back on. 'This may surprise you but I don't propose to tell that to the Americans.' The thick eyebrows lifted again in Ari's direction. 'Do you?'

It was after ten when he left the office, still irritated by the late arrival of the signal from Washington, still cursing them all under his breath.

He knew they mocked him as an angry old man – but he didn't care, didn't want office friendships and didn't trust the ones outside.

Sam didn't have a home either – he had a space to live in. He had books that enthralled him and a collection of Russian music – the only thing in the world that could still make him cry.

He also had a garage that no one knew about where he kept the most private possessions of his life. Among them, two passports in other names, bought from a Lebanese forger, who had lived in London and died, not altogether inconveniently, on a visit to Beirut; a stash of money, mainly dollars and Swiss francs, the keys to an apartment in London, acquired by elaborate deception through the good offices of a Pakistani bank – a discreet service, provided to its most discreet customers.

And a collection of telephone numbers that he had long ago believed might one day be useful.

The garage was a lock-up beneath a tatty block of flats in Central Tel Aviv and Sam walked for an hour before he was convinced that no one had followed him.

Once inside, he took a flashlight from the bare concrete wall and leafed through a notebook, encoded from the words of a poem he had written half a century earlier at school in Moscow.

The name he took away with him was Margo Lane.

WESTERN SYRIA

'How long have I been asleep?'

The girl stood over her, the thin face seemed sharper and more angular, silhouetted against the ceiling light.

'Two days, maybe longer. I thought you would die.'

Mai tried to sit up. 'I have to get out of here. They might . . .'

The girl brought her water. 'They already came. They thought you were my mother, dead just like my father. I covered you in the same way.'

Without warning the kitchen light went out. Mai could hear the girl fumbling, looking for matches. Her hands shook in the cold.

I will die here unless I move now.

The light flickered and came on again. The girl shrugged. 'We don't get much power anymore. The generators were damaged in the fighting. Someone tried to repair them – but it's not much good. Just a few hours of electricity a day. No more than that.'

Mai sat up and looked around. The pain in her abdomen seemed to come awake at the same time, coursing outwards into the rest of her body. The girl began boiling water on the stove.

'The car – the one I saw outside – could I use it?'

'This was my father's. He loved it.' She smiled for the first time. 'His mother gave it to him ten years ago and he took so much trouble—'

'But does it work?' Mai couldn't help the angry snap in her voice. It was as if she had slapped the child. The girl's smile disappeared.

'Yes, take it. I'll give you the key. Take whatever you want. It's why you came.'

'I'm sorry. I didn't mean to sound angry . . .'

The girl said nothing. She turned off the kettle, handed Mai a cup of boiling water and watched her drink. 'You should go now. Who knows if the people who came here will return? They'll get angry and desperate when they can't find you.'

In the hallway, the girl located a can of fuel and a bunch of keys, thrusting them into Mai's hand.

'You're shaking,' she told her.

'Just cold, tired.' Mai pulled the blood-stained jacket tightly around her, relieved to feel the hardness of the gun against her hip.

'I've no food to give you.' The girl shrugged. 'One of my cousins said he'd bring something today or tomorrow . . .' The voice drifted away.

'Thank you for helping me.' Mai put out her hand but the girl seemed not to notice it. They both knew that the cousin would never come. 'I'll get help and I'll come back.'

'No, please don't.'

'Why not?'

The girl took a step back. 'You can't make promises, not in a war. They don't come true. You may want to come back, but it'll be impossible. I'm telling you. If you come that's good, but it's better for me to think that you won't. Here . . .' She opened a box and pulled out a thick red jacket. 'This was my mother's – you should take it. You can't keep wearing the coat you've got.'

Mai leaned against the door. Time was running out. She knew she had to go. 'What's your name?' she asked the girl.

'Lubna.'

'What will you do, Lubna, when I leave?'

'The same as everyone else. Try to survive as long as I can.'

'Then come with me. We'll be safer together.'

'I can't leave my father.'

'He's dead – there's nothing you can do for him. We'll leave a note for your mother if she ever returns . . .'

The girl knelt down and rummaged through the piles of clothes and papers on the floor. She found a plastic bag and put a shirt inside it, along with a child's toy. In the poor light, it looked like a rubber frog.

'Is that all you have?' Mai asked.

Lubna stood staring into the semi-darkness. It seemed to Mai that her mind and body were in very different places.

'It's enough,' she replied. 'We're not going far, are we?'

LONDON

They were there when she walked in. Tribal chiefs and fawners, an expensive suit with a tie pin and a couple of overweight farm animals from the Foreign Office, glancing at their watches, because it was way past bedtime and they'd promised they wouldn't be 'too late' home.

And yet Margo thought she could see something close to excitement in their eyes, because blood always focussed the mind. That and the ritual hunt for a scapegoat.

As she sat down, Manson leaned back in his chair and stared at her across the wide conference table. 'You read the reports?'

'Thank you – they were thoughtfully provided by the driver at the airport.'

'Impressions?'

'Obvious ones so far.' She kept her eyes on Manson. 'A leak from our end or Mazurin blew it himself. We don't know yet.'

'And the Americans?'

'Not saying anything – as if they're afraid they're going to get the blame.'

'Should they?'

She could feel the irritation start to rise inside her. This was turning into a public interrogation. You put a person up against a wall, ask them a sheaf of questions they can't answer – and make them look an idiot to anyone who's watching. Golden rule if you want to succeed – tell people what you know, not what you don't know. And right now nothing was certain.

Margo's eyes tracked around the table. 'I see very little point in a meeting where we discuss our own ignorance. We need facts not supposition. Give me forty-eight hours and there'll be something meaningful to talk about.'

'That's fine – but questions are being asked now. Not tomorrow or next Thursday. A man and his wife died in very violent circum-stances in an operation that we ran.' Manson raised an eyebrow. '*You* ran, to be precise. People want to know what this means and where it's all heading.' He locked his hands behind his head.

'Which people?'

Manson threw her an unpleasant look. 'All of us.'

'All right.' She got to her feet. The eyes followed her. 'The investigation starts now . . .'

'Yes indeed.' Manson smiled. 'Forbes here will be heading that one up. We thought it better to have it handled by someone outside the immediate loop.'

Along the table, Forbes's bright red ears hoved into view.

Margo shook her head. 'The hell he will. My operation. My agent down . . .'

'Upstairs has already agreed.'

'Then you can tell upstairs that I haven't.'

There was silence for a moment. The assembled faces, she thought, had no idea that the evening's entertainment would be so absorbing. Mummy and Daddy didn't usually argue like this in front of the children.

Wasn't like the old Service, she thought – not the one she had joined so many years earlier, where the fights were quick and dirty and out of sight. And the only sign was an empty desk the day after, and a brown box on its way to someone who wasn't coming back.

Didn't happen that often these days. She was damned if it would happen to her. Damned if she'd take the blame.

But it had all been agreed in advance. She could see that now. She was the end of the meeting – not the beginning. All the decisions had been taken before she arrived. Blame defined and apportioned even as her plane touched down. There'd be no appeal. Not tonight.

Manson unlocked his hands and put his elbows on the table. 'Please wait outside, Lane.'

Margo gathered up her file. She didn't look at the faces. Didn't care to see the smug satisfaction that would be written on them. None of them had the first idea about what had happened but, hallelujah, they had taken a decision. Yes, they'd done something. Ticked a box. Put a stroppy officer in her place.

One of the farm animals cleared his throat noisily. Otherwise there was silence.

'I'll be in my office,' she said.

She stood on the Embankment in the cold drizzle, waiting for the bus home.

I should have known what was coming.

Should have seen it in their eyes.

Manson had entered her office without knocking. Hadn't wanted to sit down, so it wasn't to be a discussion. He'd come with an order.

'You're suspended for a couple of weeks. Go home, get some rest. We're going to put the pieces back on the board and try to work out who moved them. We'll call you when we need your input . . .'

'Fuck you.' She couldn't remember ever saying that in the Service, but tonight it came easily enough.

Manson feigned surprise. 'No need to get touchy about this. It's for your own good. Stops it all becoming too personal. New procedures.'

'Since when?'

'Since now.'

'I'll take it higher. You know that, don't you?'

'You can try.' Manson looked at his watch. 'Getting late and I have a busy day tomorrow.' He turned to go.

'You're scared I'm going to upset the Americans. That's what this is about, isn't it?'

He turned back to face her but didn't answer.

'Scared that your little Agency friends'll cut up rough, huh? Much easier to take me out of the equation. Bury it all – just as you did three years ago. Not in the national interest to find out what happened, is it?' Margo smiled without warmth. 'After all it's only a Russian and his ex-wife who died. The man wasn't any use to us anymore – so it's not as if we've lost anyone of value, is it?'

'You're becoming ridiculous – it may have escaped your notice but this Service doesn't exist to satisfy your personal agenda. Or your emotional needs. We all know how you'd handle this investigation. Fact is you're totally blinded by your hatred of the Americans – so you're off the grid. Now and until it's done. I'm not about to risk compromising our US operations by letting you jump up and down on their heads. Got it?'

She smiled without warmth. 'Hit a nerve, did I? Going to give me some of your best cliches about moving on, drawing a line, taking a view. Fact is, you're going to investigate fuck all – you and I both know that. Forbes, can barely find his way to the Gents. This whole thing stinks.'

But Manson was halfway through the door and he wasn't looking back.

The bus was almost empty when she boarded. At the front, a group of teenagers were arguing about who had drunk most that evening. Margo thought they were equally wasted. The girls had no coats, just thin dresses and high heels and plenty of eye makeup. They looked frozen, exhausted, but tomorrow, she reckoned, they'd be back at school.

And I'll be at home, wondering if I still have a job.

As the group got out, one of the boys stopped beside her seat. He was probably no more than eighteen, just as drunk as all the others, but the alcohol seemed to have fuelled his aggression.

For a few seconds Margo stared straight ahead and then glanced up at him.

'What you looking at?' he asked.

'Nothing,' she replied. 'Especially not you.'

He took a step closer, his knee against her hip. She could see his hand moving to grasp her shoulder. But there was something so defiant in the look she threw him, so confident, that it made him stop, and slink past instead.

She didn't watch him go. On the street one of his friends yelled out 'scaredy-cat' and a few other voices joined in.

But it was just as well he had gone. For a few seconds, no more than that, she had been ready to hurt the boy – really hurt him – just to make herself feel better.

Not a good move, she reflected. Neither clever nor controlled.

Of course, she was ready for a fight. After the last forty-eight hours, there wasn't the slightest doubt about that. But a serious fight. Not something stupid with a kid.

AMMAN, JORDAN

Ahmed cursed the traffic in the narrow streets around Shmeisani. Everywhere he looked cars were blocked by trucks, old ladies hobbled into the middle of the road, children chased balls. A hundred distractions on every corner.

We Arabs, he thought, we consider no one but ourselves. We need to cross the road – we cross. A thousand cars and elephants may be in the way, but we just don't care. We want something, we do it, we take it.

And they were his rules too. He drove without flinching. Other drivers saw the silver Nissan bearing down on them and realized instinctively that he wouldn't stop. Some could hold out longer than others – till the crash was a few seconds away – but they got the idea in the end. Ahmed wouldn't brake and he wouldn't back down. And if he smashed another car and smashed his own he wouldn't care about either.

He turned off a roundabout and headed east. Behind him were the lights of the seven hills that surround the scorched, stone city of Amman. Blocks of flats, hammered half-finished into the rocks. A single shepherd on a donkey.

But Ahmed never looked back. He drove the way he lived.

As if in a hurry to die.

ZARQA, JORDAN

The three men came from different parts of the city. One from a villa near the stinking Zarqa river, another from the suburb of Russeifa, the third from the Hateen refugee camp, where the police never visited, and the gangs decided among themselves on matters of law and disorder.

Like Ahmed's best teams, they were united only in mutual hatred and a desire for money.

Their loyalty was therefore assured until the job was done and payment had been made.

They had left their cars outside the camp, skirted the market and the rain-soaked highway, past the UN school where the girls were flooding out in white headscarves – lone symbols of innocence, oblivious to the filth in the narrow, broken streets around them.

And then sharp left, down an almost sheer drop to the blackened, concrete sprawl below, the streets barely wide enough for a single car, the sky criss-crossed by telephone wires that hung loose from crooked poles. Close by, thick black smoke from the oil refinery gushed out unceasingly over the city.

Ahmed's directions led them to a house with the words 'For Sale' spray-painted in red on the brick. An unwanted, stubby little shack, that leaned against a small warehouse, as if unable to stand on its own.

'Push the door,' Ahmed had said. 'There's no lock. But no one will come in. Wait for me. I'll come when I can.'

The two younger men rested at the table in silence. The third sat apart on a step. A week earlier he had killed fighters from both the groups that the younger men represented. And it gave him quiet satisfaction.

The two victims had thought they were so righteous, so disciplined, but he knew better, knew them for the cowards they were – one a paedophile, the other a thief. Both had deserved to die and his own faction had sent him to do the job.

Not an easy task. But necessary. Like catching rats. And he had pledged – as he did each day – to do his duty. The same way he cared for his mother, blinded by diabetes and sharing a tent with a corrugated plastic roof and five other sisters from Syria.

Every Friday he would massage her red, raw hands and feet and rub in the special cream that someone had brought him from Amman. And it made him feel good because it was the only time she ever smiled and called him a good boy and made him recall, once again, the times when *everyone* used to smile and sing and dance – long before all the killing had begun.

The younger men were chain-smoking, chucking the butts on the floor. Around them the air was stinking and stale. Every few seconds they checked their mobile phones, but the signal was weak and no messages came in.

The older one watched them through the smoke and enjoyed their insecurity.

It was quite possible that he would get the order to despatch them – only not until the job was done. Then he could shoot them like the filthy dogs they were, steal their share of the contract and buy some things he wanted.

Or maybe, as sometimes happened, no order would come and the three of them would simply walk away and never see each other again. He didn't mind either way.

Whatever took place, it was God's will.

THIRTY MILES FROM JORDAN/ SYRIA BORDER

For a moment it struck her as funny that she could think of food. But in her mind she was back in a Washington hotel, near Chevy Chase having breakfast with Harry. They had spent a night, rushed and guilty, arriving separately in the restaurant as if they were strangers, forced to share a table.

Around them were groups of kids with their dragging, slapping flip-flops and eyes half-closed. She remembered thinking that the young always look younger in the morning – their skin unmarked by time or conscience – the old, much older in the new daylight, tired and slow, as if dragged unwilling from their deathbed.

The way she felt now.

At first, the car's engine had faltered, whined and moaned as if it had hibernated for the winter and was unwilling to be disturbed. But after a few kilometres, it seemed to settle into a rhythm.

Mai could feel the tyres were wildly uneven and the steering worn.

So we're both damaged, she thought. Both on our final journey, as far as we can go.

She had wondered about whether to travel in darkness, deciding in the end that there would be more traffic by day and they would attract less attention. But she had told Lubna they would move only in short stretches.

'We're both tired. There'll be lookouts all the way to the border. People will be searching for us. Lots of people. I'm sorry.'

For a moment the girl said nothing, staring out at the flat, frozen fields and the scattered concrete hamlets. Then she turned to Mai. 'Last night I just wanted to die like my father. Now we're going somewhere and I want to get there.'

'But it's dangerous. You need to understand that . . .'

'I understand better than you do. I'm not afraid to die. Tomorrow or next week, it's OK. But just for now, we're on a journey. Neither of us knows how it will end.'

They stopped in a grey, half-shuttered village. There was bread, some olives and dried fruit and Lubna scooped money from her father's old wallet and proudly handed it to Mai.

The baker, nervous and over-friendly, tried to make conversation. Where had they come from? Where were they going? How clear were the roads? But Mai sidestepped the questions. They had come to see a relative, a very old and sick mother. Hard to help these days, wasn't it? So much tension, so much pain and suffering.

The baker nodded sympathetically and watched them leave.

Outside in the busy street, they seemed unnoticed. To all the world, a mother buying food with her daughter.

Or a widow and a fatherless child.

Either way Mai reckoned they would fit in well with the violent reality around them. She wondered if that was the reason she had brought Lubna with her. Did she care about the little creature's safety or just her own? She didn't know.

In any case, they would inch their way to the border, find refuge for the night and try to search for a crossing into Jordan. Just the two of them. Whatever happened from now on, they would live or die together.

Watching from his counter, the baker told his wife that the two strangers looked sick as wild dogs and he didn't believe they were visiting a relative.

He saw them get into their car and noted how they fell instantly on the food they had bought. It seemed to him they ate like animals, starving and desperate.

'What are you staring at?' his wife asked.

'Nothing,' he replied and continued to watch.

She drew the black hijab tighter across her hair and shook her head in contempt. 'Do something useful,' she said. 'Bring more bread from the cellar. Only a fool stares at nothing.'

TELL SHIHAB, SYRIA

Youssef had not known such fear since he'd been a child. He remembered his father screaming at him when he had played truant from school, remembered the beating with a horsewhip, and the bruises on his face that had lasted for weeks after. But this was far worse.

After the last beating, he had thought himself in the clear, safe from further humiliation. But for nearly an hour, the commander had harangued him in the basement of a villa, cursing the ground he walked on and the mother who had given him life. 'Why had the prisoner not been moved? Why was she so far west? She should have been smuggled further east to a safer area. Why had that not happened? Every 'why' came with a punch to the stomach and Youssef knew it would only get worse.

'Our people have circled the area several times. They went house to house. Soon they will do it again. Someone must have lied, someone must be covering for the woman, or she has threatened them. You should know the answers, brother. You went inside her mind. You know her better than any of us.'

The commander stuck his great, hooked nose, with the bloody veins at the side, right up close into Youssef's face and smiled as a revelation seemed to come to him. 'So we know why this filthy American spy was allowed to escape. We know this very well, Youssef, don't we? Of course we do.' He chuckled, showing Youssef a mouthful of yellow and gold. 'No one but a lunatic would leave a highly trained American operative with a single guard in an empty house. No one, that is except an enemy who was working with her the whole time and just waiting for the chance to let her escape.'

He punched Youssef twice. This time from the left side, straight into the kidneys. Youssef faltered but managed to stay upright. 'You are wrong, my brother . . .' The words came out in gasps. He struggled to breathe, to speak.

'Speak louder,' the commander shouted. 'You make no sense. Louder.'

'Nothing could be further from the truth. I was working on the woman for days, preparing for her grand execution and the television pictures that would have gone around the world. A few more hours and the whore would have confessed everything – and I personally would have cut off her lying head. This I promise you, my brother.'

The commander turned away, then pivoted like a dancer on the balls of his feet and slammed his fist into Youssef's mouth. 'I believe you, brother. If you tell me it's true, I believe you. I just have to be sure. You understand. And the more pain that you bear with such bravery and determination, the more I will believe you.'

Question, punch. Question, punch. The commander continued the rhythm until he got tired and hungry and Youssef was on his knees.

He went into the kitchen and returned with cheese and water. Sprawling in a chair, he swallowed a wedge of cheese and gave Youssef a friendly smile.

'How are you, my brother? You hungry? You wanna eat?'

Youssef's eyes had closed and his lips moved soundlessly as if he were praying.

'You see where your lies and your treachery have brought you.' The commander drank greedily from a bottle. 'This is the room you will die in, my brother. In a few minutes, when I've had some more food and said my prayers, I will get up and come over to you and cut your head off. You understand?'

Youssef's eyes remained closed.

'But it doesn't have to be that way. Confess your guilt and I will make it very quick. A single bullet. Fast and straight. There will be no reprisals on your family, I swear to you. We will bury you tonight and prayers will be said for your soul. You will feel no pain . . . if not, my brother, your death will be very different. I will cut very slowly around your neck and it will take a long time to make you die, and you will scream and scream and beg me to finish the job.' He stuck another hunk of cheese in his mouth. 'Is this what you want, Youssef? Think very carefully . . .'

Youssef opened his eyes. His body drooped, his face was white and covered in sweat.

'I have told you the truth, brother. I would not lie. As God is my witness.'

WASHINGTON DC

'Harry.'

The voice was so faint that he barely heard it.

'Harry.'

And he was on the stairs, taking them as fast as he could, because the voice was no longer hers. Her breath barely strong enough to exhale his name. It was, he thought, like a farewell cry from a traveller passing through this world, heading to the next.

He could see she was lost, disoriented. Awoken, somehow, from drug-induced sleep, eyes blinking, wet with tears.

Perhaps she had cried herself awake.

She tried again to speak but her throat was dry. He gave her water.

'I was afraid you'd gone, Harry.'

'I'm here, my dear. I haven't gone anywhere.'

'But you did go, didn't you?' The voice an urgent whisper. 'You haven't been with me these last few days. Not in your heart.'

She never missed anything. He should have remembered that, at least. Forty years, living in the same house, sleeping in the same bed, she could have read him his pulse rate without even counting the seconds.

In a wild moment of fantasy, he told himself it wasn't too late to stop. All he had to do was to meet Yanayev and tell him to order the unthinkable – end the whole saga with Mai, stop it dead where it stood.

'I was worried . . .' He looked down at Rosalind's face and saw that her eyes had closed and she was once again asleep.

Harry got up and tiptoed out of the room. He'd had no idea what he'd been going to say to her.

Perhaps he could have confessed to a minor sin or two, used a meaningless admission to mask the much larger deceit. A born liar, toying as all liars do, with scraps of truth.

And yet, however he dissembled, she already knew what that truth looked like.

LONDON

Margo lay in bed for hours, but there was no question of sleeping. A single message had been left on the answer-phone and the shock wouldn't go away.

The shock and the memories. Half-closed and put away. But never forgotten.

Sam.

At dawn she showered and dressed. But fatigue pressed down on her; the day still-born, half-hidden in mist.

He had chosen eight a.m. at London's Paddington Station – the time of bustling bodies and bags when all eyes focussed on the day ahead, seeing nothing else around them.

On his back a long, brown coat with a faded, velvet collar that smelt of cafés in Central Europe and the thick, curly hair struggling between grey and white.

But, even with a time-gap of twenty years, her eyes plucked him straight from the early-morning faces.

The self-deprecating smile, the half-suggestion from the eyebrows that he knew more about you than you wanted. A man in the middle of a crowd, but so totally alone.

Sam, you haven't changed.

Sam, from a once-locked cell in Moscow.

They left the station and sat in a small café in a cluttered, side street.

'You chose a good day to come,' she told him.

'The cold?'

'That and everything else. There's an equal chance of rain or snow. We won't know which till it happens.'

'You Brits never seem able to make up your mind.' He stirred his coffee thoughtfully.

She put her elbows on the table, resting her chin on her hands. 'So did you come all this way just to see me?'

'I was in the neighbourhood . . . hell.' He shook his head. 'Why should I deny it? Yes, I came all this way to see you.'

'After twenty years?'

'Doesn't feel like it, somehow . . .'

'I hope you've got something more important to tell me than that. This is not a day when I feel like playing games.'

Sam smiled.

It had been around five a.m. that morning when her mind had spewed up all the memories.

She could still see the Israeli intelligence barracks, the low, squat building, encased in barbed wire, pre-fabbed and dumped off a desert road, miles from anywhere; see herself sliding from the front seat of the dusty car, with the white-hot sun, glaring down on the whole ghastly enterprise.

For two days, she had watched the interrogation, veering from the subtle to the almost agricultural, a slow and visibly excruciating process, as a young Palestinian fighter was broken – first the body, then the mind, then both together.

After the first day, she had called Manson in London. 'I need to get out of here.'

'Why?'

'It's against everything we stand for.'

'Then tell them to go easy on the fellow.'

'Don't be ridiculous.'

Manson had cleared his throat noisily on the clearest of phone lines. 'We need this, Lane. There's credible intelligence that this man has information, vital to our security.'

'You mean he knows of an attack against the UK?'

'That's my understanding.'

Coy bastard, she recalled thinking. Back to the clinical office speak, the moment you're on shaky ground.

'It's still illegal. What they're doing is illegal. We both know that.'

She had waited for an answer, but the line had gone silent.

The third morning they had kept her in the outer lobby, refusing to let her through to the interrogation. Thirty minutes, an hour. She had become irritated, then downright angry.

She tried her mobile phone, but there was no signal.

And then the man who had led the team the day before had appeared in front of her in khaki fatigues and asked her to follow him.

Sam, with the same self-deprecating smile and the tight curly hair.

He had sat her down in his office and told her in heavily-accented English that the Palestinian had died. They had miscalculated. He had obviously been weaker than they had imagined.

She remembered the sudden numbness, the shortness of breath. 'You tortured him.'

'Yes.'

Such a simple, unadorned admission, she had thought; in a desert outpost where life and laws counted for nothing, where humanity was left God alone knew where, and only the information had value.

Sam pushed a piece of paper across the table. 'The names of his associates, the address in south London where they are headquartered, the plan and the rough timetable for its execution.' Sam had lingered over the final word for effect. 'I suggest you pass this to your superiors without delay.'

She had got up to leave, but he had blocked her way to the door. 'You could say thank you.'

'I could,' she had replied, 'but I'm damned if I'm going to.'

Keep it normal, she thought. Order tea and a croissant. Don't show any sign that you're ill at ease.

Sam was staring at her, expressionless.

She knew the technique: arrange a meeting, say nothing, hope that your interlocutor will give something useful away, just to fill the silence. But she wasn't going to play that game.

'We could sit here all day, like this . . .' He glanced out of the window.

'And then you'd have wasted your time coming. As far as I remember you're not a man who likes wasting time.'

In that moment, he seemed to make a decision, pushing away the coffee cup, wiping a few drops from the table top with his napkin.

'I've been here a few times since we last met. I often thought of getting in contact with you – but I never did.'

He paused as if expecting her to say something – but she didn't.

'I never did, because in the first few years, I thought you were stuck-up and judgmental – a typically hypocritical Brit, going round the world, condemning other people who, for whatever reasons, didn't seem to meet your exalted standards.' He closed his mouth and sniffed loudly. 'Your *so-called* standards.'

'And you stayed at home, torturing and killing people in the name of self-defence and convincing yourself that in each and every situation you were the ultimate victims.'

Sam smiled. 'You haven't changed a bit.'

'Nor have you.'

'But that's where you're wrong, Margo Lane.' The smile stayed where it was. 'I've changed a great deal. And that's why I came here to see you.'

She sat back in her chair and stared at him. The kind of expression, he thought, that people seem to reserve for second-hand car dealers when they make their initial offer.

'So you've seen the light. That's it? New Sam? New Israel? You're turning the page.'

The smile tapered off. 'It's not that simple, Margo Lane . . .'

'Oh I get it . . .'

'No, I don't think you do. Hear me out. Please. I came a long way to say this to you.'

She nodded.

'What happened twenty years ago . . . we can argue about it. The Palestinian shouldn't have died and I'm sorry he did. But a great many lives were saved as a result of the information we extracted. British lives. On British streets.'

She opened her mouth to speak but he held up his hand. 'Wait a minute. Please. I'm not saying that torture is always justified. To be perfectly honest with you, the excuses are always produced that we had no other way . . . the man had information that could save lives, the bomb was ticking . . .' The hand went up again. 'This is very rarely true – sometimes our people exaggerate – we both know this. But it was true when we met twenty years ago.'

She had stopped trying to interrupt. He could see that her temper had calmed.

'When I said to you that I've changed, this is absolutely true. I have changed fundamentally and in ways you could not even imagine. So have many people in the Israeli intelligence service. Why do you think that all the former heads of Mossad and Shin Bet are in the peace movement? Mm? Why did six of them go public in a film and declare that we – Israelis – are making life intolerable for millions of Palestinians on a daily basis? That's change, Margo Lane, real change – by my standards and by yours.'

'Just words, Sam,' she said quietly. 'Just words.'

He shook his head. 'The fact is that successive governments in Israel are leading the country to isolation and ruin. Politics are dominated by settlers who are nutcases and won't listen to reason of any kind. I love my country and that's why I'm speaking to you. After all these years we have no peace, no friends, growing boycotts and sanctions and a human rights reputation that's sinking fast . . .'

'You still have America . . .'

'For the moment that's true. But our perception is that this will not last forever. Patience with our policies is wearing thin, especially among Democrats. We also have a prime minister who seems to enjoy sticking his finger up their arse whenever he has the opportunity. So there's no guarantee the relationship will be the same in five years' time. We have to think ahead . . .'

'And you've come looking for friends in Europe . . .' It was only half a question.

'Of course I have. I've also come with a little token of good faith.' His eyes locked onto hers and held steady. 'From what I hear, maybe I arrived at the right time.'

And then he had said his piece. The story of an American operation in Syria that had gone badly wrong, the US national security adviser who had needed an urgent favour from the Russians – the Russians who had insisted he pay in kind – and the cold, unvarnished fact that he had done exactly that.

The price, paid in full by Arkady Mazurin.

She wrote furiously as he spoke. Half shorthand, half longhand, with scrawls and arrows and numbered pages in her notebook.

And when he had finished, he could see the lines of disbelief forming across her forehead. He watched her stop writing and run a hand through her hair. The emotions were colliding inside her. Anger and amazement, of course – and yet her self-control, her steel were impressive. He reckoned she was a formidable enemy.

'Allow me to imagine your thoughts.' He leaned across the table. 'Sam has taken leave of his senses. Sam is a fantasist, or just a liar, like so many of us in this business. Your superiors will say it, even if you don't. It's for that reason, that I'm going to do something I've never done before: reveal the identity of our source, who is personally very precious to me and who I have known and respected for many years. I would never do such a thing, unless it was vitally important, but I know you'll treat the information with the utmost care.'

'How do you know that, Sam?'

'I'm not a bad judge of character.'

A few moments later he stood up and the self-deprecating, little smile had returned.

'I'll remain here in London for a few days. I'll pass on whatever I can. Seems to me you'll need some up-to-date information . . .' He paused for a second. 'If you do what I think you'll do.'

'And what would that be?'

'In your position you don't have many choices.' He held out his hand. 'I don't expect any thanks, this time.'

She tilted her head, acknowledging the shared memory.

'Just as well.'

ZARQA, JORDAN

Ahmed surveyed the three men with evident distaste.

What he most disliked about them was their hypocrisy, the veils of piety in which they wrapped their violence and greed – the endemic self-delusion that they were somehow God's appointed judges on earth, licenced to determine who should live and die.

Ahmed had never objected to violence – but he didn't cloak it in righteousness.

He used it because it was essential to the job, designated by his masters. An alternative tool for the time when warnings went unheeded and bribes were inadequate.

So he knew what he was – a fixer, a facilitator, who was simply too violent and ruthless to cross. And most people – including the scum in front of him – knew that too.

For now, though, he would humour them, treat them with the kind of respect they didn't deserve, but make sure they knew the penalties for disobedience.

He dragged his chair closer to the table. 'Thank you for coming and I apologize for making you wait. All three of you have worked with me in the past as individuals – this is the first time you have come together as a group.' His eyes moved across each of the faces. 'You represent, shall we say, very different interests. If that's a problem for any of you, then you should say so now. You can walk out of the door and forget you were ever here. Should you decide to walk later, after hearing about our project, this would not be tolerated. Do I make myself clear?'

The men glanced at each other, then back to Ahmed.

'We're going into Syria to bring out a woman that my associates wish to interrogate. They will pay good money for your services – what's more they will pay you in cash, once she has been delivered safely across the border.'

'How much?' The older man leaned back in his chair.

'Thirty thousand dollars each. All three of you have worked with me before. You know that I keep my word.'

'Who's this woman and where is she?' It was one of the younger men from the Al-Qaeda affiliate.

'She's American. Her last-known position was some thirty kilometres from the border. But there are people after her – so I have only a vague idea where she is now. You three are going to help me get to her. You all have groups in the area – some of them will be hunting her as we speak. You need to use your contacts . . .'

'Wait a minute.' The older one shook his head. 'You want us to betray our own brothers, so you can take an American bitch to safety? I don't go round helping Western whores to escape. She's a spy, isn't she? Uh? . . . Fuck you!'

Ahmed studied the man's face. It was just possible that he had underestimated his stupidity. He ignored the outburst. 'As I said, the fee for each of you is thirty thousand dollars in cash.'

'Fifty!' The older man's index finger jabbed the air with excitement. 'Fifty thousand to get the bitch out and across the border.'

Ahmed's eyes swivelled towards him. It was clear his objection had been purely tactical – a simple attempt to extract more money. But now he would be the one to pay.

'You can leave,' he told him, abruptly. 'You're no longer required. Get out of here.'

For the first time, Ahmed saw fear in his eyes.

The man hesitated. 'OK, OK . . . thirty is fine . . . not a problem . . .' He glanced at the others, as if seeking their support, but they wouldn't look at him. 'I was just joking . . . it's OK.'

'You don't seem to understand what I said.' Ahmed got slowly to his feet. 'I don't want you here anymore. Go.'

'But you said no one leaves once they know the mission . . .'

'Yes, I did say that.' Ahmed shrugged. 'So maybe you shouldn't go after all.'

The man seemed to relax but for no more than a few seconds. He saw Ahmed turning away and realized far too late that he was pulling a gun from his right pocket, swinging it around with industrial speed and precision. Even as the man struggled for his own weapon, Ahmed's two bullets spat into his forehead from barely a metre away. His body slumped in the chair and fell sideways onto the floor, face down.

Ahmed stood over him and fired a third shot just below the nape of the neck. He knew the man was already dead, but he needed the others to remember what they'd seen.

He replaced the gun in his pocket and turned back towards them. They were sitting expressionless and in silence, eyes focussed in the middle distance. As he watched, one of them leaned forward and drank slowly from a glass of water on the table in front of him. The other yawned and rubbed his eyes. Ahmed was satisfied that the killing had been of no concern or even interest to them.

They were exactly the kinds of men he wanted.

TELL SHIHAB, SYRIA

Mai had turned on the car engine – but in that moment the pain seemed to attack her simultaneously from different angles. She fell back against the seat, breathing hard, fighting for air.

'What is it? What's happened?' The girl grasped her hand.

'Wait . . . just give me a moment . . .' The pain was spreading out across her abdomen, her hands seemed cold and numb; in a few moments she knew her body would be overcome by weakness and go into shock.

I can't let that happen.

Her eyes must have closed for the next thing she remembered was the sight of hands, banging on the window. She thought it was a dream but the banging got louder. With one eye open, she looked outside, took in the black hijab, the nervous eyes, the shouts to open the door. Lubna was telling a woman to go away.

'Wait . . .' Mai struggled to sit up. 'Open it, let her in. In the front . . .'

A slap of cold air and the car seemed to fill with black, flowing veils.

Mai turned stiffly and stared at the woman. 'I know you. I'm sure I do . . . The bakery . . . you were there.'

'Yes . . . My husband's the owner. He sold you food a few minutes ago.'

'I remember . . .'

'But you need to get out of here. Now! I don't have time to tell you why, but I think you're in danger. Please leave here while you can . . .'

Mai reached for the steering wheel but her hands never got there. 'I can't do it . . . I'm sorry . . .'

Beside her the woman began giving orders to Lubna. Together they pulled Mai over into the passenger seat. The woman sat behind the wheel and the car jolted slowly forward.

'Where are we going?' Lubna's frightened whisper from behind.

'I'll take you somewhere safe. You need a place to stay. My brother will help us, I promise.'

As she lay on the passenger seat, Mai could feel the woman's black chador, stroking her face as she moved the wheel.

'Why did you say we were in danger?'

The woman glanced sideways at her. 'My husband was watching you. He was very curious about who you are and where you're going . . . I've no idea if he will start asking questions.'

'But what about you? Did he see you leave?'

'I hope not. I sent him to the storeroom to get some supplies.'

'You're a very brave woman.'

The baker's wife stared straight ahead at the road. 'I'm not brave at all,' she replied. 'All the brave people in Syria are dead.'

THIRTY KILOMETRES FROM SYRIA/JORDAN BORDER

When he awoke, Youssef sighed with relief.

He had been badly beaten, but eventually the commander had believed his story.

After fulsome apologies, he had driven Youssef to his own house, where his wife had treated his bruises and given him food and water. God had not deserted him, after all.

Before he had slept, he had promised to help the commander find the American woman.

For more than twenty-four hours, patrols had been going house to house in the area, searching for her. There were lookouts and informers everywhere. Someone was certain to notice her. The commander seemed confident.

'I am bringing in one of my best men from Jordan.' The yellow and gold teeth appeared in a broad smile. 'We have plenty of supporters there. Even public demonstrations have been held for us. In Ma'an and other areas. Don't worry, together and with God's help we shall corner the woman and destroy her.' He had patted Youssef on the back. 'We'll get her across the country to Raqqa and interrogate her. And then you will finish it.'

Youssef had simpered and bowed a few times, anxious to show that he was appreciative of such a privilege.

It was hard to forget, though, that just a few hours earlier, he had been promised a similar fate.

LONDON

'Why the urgency?'

Manson ordered coffee and threw Margo an unpleasant look. She had arrived earlier at the restaurant in Covent Garden and was halfway through a three-course lunch. The timing was perfect.

'Some important information.'

'So important it couldn't wait for the investigation?'

'Yesterday, you were keen on getting answers now. Today, it seems you don't want any.' She put down her fork. 'Or have I got that wrong?'

'Don't be too clever. We work on the same side, remember?'

'I'm trying to.' She picked at her food, speared a prawn and pushed the rest of it away. 'I had a visitor from the Israelis. Mossad. He seemed to know quite a bit about what happened in Moscow.'

Manson's eyebrows flickered. 'Mossad? How the hell do they come into this?'

'Long story.'

'Then tell it.'

'There's a price. Proper investigation and a proper response team. Headed by me.'

'Done.'

Ten minutes later Manson rose abruptly and put on his coat. But a thought seemed to puzzle him. He frowned and sat down again.

'This story you got from the Israeli . . . Why would Harry Jones risk betraying our agent just to get this woman out of Syria? If she was so valuable, why send her there in the first place?'

'The Israelis assume there's something between them. A personal commitment of some kind. A debt maybe . . .' Margo raised an eyebrow. 'Who knows, perhaps he fell for her . . .'

'What, Jones? With his tweeds and bow ties. Don't be stupid.' Manson snorted derisively. 'Besides, his wife's got terminal cancer so . . .' He stopped mid-sentence.

'So maybe he went looking for comfort elsewhere.' Margo raised an eyebrow. 'Wouldn't be the first time.' She took an envelope from her bag and pushed it across the table.

Manson removed a small black and white photo, passport-sized, and stared at the face in it. 'Name?'

'Mai Haddad. Harry Jones's special interest.'

He glanced again at the picture. 'I assume there's very little to know about her.'

'Yes. All references comprehensively removed from open sources and most classified ones as well. Someone from Defence Intelligence met her on a briefing trip to Washington five years ago – filed her name. But that's it. It seems someone swept up very carefully after her. So she obviously matters.'

'In more ways than one, it seems.' He got up. 'You *have* been busy.'

She watched him pick his way through the restaurant and went back to her food.

Manson wasn't important. Nor was Mai Haddad.

The only thing that mattered was to make Washington pay for its betrayal.

'Prime Minister?'

Wally Sears, chairman of the Joint Intelligence Committee, put his head around the study door and raised an eyebrow.

'Yes, come in, Wally.' The prime minister pushed away the papers on his desk, got up and gestured towards the sofa. Sears was one of only a handful of advisers who didn't need an appointment. He had known the prime minister since they had shared lodgings at university. 'You're like that three a.m. call that I've come to dread. I take it this isn't a social visit?'

''Fraid not. Manson, one of the senior directors at Six wants to see you. Says it's important. But I have an idea what it's about, so I wanted to get in first.'

'Why Manson? Why not C?' The PM passed him a glass of whisky and poured another for himself.

'Chief's ill. Appendicitis.'

'Isn't he a bit old for that?'

Sears tried to smile. 'It's the Americans.'

'Oh God. Go on.'

'I need to tell you a little story. You're not going to like it.' He could hear the prime minister's intake of breath. 'Three months before you came into office Washington screwed us over with one of our Russian sources. He was someone we'd begun to work in the US, and in the short time we had him, we got some of the highest-grade intelligence we'd seen for years. We were in the process of assessing it – and him – when he was extracted by his own people, taken back to Russia and shot.'

The prime minister removed his glasses and laid them on the armrest. 'What went wrong?'

'The Americans let it happen. One of their assets was blown in Moscow. So they did a deal with the Russians – they were allowed to get their agent out, provided they blew one of ours.'

'For God's sake! . . . why wasn't I briefed about this?'

'At the time it wasn't high on our list of priorities . . .'

'Then it's a bloody strange list of priorities.' The prime minister put down the glass. 'If our closest ally is selling out our agents on the open market and you don't happen to think it's worth telling me, there are some pretty poor decisions being made around here.' He eyed Sears angrily. 'So what's happened this time?'

Sears bit his bottom lip. 'It appears they've done it again.'

The prime minister got up from the sofa and went over to the window. 'I can't tell you how angry this makes me. The fucking bastards are always talking about values and integrity – and then they go and do this to us.'

'Come on, Alec – what did you expect?'

'Better. I expected better. Especially since successive governments here have fallen over themselves to help with everything from the Iraq disaster to all the bloody listening devices and surveillance. We took a lot of flak for that. For them.'

'It's who they are. Christ knows, go back to the war. You know as well as I do that without Pearl Harbour there'd have been no Americans on the Normandy beaches or anywhere else in Europe. Roosevelt's grandson said it the other day: "my grandfather had no intention of entering the war – he was quite prepared to see the swastika flying over Europe" . . .'

'I don't need a bloody history lesson. And I'm well aware of who I can't trust. Which is pretty much everyone these days, especially the wankers in my own party.' The prime minister returned to the sofa. 'But I can't simply ignore this. It's huge. Puts the whole alliance at stake.'

'You can't allow it to.'

'It already has. Straight fucking treason. No way round it. If I ignore this they'll keep on doing it, and then we're finished.'

'So raise it with the president – you're due to see him next month. Have a private chat.'

'Private chat? For God's sake, Wally, think this through.' The prime minister reached out and poured another whisky. 'I push it under their noses and they deny it point blank. What then? You know how prickly and defensive they are. The relationship's over.'

'Listen, Alec. It's business. That's all. Americans understand that.'

The prime minister shook his head. 'So how does this go? A little shouting match in the Oval Office, we throw pillows at each other and then he offers me a jelly baby, slaps me on the back and we're friends again? Bollocks. It isn't going to happen.'

'What if it's a rogue operation – sanctioned by no one except the national security adviser?'

'I can't take that risk. I'm supposed to safeguard the security of this country. It's what I was elected to do.'

'Don't be a pompous prick, Alec. You're here to shovel the shit. That's it. Holding your nose while you do it. You're shit-shoveller-in-chief. Get used to it.'

'That's just great. Fact remains, though, that if our closest ally is getting our agents killed and giving away our secrets, I've no choice but to put some distance between us . . .'

'And if you do, it could backfire badly on us . . . This is a bomb, Alec. A big one. If you can't live with the fallout, don't even think of using it.'

For a moment, the two men stared at each other in silence. Outside in Parliament Square Big Ben chimed eleven thirty. The prime minister got up and rescued his jacket from the chair behind his desk. 'I'm not going to speak to the president for the moment. But you tell Six we need a way to stop this US operation in its tracks. I'm damned if they're going to profit from the death of our agents.'

Margo took the 113 bus north from Victoria and got off at the top of the Hendon Way. When she needed to think, she went back home to do it. The last place, she often told herself, where life had been open and real.

Manson had called her in and explained it all in a collection of blunt monosyllables. The prime minister wanted a plan; Washington's betrayal had to be confronted and their deal with the Russians aborted.

'One more thing, though.' He had got up, circled his desk and stopped right in front of her. 'Just so I make myself perfectly clear. The instruction is not to destroy the Western alliance, however much you might enjoy doing that. It's to disrupt this American operation and leave them with the unshakable conviction that this can never happen again. Do you understand?'

She had nodded.

'I need to hear it.'

Margo didn't move.

'Go on, get out of here.' He didn't hide his irritation. 'You'll be briefed at ten a.m. tomorrow.'

She crossed the Finchley Road, now clogged in traffic. In years gone by she had alighted from the same bus with her school satchel, stuffed with exercise books and homework, and the pullover with the ragged sleeves that she had always bitten and chewed to destruction.

Now, she reflected, the homework was rather different.

In through the garden gate, up the three steps and suddenly the house was all around her like a blanket. A thousand memories threw themselves at her and Mum and Dad were putting tea on the table, hunks of cake conjured from an ancient tin.

Conversations had always been with Dad. Mum just sat there, trying to smile; same face that Margo remembered throughout her childhood, the reassuring one, the one slightly dampened by tears, the one that promised, however bad the situation, it would always end well.

They finished tea and sat looking into the garden.

'We can't just let it go, Dad.'

'Is it you saying that – or the Service?'

She reached across and squeezed his arm. 'Both, I suppose. They've betrayed us twice. First Mikhail, then Arkady. One I liked and the other one I'd probably never have liked. But they were my responsibility. That means something. Has to. Otherwise I'm finished in this job.'

She knew it was wrong to tell them the story. The men in grey suits would throw every book they could find at her for that. But so what? There had to be someone to trust. And Mum and Dad would have swung from the gallows before telling a soul what she'd said.

'This woman in Syria . . .' Dad stopped for a moment. 'The American agent – what if she makes it out?'

'Then they'd win. Winner takes all. We can't let that happen.'

'But it's not her fault, is it?'

'They put her in harm's way . . .'

'And you'd make sure it reached her.' He stopped suddenly, seeing her recoil, realizing he'd gone too far. 'I'm sorry – I didn't mean to say that. I don't know the facts or the context . . .'

'It's OK, Dad. It's OK.' She tried to smile at him, but her lips wouldn't move. His words had caught her like a blow to the head. All the excuses, the self-justification, the notion of the greater good – and Dad had punched a hole right through them. As he always did.

'I have to go.' She got up and kissed them both. In that moment she thought they looked very old and forlorn and the tears on Mum's cheeks were fresh.

'Please don't go like that.' Dad holding her arm. 'I'm so sorry I said what I did.'

'But you were right. You've always been right. The very first day I went to the Service, and I was full of idealism and crap – all the stuff about Queen and country, the sacred duty to protect democracy and you remember what you said? You told me what a bunch of shits they all were and I should watch my back. And it took me years to realize how true that was – and is. I work in a dirty business, Dad. Fact of life. I do horrible things so as to stop even more horrible things from happening. It's what I keep having to tell myself.'

He hugged her, unwilling to let her go. Hated himself for asking the silliest of all questions. 'Will you be OK?'

'I'm a fighter, Dad. You know that. I don't ever give up.'

ZARQA, JORDAN

The two men nodded to Ahmed and hurried out into the narrow street. The wind was furious, flinging rain at their faces, driving rivers of dirt along the cracked, uneven road.

Neither had even glanced at the body, left behind on the floor. The victim had meant nothing to them. If ordered to shoot him, they would have done exactly the same as Ahmed.

Over time both had come to understand that their world was infested with enemies and that killing them was a sacred duty.

It gave them a role and a status – and a bright, guiding star in the darkness around them.

They came from different tribes that had shifted for generations across Jordan, Syria and Iraq, sucking in the angry and resentful, barking and growling at each other across the wastelands of their impoverished towns and cities.

From time to time they fought – or got bored and made fragile peace.

For now, as so often, they resided in sullen standoff, aware that fighting could break out again between them at any time. Provocation might come in the form of a careless insult or an accidental killing. Everywhere lay tripwires, some cultural or religious, others more simple – the carve-up of a criminal enterprise, the endemic jealousy between crooks and killers.

And there was the crime of sowing *fitna*, the Arabic word for strife or division – an accusation – that covered so many misdemeanours, both real and imagined, and could so easily get you killed.

The two men agreed they would hunt together – but it wasn't out of trust. On the contrary, they would watch each other's every move, day and night, to ensure there was no betrayal before the job was done.

'Today we are brothers,' said the one from the Hateen refugee camp. He was small and wiry and spoke from the right side of his mouth in short, guttural gasps.

'And tomorrow?' The other man grinned and slapped him on the shoulder.

His companion didn't return the smile. 'Tomorrow there'll be apricots,' he said. 'We'll see who gets the bigger share.'

From the upstairs window in the shack, Ahmed watched them leave.

For him, Zarqa was the story of everything that had gone wrong in the Arab world. Crime and child prostitution were endemic. Every extremist stripe in the region had embedded its cells and assassins there. From morning till night the mosques shook with hatred and invective. Broken roads and houses lay festering and unrepaired, while in offices high above the filthy alleyways, fat, lazy officials stuffed their wallets with bribes and protection money. The city was a running, incurable sore.

So there was no way to trust anyone who had grown up there. Ahmed had told the men to arrange a rendezvous within eighteen hours. For now, their greed would keep them focussed and busy.

In the end, though, they'd betray everyone – him included – the way they always did. They couldn't help themselves.

TWENTY KILOMETRES FROM SYRIA/JORDAN BORDER

Mai could feel the hands gripping her, the cold rush of air outside the car and the voices, nervous and high-pitched that seemed to float in and out of her hearing.

And then there was the softness of a mattress beneath her, a pillow and the long-forgotten smell of clean cotton.

Someone took her left hand and held it tightly. The grip was reassuring.

'Can you hear me?' It was Lubna, right up close, whispering. 'They've gone to find a doctor. They want to help us.'

Gradually she opened her eyes and took in the surroundings. They were in a small bedroom with a makeshift curtain across the window. An electric heater whirred in the corner. She could see a child's cot, standing at a crazy angle, because the wooden legs had collapsed.

The baker's wife came into the room. 'How are you feeling?'

Mai nodded. 'Where are we?'

'My brother's house. He's an honest man, but he's scared of you being here. He has a young child. I told him we would go once the doctor arrives. But we don't have long.'

'And your husband?'

'I don't trust him. Or his friends.'

'What friends?'

'Jihadis, killers. People who fill his head with nonsense. I have nothing to do with them. All they know how to do is murder.'

Mai was wide awake now. 'I don't want to put your family at risk.'

The baker's wife sat down on the bed beside her. 'We're all at risk. No one remembers a time when we felt calm or happy or certain of anything. But there is still right and wrong. And some of us even remember the difference. I don't know who you are – but I won't betray you.'

Someone knocked at the door and an elderly figure in a black anorak and dark pullover shuffled nervously into the room. Mai took in the wisps of grey hair and the pale skin. He wore thick spectacles, with the frames bound together by sticking plaster. She thought he looked just as sick and tired as she did.

He sat on the bed. 'I was a doctor a few years ago. I retired, but there's no one except me in this district.' He held up his palms and shrugged. 'So my retirement has been postponed. You speak Arabic?'

She nodded.

'I don't wish to ask questions, because it is better for both of us that I know nothing. But I need an idea of what happened to you – the bare outlines.'

'I was tortured over several days – sometimes I was badly beaten.'

'I understand.'

She could see the sadness in his eyes and wondered how many such stories it had taken to implant it.

He examined her without comment, noticing how she winced when he touched her swollen stomach.

'You feel light-headed? Difficulty in breathing?'

'Yes. I'm very tired.'

He turned away and reached into the side pocket of the anorak. 'I have nothing to offer you except painkillers.' He placed a small bottle on the bed beside her. 'They will work for twenty-four hours, maybe thirty-six, but you need to be in hospital. You have internal bleeding from the beatings. I don't know how serious it is – but the signs are bad enough. You should have specialist care.' He stopped and rubbed his eyes. 'I can't offer you that – there are no facilities here and no money for them. I'm sorry there's so little I can do for you.'

He sat on the bed for a moment, then straightened suddenly and got up, as if he had made a decision.

'I have to be truthful with you. Wherever you're going, you need to go quickly. If you don't get the internal bleeding stopped within two days, you'll probably die. I'm very sorry but you need to know this.'

Mai gave a thin smile and patted the old man's hand. A few weeks ago his words would have come as a terrifying shock. Now they seemed so mundane, so ordinary. Whichever way she looked at it, there was nothing special about her case. The whole of Syria was facing the chopping block. Blood on the streets. Death at every corner. Escaping it, would have been little short of miraculous.

After the doctor had left, she managed to prop herself up against the wall.

In the distance she heard shouts and angry voices. A woman began crying. Doors slammed.

Would the country ever dry its eyes and hold a normal conversation?

Of course, one fine day across a wooden table in a burned-out building, a collection of posturing liars would sign a peace treaty – but no one would respect it.

We Arabs don't do compromise.

For decades to come they would queue up to die in feuds and vendettas.

In the twisted, senseless philosophy of the time, dying was much, much easier than staying alive.

No requirement to live with guilt or shame, no need for explanations, duties or responsibilities. No accounting necessary for your sins or your mistakes.

A hole in the ground got you out of all that.

Maybe that explained why she could accept it so easily for herself.

WASHINGTON DC

t was three a.m. when Lydia tiptoed out of the bedroom. Vitaly hadn't moved for more than an hour, exhausted by the events he had set in motion, fearful that they could end up destroying him.

'If anything happens to me,' he had said after switching out the light, 'don't go back to Moscow and don't stay here either. Trust nobody. Especially people from the embassy.'

'But why are you so worried?'

'Because I know what they're like. Moscow is beside itself at the potential of this operation. But if it goes wrong they'll be looking for a big scapegoat and when they find one, there'll be no mercy.'

Inside the study, Lydia located Vitaly's briefcase and snapped the locks.

There were several messages from Moscow. It seemed Vitaly had suspected he was being kept out of the loop – so a friend in the Foreign Ministry had supplied him the latest information from Ahmed.

She could sense the urgency in the texts – sharp stabs of information, the caveats and qualifications, the talk of sources who lied frequently but sometimes, tantalizingly, told the truth. The impossibility of knowing for certain which they were doing and when.

Some facts lasted an hour, others barely a few minutes. Rumours came and went, a dozen a day.

'We believe nothing that we hear and only half of what we see.' Ahmed's judgement as the people of Syria and the tribes and the proxy fighters from a hundred different places around the globe, fought, stumbled and died across the country.

His team had crossed the border from Jordan, heading for a tiny, grey village that might already have been destroyed. No maps could reflect the physical realities in a fast-changing civil war. And yet, if she was still alive there, crouching in a cellar or an attic, or outside in cold, rough country, an American woman was running for her life against the odds, as the men of violence scoured the villages along the border.

Standing in the cold, dark study, Lydia could feel her pulse begin to race. She photographed the key messages and had begun replacing the papers when a single paragraph from the Federal Security agency in Moscow caught her eye. Once the American woman had been extracted, Vitaly would be recalled to Moscow to brief the intelligence chiefs. The talks were to have a single focus: how to blackmail Harry Jones.

Maybe Vitaly was right to be worried. The stakes were rising fast.

Lydia went back to bed but she couldn't sleep.

LONDON

'Sam.'

'Margo.'

He had arrived first at the café at St Pancras Station and was halfway through a sandwich. He started to get up, but she waved him back into his seat. 'What news from your contact?'

He finished his mouthful. 'The Russians are still trying to locate the woman. Once they have her, they intend bringing her over the border into Jordan.'

'How long?'

'Not sure. Maybe in the next twenty-four hours.'

'OK. I need to see Manson.'

'And then?'

She looked hard at him across the table and breathed in deeply. 'And then I'll get my orders.'

'If they send you to Jordan, I could be of help to you.'

'How?'

'I've worked there many times – and behind the scenes we have some good contacts.'

She got up to leave. 'You people . . .'

Sam looked puzzled. 'What?'

She shrugged. 'The deals you all do. Government to government. Out of sight, never mentioned in public. You wriggle, you manipulate, you buy weapons, you sell weapons. And you go on doing it year after year. You live well and prosper while everyone else does the dying. Take a look out there, Sam. More and more people are dying – and you say you want to stop this? You want to stop propping up Arab dictatorships that do your dirty work for you? When you go home after all this, are you really going to do things differently – or are you just going to call in another debt when you need it from me? Which is it going to be?'

He stared at her intently but he didn't speak.

'You know what I really love about the Middle East, Sam?'

He raised an eyebrow.

'Absolutely nothing.'

As she spoke, Manson stared out of the window towards the Houses of Parliament. It occurred to her that he had already made up his mind what to do – the only remaining question was when.

'OK.' He turned back to face her. 'You need to get yourself to Jordan.'

'I'm booked on the 14.35 to Amman. I'll be in there by tonight.'

'Will the Israelis keep you up to speed?'

'They say they will.'

'Fine – we'll have you met at the airport and given some equipment.'

'That's it? How about discussing what I'm going to do there?'

Manson raised his eyebrows. 'I don't have a lot to say about the details. At this point you seem to know more than anyone else in this building about the situation. So get out there and finish this thing.'

She stood up. 'No, no. Just hang on a minute. I'm not going anywhere until you define "finish this thing".' Her cheeks had reddened, the anger just below the surface. 'This time you're going to have to spell it out – words of one syllable. I don't want any room for misunderstandings here. No word games.'

'How clear can I be? Washington's operative does not make it home. Is that understood? How you achieve that is up to you. You're cleared to use any and all available means to prevent her getting back to the US . . .'

'Cleared by whom?'

'Upstairs, of course.'

'Including killing her. Is that what you're asking me to do?'

'Any and all available means.'

'I asked if that included killing her.'

'Is there something about the grammar you don't understand?'

'I want it in writing. All of it. Every word you said.'

Manson turned his head away and opened a file on his desk. 'We're not in the movies, Lane.' He looked down at the papers and began leafing through them. 'Just go and do your fucking job.'

They kept him waiting in the secretary's pool for more than twenty minutes. Typical Downing Street, he thought. Full of arrogant, young tossers who didn't even wear a tie and knocked off at six, thinking they'd had a hard day.

'Mr Manson?'

He got up. The secretary was holding a door open into a corridor.

'Mr Sears will see you now.'

'My appointment was with the prime minister.'

'As I said' – she raised an eyebrow, the voice a little firmer – 'Mr Sears can see you now.'

Sears didn't get up when he entered. Manson had met him only once before but he knew the type – back-room ferret, civil service string-puller, happiest in the shadows where decisions were 'nodded through' and sunlight rarely shone. He'd have good instincts, but only about self-preservation. He would know without thinking when to have an urgent appointment out of town or a sudden, critical attack of flu; how to scrape the excrement off his own shoes and make it stick to someone else's.

He sat down across the desk. Sears looked up but waited a few seconds before speaking.

'Let me just explain what we're doing here and how I shall write up the notes of our conversation.'

'I beg your pardon. At our last meeting . . .'

'I always think it's useful in these circumstances to work back from the destination we all want to reach.'

'I see.'

Sears smiled without warmth. 'I felt sure you would.' He pulled out a sheet of paper from the desk drawer. 'The line we're taking is that you came to tell us about an American operation taking place in Syria – that's to say the extraction of one of their agents via Jordan. We decided to send an officer just in case we could be of assistance, given our long-standing, amicable ties with the Jordanian government and our wish to offer any and every help to our allies.' He looked up. 'And that was all that was said. You didn't have a cup of tea. You didn't discuss any other business and the meeting ended' – he looked at his watch – 'at six minutes past three.'

Manson's face remained expressionless. Tracks were being covered, stories re-written, just in case it all went to hell and ended up with questions in some ghastly parliamentary committee. Sears wanted the story straight in advance. He wasn't seeing Manson to get a briefing, he wanted a 'get out of jail' card – with 'I knew nothing' printed in capital letters on the front of it.

Manson got up. He should have expected it, thought he knew all the bloody politicians by now – but Sears's confidence and duplicity took even his breath away.

'You won't want to hear this—'

'Then don't tell me.' Sears's cheeks had reddened.

'. . . but I'm going to anyway. As we discussed the last time we met, we've sent in one of our operatives. Very capable woman, as it happens, but it's a risky business and I'm not sure she'll complete the mission, even if she gets the chance.'

'I really must be going.' Sears stood up and put on his jacket.

'She wanted detailed, written authorization which I, of course, was not in a position to give. So I have no idea whether she'll go through with any of this.'

Sears pushed past him. 'Then you'd better go and finish it yourself.' The eyes stared straight ahead, the voice was hardly more than a whisper, but as Manson reflected later, the anger in it was quite unmistakable.

He smiled at the man's discomfort. High time he grew up.

TWENTY KILOMETRES FROM THE SYRIA/JORDAN BORDER

If you have a story to tell about suspicious strangers on the run, then it doesn't take long to get an audience. Not in Syria.

Within an hour, the baker had told his embellished, intriguing tale about two female fugitives to at least a half dozen people – one of whom made a phone call to a very interested party.

Just after midday, two men in jeans and hoodies pushed their way into his shop, waited till all the other customers had gone, and told him to close up.

The baker did as he was told, careful not to look the men in the eye, but his cheeks were flushed with excitement. Powerful people wanted to listen to his story. Sheikhs, he called them. Men of authority and principle who were committed to fight and kill the enemies of his religion. Now, at last, he had a chance to prove himself.

It was only when they bundled him, ungently, into the back of their car and pulled a balaclava back to front over his head, that some of the baker's excitement wore off.

No one spoke to him on the journey and when the car stopped, the two men left him where he was, ordering him not to move. In the distance, he heard the occasional car but he realized that he was far from anything or anyone that he knew. In recent years, he had seldom left the little town and the shop.

His two children had gone off to fight – who hadn't? But he didn't know what group they belonged to, or even if they were still alive.

Perhaps he should have kept his mouth shut about the women, and yet it was a long time since anyone – especially his wife – had listened to anything he said. A long time since he'd had a story to tell. And the women had definitely been suspicious. The older creature, sick and in evident pain. The younger one silent and in shock. They were on the run. Had to be.

He heard footsteps getting close. The car door opened and a hand yanked him out of his seat.

'Where am I?' he asked. But whoever was attached to the hand didn't answer.

He was led into a building. The air was cold, stale.

'Sit on the floor.'

'I can't see.'

He was pushed onto the stone tiles. Only then did they remove the blindfold.

The commander was sitting silent in a chair opposite him. A single desk light on the table beside him.

'Tell your story.' The voice seemed further away than the man.

The baker nodded furiously, trying hard to order his thoughts. He should not waste the time of a sheikh, but this was unexpected. There was no warmth or friendship here. No greeting. No hand to shake.

'I told it to one of your people, I think . . .'

'Tell it again.' The voice was quiet but strong. A voice that gave orders.

'Two women were in my shop today. They looked odd, out of place.'

'Why?'

'Sick, desperate somehow. Running from something.'

'This is Syria. Everyone's running. Why do they matter?'

'The older one wasn't from here. Different Arabic. Syrian, but maybe she'd lived abroad.'

'And the younger one?'

'Local. I'm sure of it. Tired, hungry. Both of them.'

'Where are they now?'

'I don't know. I went to get some supplies from the basement. My wife asked me to. When I came back, they'd gone.'

'Did they speak to anyone else?'

'Only my wife.'

'Then we will talk to her.' The commander turned away and looked into the darkness as if throwing the idea to someone in the shadows.

'I tried to call her . . .' The baker stopped. Something in the commander's voice worried him. He shivered suddenly, not knowing if it was from fear or the cold.

When the baker had been led out of the room, the two men from Zarqa emerged from the darkness behind the commander.

'What did you think?' He looked up at them.

The younger man shrugged his shoulders. 'Hard to tell. The fellow is stupid and looking for attention.'

'But is he lying?'

'Why would he lie? Maybe he was just nervous.'

'But his eyes were all over the place. One lie, chasing another . . .'

'Listen my friend' – the older man from Zarqa put a hand on the commander's shoulder – 'we'll take the baker back home and talk to his wife. If there's anything in his story, we'll find out.'

'Do it quickly. The hours are passing and the American spy has still not been found. This is the first and only lead we have.' The commander got up from the table and stared from one face to the other. 'Understand this, my brothers. It will go very badly for us all if she gets away.'

LONDON

'Did you fix the thing we talked about?'

'It's not that easy. Events are moving fast on the ground . . .'

'I don't want excuses.'

'I'm giving you facts, Alec. This is highly delicate – the whole thing . . .'

'Then go off the books . . . use some of the former Service people . . .'

'There's no time for that. And no time to find someone who'd keep their mouth shut. This thing is highly toxic – it leaks and the whole alliance is finished. I shouldn't even be talking to you about it, in case you get questioned.'

'I'll handle the questions.'

'I'm not talking about the press – or even one of those bloody silly committees. I'm talking about a possible criminal enquiry.'

'I know what the risks are.'

'Do you really, Alec? This isn't about losing power, political disgrace . . . it's about authorizing a termination.'

'I didn't use those fucking words . . . in case you've forgotten. I said make sure the operation is stopped.'

'So how else do you think we stop it? Blow a whistle? Set up a fucking traffic light? Sorry, Alec. It's dirty hands' time. And if this goes ahead then yours'll be as dirty as anyone else's.'

The prime minister swivelled his chair and stared at a portrait over the fireplace. It was one of his predecessors, who looked considerably happier in the job than he was.

Sears stood up and approached the desk. 'I can abort this now. One phone call and it all comes to a grinding halt. The MI6 woman is recalled. Manson gets stood down. We go back to square one—'

'. . . with the Americans, blowing our agents and screwing us with impunity?'

'You can do this through diplomatic channels. Much safer option.'

'We both know that isn't going to work. They'll deny everything and all we'll have done is stir up a bloody hornets' nest.'

'So what do you want to do? Our agent lands in Amman in two hours' time. After that, she's on the ground and may even be out of reach . . .'

Sears went back to the sofa. 'It's your call.'

BA 737 EN ROUTE TO AMMAN, JORDAN

She didn't look round. Didn't need to. Sam was ten rows behind her. They would meet later at the unremarkable and hopelessly inefficient Landmark Hotel in Central Amman. No further contact till then.

She knew he'd be sleeping. Sam was untroubled by 'big' thoughts: the mechanisms by which you hastened the death of some people and delayed it for others. It's just timing, he had told her. A little bit more time or a little bit less. Such a fine calculation, depending on the intersection of so many random and uncontrollable events.

Recalling his words, part of her envied him his cheap and easy philosophy. The elegance with which he could finesse the taking of a life and the finger on the trigger. The entire, time-honoured rationale of the powerful, confronted by the weak.

It's your fault that I'm killing you. You brought this on yourself by resisting oppression, left me no choice, drove me to it. The responsibility is yours.

Murder converted neatly into suicide. And no shortage of useful idiots to believe and retell your version.

Margo closed her eyes, listening to the miles rush past beneath her. So what would she do when the time came to confront the American woman, when the thinking had to stop, when the choices were distilled down to the final two?

All she knew was that she would walk to the edge of the cliff, stare into the darkness beyond and find out.

As Sam had said, such a fine calculation.

LONDON

He hadn't allowed time to go home. Stopped the car on its way to Northolt airport along the Great West road, bought a couple of shirts and some underwear, didn't know how long he'd be away.

They had his name at Security and directed him to a small private terminal.

He could see the plane refuelling close by – a white Gulfstream, owned by one of the Service's shell companies, registered God knew where.

'Mr Manson?'

The man approaching him wore a blue pilot's uniform but there were no markings on it.

'I'm Phillips. Flight Lieutenant. But for obvious reasons not wearing my usual stuff.'

They shook hands. Manson didn't want a conversation but as always he wanted it clear who was in charge.

'You've filed a flightplan?'

The pilot stiffened slightly. 'Only to Cyprus, so far. We'll declare the onward route into Jordan, once we're further south. No point alerting anyone in advance. By the time we're out over the Med, we'll get lost in the commercial corridors and I doubt anyone will pay any attention.'

'And the final destination?'

'It's a military airfield. There are one or two we could use close to the Syrian border. Your people are taking care of that. I'll just fly where I'm told to.'

'Co-pilot?'

'Yes. One of ours. No inflight service, I'm afraid. You'll find a fridge and some sandwiches. That's it.'

Phillips led the way to the aircraft. Manson didn't bother to greet the co-pilot. He strapped himself in, loosened his tie and checked his messages on his phone.

He hadn't been involved in a live mission like this for many years – and never behind the back of a serving officer.

Sure, there were things you didn't say to people, facts and details you might withhold for short-term expediency. But to run a parallel operation, without informing a senior, serving officer, was taking a monumental risk.

Did he really think Margo Lane would disobey a direct order? A woman with an outstanding track record like hers?

And yet everyone had a line they refused to cross. He'd seen it enough over the years. Even if you never knew where it was drawn, that line existed.

For him, though, it was a very different game. No question. He'd lived his professional life in the grey zone and been happy there – the no-man's land between what you could do and what you knew you shouldn't.

Manson had never found it difficult to look in the mirror and see himself as he really was.

Practical, ruthless and unencumbered by inconvenient principles.

He didn't like Lane – he could admit that easily to himself. Didn't like the way she would bring out her conscience and wave it in his face, didn't like her assumption that she alone had a moral compass and everyone else made it up as they went along – or didn't bother. Didn't like the fact that, even with her incessant questioning and arguing, she was a brighter, more capable, more creative intelligence officer than he had ever been.

TWENTY-FIVE KILOMETRES FROM JORDAN/SYRIA BORDER

They could have asked the baker for the keys to his shop but the men from Zarqa couldn't be bothered.

Without waiting, the younger man slammed his shoulder against the main door, shattering the metal clasps that held it, and sending it crashing to the floor.

When the baker protested, he was punched hard in the face and told to sit on the floor and stay quiet.

The two men searched the shop and the apartment above it, but found no one.

'Where's the wife, old man?' The figure from the refugee camp, grabbed the baker's chin, jerked it upwards and peered unkindly into the man's eyes.

'I don't know. She said nothing. Maybe she's gone out looking for food.'

'Does she visit anyone? Has she friends?'

'She doesn't—'

The man from the refugee camp took a step closer. 'She doesn't what?'

'Doesn't tell me anything. She has a brother, though, lives three kilometres away, I haven't seen him in years.'

They dragged the baker to his feet. 'Call her.'

'I can't . . .' He wiped the blood from his mouth with his sleeve. A thin red trickle had oozed onto his chin. 'She has no phone.'

They took him back to the car.

'You remember the way to her brother's?'

'I think so. Inshallah, I will remember.'

'You better hope, for your own sake, that you do.'

The older man stood for a moment beside the car, watching the road in the direction they had travelled.

His eyesight was sharp and he was pretty sure what he had seen. A white pickup truck, about half a kilometre from them, had pulled off the road but most of it was still visible behind some trees. The same truck that had tailed them at a distance, ever since they had left the commander.

He wasn't surprised to be followed. There was no trust between any of the groups. Whole towns and districts changed sides overnight. Fighters and factions came and went, winning and losing land and winning it again. Sometimes you battled the same faces who had stood alongside you as comrades just a few days before.

In truth, the only way to be certain of anyone, he decided, was to kill them.

The painkillers had been stronger than Mai imagined. From time to time she could feel herself drifting in and out of consciousness, as four or five sets of hands lifted and carried her to the car.

She forced herself to sit up and look around.

Night was falling, turning the landscape to grey. A young boy was driving sheep along the main road, with a dog herding the strays. For a moment she remembered what a normal life had looked like. Land and animals. Peace and laughter. A night beside a fire.

The baker's wife slid into the driver's seat beside her. 'We're not going far. Too dangerous to travel at night. But I know a retired schoolteacher who lives nearby. He'll put us up, if I ask him.'

'And if he doesn't?'

'It would not occur to him to turn us away.' She touched Mai's sleeve. 'People were good to each other before the fighting started. I had a lot of friends. Then it became difficult. Nobody wanted to talk anymore because families were divided. Fathers and sons even – some of them fought on different sides. But I know this man. He's a good person.'

The car moved off into the shadows. In the back seat Lubna hummed a children's song.

Mai put her hand in the zip pocket of her jacket and felt the gun. She had almost forgotten it was there. Holding it was a small comfort.

She thought about the doctor, his patched-up spectacles and the tired, slow-moving eyes behind them; Lubna, who had helped her without a second thought; the baker's wife, driving into the night with a couple of endangered souls for company – they had proved to her that against all the odds, kindness and bravery could survive.

And yet that kindness would offer no protection from the men who were hunting them in the darkness, who might ambush them at the side of a deserted road or run them to earth in a dugout like animals.

At that point, only the gun would count.

WASHINGTON DC

Harry Jones could feel the doors closing. The silence from the White House told him everything he needed to know. Not the silence of respect for a senior official whose wife was dying, but the quiet that surrounds a man under suspicion, a man who has moved imperceptibly from sunlight into the shadows.

It didn't matter what had triggered it. Probably his frequent meetings with Yanayev. Ambassadors – especially Russian ambassadors – were under blanket surveillance and eyebrows in the FBI and the Agency would have been raised more than somewhat by Yanayev's encounters with a senior White House official.

Somebody would have told the president, because he alone had the power to order Harry Jones into quarantine – Jones with his intimate knowledge of US capabilities and assets across America and around the world.

Even now they'd be watching him from somewhere near the house. Probably a mobile command centre, monitoring his phone and computer, standing by to cut him off if he became a security risk. Armed, as usual, to ridiculous excess.

And Harry knew that the president, moody and irascible as he was, would be unwilling to think the worst of him; he would have told the agencies that Harry's wife was desperately ill and that he wouldn't want the two of them separated. Not at this stage. Not until the evidence against Harry was solid.

The nurse met him on the landing. Rosalind was sleeping deeply, her condition unaltered. When the doctor had visited that afternoon, Harry had asked him if she should be moved to hospital. But the man had simply touched his arm and told him there was little point. She was comfortable at home. She had no pain. It wouldn't be long.

He sat in the kitchen and stared at the television. He was glad that Rosalind wouldn't live to see his disgrace, to see him put on trial, to see the handcuffs on him and the cameras in his face. She couldn't have stood that. The friends who would shun her, the phone that would never ring, the knowing looks in the local shops. It would all have been way, way too much for her.

And Mai? He could see her face so clearly in front of him, half covered by the black, wavy hair, the chipped front tooth, the sudden smile that could blaze at him when he least expected it.

He remembered an afternoon when they had driven out to the Shenandoah mountains and Lost River State Park, remembered word for word what she had told him.

'I feel so American here. But when I was last in Syria, I was an Arab again – which meant I was a donkey, staggering under the weight of the great lie. Whose lie? All the lies and the hatreds and the duplicity that cut through the heart of our people. The arrogant refusal to accept blame. The obsession with self.'

The pathway had become steeper through the forest. He had taken her hand and held it.

'But with all our faults, I can't help thinking there are two Gods – one who gave *you* forests and lakes and precious silence – and another who decided to give *us* something terrible, the barren land, the constant betrayal and the endless killing.'

She had stopped and looked straight into his eyes.

'You brought me to this park, Harry. I could stay in this park forever.'

And he had known then that this wasn't the throwaway line of a daytripper.

Behind it, a depth of longing and despair, quite outside his own experience.

When she had said: 'I could stay in this park forever,' she had meant exactly that.

Harry got up and switched off the kitchen light.

If Mai could be saved, then his own downfall would at least have some meaning.

Whatever had happened to her, he had to know.

RAMTHA, JORDAN

Ahmed had grown tired of waiting. As the sun set, he had parked on the outskirts of the town near a cemetery and had watched the gravediggers scoop out four fresh holes in the rough, cold ground, before going home, leaving their spades upright in the piles of earth.

Behind them, across a fence, sat the town's licencing office for cars, a tattered Jordanian flag attached to an upper window, the dreary building deserted. In the distance he could make out the gaunt arrays of spotlights at a sports stadium, but that too was in darkness.

He got out of the car and shivered. Inside the cemetery he bent down and examined the graves with a small flashlight. They were simple rectangles of bricks or stones with the names spray-painted in black.

Mohamed Abdel Rahm – brave martyr, born 1978 – died 2013
Mariam Shukhair – no date of birth or death
Hassan Mohamed Attiya al Yateen – born 1968 – died 10.6.13

So some of the dead were being brought from Syria and buried out
of sight in Jordan. No doubt the names were false. At any rate there
was no time or requirement for fulsome tributes. The place was a
production line. And at the end of it – four open holes in the ground
waiting for the next incumbents, dead already or dying just a few
kilometres away.

Ahmed returned to the car and switched on the engine.

Once, in recent history, it seemed the town of Ramtha had had
a life. There would have been crops to harvest and plenty of other
produce to sell. The stadium would have brought visitors and young
people. Now it was just the dead, arriving to be buried.

Perhaps the two men from Zarqa were already among them.

He tried their phones again – but there was no connection. At
best the phone system was overloaded – often, like everything else
in the region, it gave up completely.

As he drove back into Ramtha his headlights picked out some
graffiti on a wall. *'My mind is tired and my heart is crushed.'*

He passed half-finished buildings with blankets stretched across
the entrances instead of doors. A dog sniffed the legs of a child that
were poking out onto the street.

The town slept in its poverty and distress.

AMMAN AIRPORT

A driver had been waiting for her at Arrivals and on the back
seat of the car was Manson's promised gift. She didn't need
to open it. It had the weight of an automatic with several
clips of ammunition. Local embassy issue, she assumed. And somewhere in the pack would be the arse-covering piece of paper to fill
in if you used it or lost it, or returned it in less than pristine
condition.

She stared out the window at the darkened landscape. In her

world everything had a paper trail – except the things that were really important.

Like her mission in Jordan. Like the instructions from Manson.

She checked into the Landmark Hotel and waited for Sam to arrive.

He was only minutes behind her. As she opened the door to him, she noticed he had changed clothes. The Central European coat had been replaced with a black anorak and his mood had changed as well.

Laid-back Sam had a new light in his eyes. The man was enjoying himself, fired up, she reckoned, by the mission and the chance of violence.

You're not like me, Sam. You live for this . . .

'OK. I've got a car outside. Let's go.'

She raised an eyebrow. 'Where to?'

'Our source says the best guess is the border village of Al-turo, near Ramtha. If the Russian can extract the woman – signs are he'll take her there. We might get more information en route.'

Margo pulled on her coat.

'You have a gun?' he asked.

She didn't answer. Didn't want to go down that road with Sam.

When it came to the really difficult decisions, you had to work them out for yourself.

You didn't hunt in packs or committees. Not in the world where she lived.

You didn't care and share. You just got on with it.

She remembered years earlier how she had blackmailed a Bosnian Serb before turning him into a double agent.

'If you tell me what I want to know,' she had whispered to him, 'I will keep it secret from everyone. But if you don't tell me, I will go out and inform the whole world that you did.'

The Serb had cowered in fear – but he had talked. And she had kept her promise right up until the day he had lied to her.

His body was never discovered.

So was she really any different from Sam? Or had the passing of so many years made her softer.

He opened the door and held it for her. 'Shall I wish us luck?'

'Don't bother.' She glanced at him. 'We're going to need something better than that.'

FIFTEEN KILOMETRES FROM THE SYRIA/JORDAN BORDER

They had all been forced into the kitchen – the baker, his brother-in-law, two of their children and the old doctor with the broken spectacles.

In front of them, the younger man from Zarqa produced a gun but none of them showed a trace of surprise.

He thought they had probably seen plenty of guns in recent years – hadn't everyone in Syria? – but he knew no other way to get their attention.

'We're looking for two women in a car – and' – he pointed to the baker – 'and *his* wife. Not to harm them, not even to ask them questions – but to help them. That's all.'

The doctor began to laugh. 'You really expect us to believe you? You come out of the darkness, you wave a gun at us and you say you just want to help. An odd way to help, isn't it?'

'Listen to me.' The man from Zarqa wasn't used to verbal persuasion. By this time, he reflected, he would normally have shot someone – at least through the foot – which always seemed to make information flow more freely. 'Listen carefully. If we don't find them, somebody else will and those are not people they want to meet. OK?' His jaw jutted towards each of them in turn. He would lose it in a moment, he thought. Didn't do self-restraint. Not with fools who stood in his way. Never had.

'I have nothing to—'

'Tell him.' It was the baker who raised his voice. 'Tell him what he wants to know. It's the only chance for my wife. She doesn't know how much danger she's in. Doctor, please . . .'

The doctor lowered himself painfully onto a wooden stool. He drew a rag from his pocket, blew his nose and glanced over towards the baker. 'This is Syria. It's dangerous to speak – maybe it's just as dangerous to stay silent. I don't know anymore. But if this is what you want . . .' He sighed. 'Your wife came here, another woman was with her and a child – a girl – maybe thirteen or fourteen.' He grimaced. 'I find it hard to tell ages these days . . .'

'Where did they go?' The older man from Zarqa took a step forward. 'How long ago was this?'

'Maybe an hour . . . maybe a little less. They were looking for a place to spend the night. I—'

'Where?'

'I don't know – but your wife . . .' His eyes alighted again on the baker. 'She spoke of a teacher and said he wouldn't let them down.'

'What teacher?' The man put away his gun.

'I know who it is . . .' The baker got to his feet and put a hand on the doctor's shoulder.

The old man looked up at him, shook his head but said nothing. Neither of them expected to meet again.

Outside, the three men climbed back into the car and the driver produced a map. 'Show me where this teacher lives.'

From the back seat, the baker leaned forward, drawing his finger along a section of road, close to the border.

'What's there?'

'Some houses, nothing more. The teacher lives alone. All his family are dead.'

The two men in the front exchanged glances. The younger one produced his mobile phone, sent a text message, then turned back to the driver.

'Are they still following us?'

His companion let in the clutch and the car jerked forward, bouncing across the potholes.

'Of course they're following us. They're crazy for this woman's blood.' His eyes fixed on the road ahead. 'And if they don't get it, you can be certain they'll want ours instead.'

ISRAEL/JORDAN AIR CORRIDOR

'Ten minutes and we'll be in Israeli airspace.'

Phillips had come through from the cockpit and was leaning over him. Manson struggled to open his eyes.

'What did you tell them?'

'We're flying in urgent blood plasma for the Jordanian royal family. The Israelis don't seem too concerned. This plane's from a charter company that's pretty well-known in the region. It's done similar things for some of their own VIPs.'

'And the landing?'

'Al Mafraq airbase – north of Amman. There was a choice of two in the area. Your people took this one. I gather there's some kind of Jordanian team waiting for you. You expecting that?'

Manson nodded and watched the pilot return to the cockpit.

He pulled a satellite phone from his overnight bag and made a call to London. Margo Lane, they told him, was en route to the town of Ramtha, close to the border with Syria.

From there she would make her way to the village of Al-turo.

No, the voice on the line was quite adamant, she had said nothing at all about her intentions after that.

Bugger the woman. He whispered it silently, cut the connection and leaned back in his seat. He thought he knew now what she would do. Remembered that he'd looked at her file in detail over the years, read what the trainers had written, the psychological profile, reaction to authority, likely responses under specific pressures. A lot there. And all of it had pointed in one direction.

Margo Lane would kill in self-defence – but she didn't do executions.

More than fifteen years had passed since her training and he doubted that any of her convictions had changed. Especially that one.

She would know perfectly well the difference between legal and illegal orders, because she was paid to know and paid to think. She wasn't the kind of zombie thug who could do strategy one day and slit throats the next.

But Manson knew *he* could – if it came to that. And the little boy Sears, sweating away in his Whitehall office, intent on covering his tracks, had known it too.

He cleared his mind as the plane descended towards Jordan and thought of the team that would be waiting for him.

He didn't know them. Would never see them again once it was over. Didn't need their names, couldn't have cared less if they had fathers or herds of sheep or queues of girlfriends. Hoped he wouldn't even see their faces in the short ride to the border. In any case there'd be no chit-chat, no tedious banter to ease the wait.

They were strangers, designed to stay that way.

HIGHWAY 25, JORDAN

Sam was silent on the drive and she was grateful for that. Gradually, the traffic began to thin as they headed north and the steep hills gave way to country that was flat and desolate.

They passed the filling stations and cafés, the police cars tucked into the side of the road, their lights off, watching them go by. Snapshots rolled by: two men playing cards under a paraffin lantern. A boy in a striped shirt waved from a fruit stand and threw a banana in the air. She caught a glimpse of three children, laughing on their way into the night, careless, unaware of danger.

Such a long time since she had felt that way.

By the morning, she thought, there would be something else to try to forget. Whatever happened. Another slab of life, not to be revisited. Like a gallery that's shut. Exhibit closed. Permanently off limits. One more guilty secret deep in the unprintable and irretrievable archives.

Only she would always know it was there.

The successes in the job never compensated for the losses. How many people in the Service had told her that? Success was a drink in the bar or a pat on the back in a sixth-floor office or a miserly civil service bonus of 250 pounds at the end of the year.

But failure – despite all your efforts – never went away.

Like a deformed leg or a birth scar on your cheek. Or the lousy, immovable view from your bedroom window when you pulled back the curtains. A brick wall that would forever obscure the sunlight.

She didn't want this day, didn't want the decisions it would force her to make, but now there was no way to stop it.

LONDON

'Where is she now?' The PM took off his jacket and slung it over the back of his chair.

'I don't know. I don't know who *she* is, I don't know where *she* went. I don't know anything about it.' Sears raised his eyebrows and stared expressionless across the study.

'Don't play games with me. Deniability is one thing. Betrayal is something else. I'm not going to betray an agent that we sent to do our dirty work for us.'

'Fine.' Sears smiled without humour. 'I wondered if you'd have a little attack of conscience before all this was over. Pity your conscience didn't click in a little earlier. And then we wouldn't have to be sitting here in the middle of the night wondering . . .'

The prime minister crossed the study and stood over him, fists clenched. 'We may have known each other a long time, but don't ever speak to me that way again.'

'I'm protecting your back . . .'

'Or maybe just your own.'

'Listen to me, Alec. You're a good man, always have been and I admire you for it. But the interests of this country are not well-served by you putting yourself in the firing line, just to do the decent thing. You made the decision that the US operation should be stopped. I didn't agree – but we'll live with that. Only remember one thing – our entire relationship with the US could be on the line over this – and if it goes wrong you're going to need that deniability. Not for you. But for the country.'

'So I scuttle away into the shadows while one of our agents puts her life on the line. Is that what you want?'

'Let her do her job, Alec. That's it. That's what she signed up for. Besides' – he raised an eyebrow – 'it's far too late to turn back now.'

RAMTHA, NEAR JORDAN/ SYRIA BORDER

t was two a.m. when the text came in. The men from Zarqa had a lead on the American and were tracking her towards the border. No other details.

In the darkness of the car, Ahmed nodded to himself and shut his phone. He would wait for them to come to him. He scanned the map. But he already knew which way they would travel, knew they would make use of the small amount of natural cover, just as the contact had done. Knew they would choose the undulating fields, close to the village of Al-turo, the clumps of trees and ditches. Knew it would be slow and dangerous.

In two hours, maybe three if they were lucky, they'd bring the woman across the unmarked border, dodging the Jordanian patrols, praying the sky was still dark.

He checked that both automatics were armed. Beside them lay the machine pistol in the floorwell by the passenger seat. A small zip bag contained spare magazines. All serial numbers and markings had been carefully chiselled away. The kit was clean.

It was his discipline. His set of unbreakable rules.

When the world around you went to hell, only rules could save you.

He picked up the phone again and told the contact to wait on the Syrian side of the border, in case things went wrong. The next few hours would be crucial.

FIFTEEN KILOMETRES FROM THE JORDAN/SYRIA BORDER

Youssef took a last look around the kitchen. Nothing moved. He had shot one of the young boys first – a tiny creature, no more than five years old, much like his own son – but he had done it without any qualms or reservations. And the boy had fallen silently into a woodbasket.

As expected, the doctor had broken down in horror at the violence and told Youssef everything he wanted to know: where the men from Zarqa had gone and where the American spy was likely to be hiding.

Of course the old man had begun begging for the life of the other boy and his father, crawling across the floor, tugging stupidly at Youssef's trouser legs, but by then Youssef was no longer listening.

He simply shot the three of them where they were – a bullet each in the forehead. Precise and effortless. Just as he had done so many times before.

They hadn't even tried to run, so perhaps they had simply accepted their fate. It wasn't his fault that they were on the wrong side.

Outside in the white pickup truck, he told the commander what he had done and received a pat on the head.

The earlier unpleasantness between them had passed and Youssef felt sure that he had acquired a useful comrade and friend.

He felt proud and elated. But what he looked forward to more than anything was the abject terror on the American woman's face when she would see him again and realize that this time there was nowhere to run.

He knew she was close. So close he could almost touch her, smell her.

He began to giggle uncontrollably.

SIX KILOMETRES FROM
THE JORDAN/SYRIA BORDER

'I don't see them anymore.' The younger of the two men from Zarqa turned round and stared into the darkness.

'They're coming. You can be certain of it.' His companion reached into the back seat and shook the baker. 'How far to this teacher's house?'

'One kilometre, I swear. No more.' The man was shaking with fear. 'There is a turning soon. I will tell you.'

The car banged and shuddered over a pothole but they kept moving along the empty road. They passed a garage with burned-out cars in front of it. A tanker lay rusted and overturned in a ditch.

'Turn here, turn here . . .' the baker shrieked out and the driver swore at him.

They lurched down the unmade road.

'Pull off into this field – on the left. Go on . . .' The older man grabbed the driver's arm.

'What in God's name . . .?'

'We need to surprise them, stop them getting to the American woman.' His companion looked blankly at him. 'You understand nothing. We have to kill them here otherwise there's no chance of making it to the border. Get the car out of sight.'

He got out and walked back to the road to check if they could be seen. No sign of a moon, the clouds hung low and motionless over the fields.

The driver joined him. 'I've messaged our location to Ahmed.' He jerked a finger towards the baker. 'What do we do with the old fool?'

The man from the Zarqa refugee camp sniffed the cold air and wiped his nose on the back of his hand. 'Who cares? If he makes any noise, shoot him.'

MAFRAQ AIRBASE, JORDAN

They had made his plane circle in high winds for more than half an hour and Manson was visibly angry.

A Jordanian colonel, in black fatigues, greeted him at the foot of the steps and led him to a single-storey complex.

Looking back, Manson noted that the runway lights had already been switched off and that the airfield, iced-in and deserted, was virtually in darkness.

Only a handful of bulbs were burning in the briefing room – he didn't know if it was because the place was a dump or they'd switched them off intentionally.

It didn't matter. He'd take charge the way he always did. Someone had to make the fucking decisions when everyone else ran for cover.

To him it was a business meeting. Nothing more. The business, just a few miles across the border and into Syria. All to do with logistics and interventions, cordons and corridors.

And yet for a moment he felt curiously exposed in front of them, a long way from the numbered corridors of Whitehall and their comforting blanket of deniability.

He left the life and death stuff till the end; then told them in slow, almost ponderous phrases, what he wanted – and what he couldn't accept. On a screen behind him, they flashed up a black and white picture – grainy and enlarged – with the unmarked, oval face of a young woman, shrouded by wavy black hair and sporting, he told them, a chipped front tooth.

Whatever happened that night, she would not be leaving the area. The tatty little town of Ramtha, of minimal importance to a largely indifferent world, was to be the final, irrevocable stop on her journey.

'Do not misunderstand me on this. My orders have been verified and confirmed – and the subject is now closed.'

He looked across at the colonel. There was no sign that he had heard or registered anything at all.

Manson stood for a second in silence, then raised his eyebrows at the dark shapes in front of him. 'Questions?'

For miles around, it seemed, there was absolute silence.

FOUR KILOMETRES FROM JORDAN/SYRIA BORDER

Half the schoolteacher's house had been destroyed. Two rooms, one on top of the other lay open to the elements, their brick walls torn apart by the sheer force of a blast. A wooden beam hung crazily from a shattered ceiling. Shreds of blue wallpaper fluttered in the wind.

They discovered him sheltering by the kitchen stove. Mai could see the head bowed in submission, a thick woollen scarf wound around his neck, but when she spoke to him the eyes seemed bright and alert.

'Why wouldn't I help you? The war has taken from me most of what I loved. And now, like everyone else, I'm ready to die. I have nothing more to lose.'

'You could have gone to Jordan when it was open to the refugees. You're only a kilometre or two from the border.'

'Maybe. But I'm too old to start anything new. Besides—' he grinned – 'you can go for me. I'd be happy to know that you got away from all this . . .' His right hand gestured vaguely towards the world outside. 'Perhaps you'll send me a postcard.'

They helped Mai onto a makeshift bed, supported by packing cases and wrapped their coats around her. A single candle flickered in the draft from the window.

Lubna brought her water and a painkiller.

'How do I look?' Mai whispered.

'You look as you are.' The girl tried to pull away. 'You look tired.' She opened the box of pills that the doctor had given her. 'Three left. That's all. Enough for twelve hours. Then we'll need more.'

Mai let go of her and sank back onto a cushion. She knew what
'needing more' meant. It meant that the girl had learned very early
how to lie, how to deliver bad news; what you were supposed to
say when the words, like everything else, were running out.

For a moment she thought of writing to Harry, while she still could
– just a line or two that would help him to let it all go. Let her go.

He would want a conclusion. Harry, with his ordered thoughts.
Beginnings, middles and ends. So Harry.

But perhaps it was better to say nothing. No aftershocks from the
grave. No final, unexpected words to haunt and torment him in
the years to come.

Life should always end quickly. Only the jolt of finality made it
bearable.

She shut her eyes and tried to think around the pain, to push it
to the edges.

The teacher brought her a cup of water.

A thought struck her. 'Where did you study?' she asked him.

'Beirut.' A half-smile at the memory of it.

'What did you learn there?'

'Learn?' The teacher shook his head and reached out to touch
her arm. He tried to smile and the old eyes roamed around the
semi-darkness of the kitchen and the anxious faces. 'I didn't learn
anything,' he said quietly.

Youssef drove. His hands wet from excitement on the steering wheel,
his shirt drenched in sweat. The commander told him the truck had
belonged to the Americans. 'Built for someone important from the
CIA, strong as . . .'

But he never finished the sentence.

Youssef heard the shots before he saw the attackers – two maybe
more, grey, faceless shapes, caught in the truck's headlights, firing
straight at them with semi-automatics from ten or fifteen metres.

His instant reflex was to stop the truck. Any moment he'd be
dead. The gunmen had surprise and overwhelming firepower. There
was nothing to be done.

But in a second, he could hear the commander laughing, as the
bullets ricocheted harmlessly off the bulletproof windscreen,
clanging on the steel bonnet.

'Drive brother, drive . . .' The commander punched his arm and in a lazy, almost casual fashion, lowered his side window and sprayed the men with a machine pistol. They fell instantly by the side of the road.

Youssef rolled the pickup a few yards on and then stopped. The commander got out and fired two more shots at each of the bodies.

Back in the vehicle, he was still smiling.

'You see! God is looking after us, my brother.' He tapped the window. 'Bulletproof glass! Drive on. We've got work to finish.'

THE LAST DAY
AL-TURO – JORDAN/SYRIA BORDER

S am had broken the glass and forced the door of an old shack, full of agricultural machines, and a pungent smell of oil and chemicals.

It was close to the brow of the hill – around 500 yards, she reckoned, from the nominal border.

They had concealed the car behind a hedgerow, but it wouldn't provide much cover – not if they were still there at dawn, not if anyone was looking for them.

Margo sat on a wooden bench, letting the cold sink in, relying on it to fight the tiredness.

She pulled out the automatic, slammed the magazine into the grip and checked the safety catch. As Sam watched her, she screwed on the silencer and laid the gun carefully on the floor.

For a moment she wondered what her parents would make of the scene in front of her. Bizarre beyond belief. Light years outside anything they could imagine. Their daughter with a weapon and lethal intentions.

She shut her eyes and tried to think of other things. She imagined walking through the house where she had grown up. The floorboards still creaked in the places she had trodden as a teenager, tiptoeing back home in the early hours of the morning, trying so hard not to wake Mum and Dad.

The dog she had grown up with didn't bark, just snuffled in the darkness, lying on his mat under the stairs. His tail thumped against the wall.

On the first floor she glanced into their bedroom – both parents were asleep. Some intermittent snoring, Dad restless, half-covered by the duvet, Mum deeply comatose with the covers wrapped tight around her.

The light from the streetlamps sent shadows across the room, odd shapes that made her think they had moved the furniture. But it was still the same.

She touched a bedside table, moved onto the glass door handle and then the great 'throne' – a carved mahogany monster that had somehow survived generations of Mum's family to sit, in rather diminished circumstances, on the landing of a semi-detached, four-bedroom house, off the Finchley Road.

She touched it too and the wood was cold just as it always had been. Even in summer.

In that moment she too heard the shooting, way out in the distance across the dark, frozen countryside of Syria, with its moving, seething armies of ghosts.

Ahmed heard the shots and sprinted for the cover of the gully. Three hundred metres across the farmland and he caught a glint of light on the road ahead. It had to be the contact's car.

They didn't greet each other. The contact was shown the text message. He nodded, pushed the car into gear and headed away from the border.

An empty road, back into the darkness of Syria.

When Ahmed had called him, it hadn't occurred to the contact not to come. He didn't know the extent of the danger ahead, but assumed simply that there would be violence along the way and he would encounter people who would wish him harm. Not a subject to dwell on. It was a daily business and he had grown used to it. Whatever you did in Syria, the odds were lousy.

He threw a quick glance at Ahmed. 'Are we expected?'

'Maybe.'

'How many of them?'

'I've no idea. We'll do what we can.'

The contact said nothing for the next kilometre. In the past he had been silent in Ahmed's company, intimidated by the man's coldness. But tonight, for some reason, his curiosity seemed to boil over.

His eyes swivelled towards Ahmed, his voice no louder than a whisper. 'Why do *you* do this, my friend? I want to know.' He pointed a finger at his head. 'Me? – I've got nowhere to go. My wife who hates me is here, and all the rest of her insufferable family . . . I can't just leave them . . .' He was silent for a moment. 'But you don't have to stay . . . this war's insane . . . beyond anything we could imagine. You could go now, this minute . . . turn the car round, disappear . . .'

He had half expected Ahmed to hit him, but the man's face showed no reaction.

'I'm a fighter. That's all. I don't know anything else . . .' The words, barely audible above the noise of the engine.

'But you don't believe . . .?'

'No . . . I don't believe – not in anything. You're right, I could get out of here, but the world is full of wars – so wherever I went there'd be a battle. I might as well stay and fight here.'

The contact nodded and drove on. He was pleased to have had an answer and faintly gratified to learn that the rest of the world was as suicidally destructive as Syria.

It struck him that this was the first remotely personal exchange he had ever had with Ahmed. And, in all likelihood, the last.

There were six men in black, fanned out over a mile along the border, black balaclavas and fatigues. He hadn't looked at their faces, wouldn't have learned anything if he had. They'd absorbed the orders and would process them in their own way.

And when it came down to it, he knew that his briefing would count for very little. This wasn't a unit that would bother too much with details. There'd be no time and no light for proper identification. Not much incentive to think and wonder. They would shoot at anyone who came their way.

Manson heard the gunfire in the distance – but could see no movement beyond the puffs of mist.

He climbed back into the army Land Rover. The colonel who'd greeted him passed him a plastic mug of tea. From the dashboard, the radio spat intermittent static at them.

He was glad the final phase had started. Hated waiting around, second-guessing himself and everyone else. The border was now a killing zone.

Margo Lane would know that too.

Sam replaced the infra-red binoculars in his pocket and turned away from the broken window. 'We should get out there.'

She shook her head. 'In a little while. Best view over the terrain from here. I'm only waiting for the American woman. Nobody else matters.'

Sam went back to the window.

He wondered if he should tell her about the movement that he had seen just before the shooting – the faintest, blurry impression of two figures, crouched for a second in the no-man's-land and then lost in the undergrowth.

Had he imagined it? He dismissed the question.

He had no imagination. Never had a use for it. Always reckoned it would impede his judgment and cloud it with emotion.

Instead he trusted his senses, nurtured and honed over decades.

So he had a good idea what he had seen. And an even better idea what lay behind it.

Someone else had arrived to finish the job. British or American – or another interested party. It made no difference.

He looked across at Margo, but said nothing. Whatever happened, the whole enterprise had to end tonight.

Mai knew what she had heard – a brief gun battle and then the final shots of the executioner into the back of the victims' head.

Just to make certain.

The double tap, as the soldiers called it.

She sat up, retrieved the pistol from her jacket, then turned and looked around the kitchen.

They were watching her in silence. Lubna, the baker's wife, the old schoolteacher – her tiny team of helpers, waiting for advice, instructions – or some words of comfort.

But there was no fear in the faces. No sense of alarm.

'Somewhere I have a rifle . . .' The schoolteacher opened a cabinet and began rummaging inside.

She smiled at them and stretched out a hand to Lubna. 'You are the best people I ever met. I'm sorry I brought you to this. Please . . . I shouldn't even ask you this . . . but please forgive me.'

'There's nothing to forgive,' whispered the baker's wife. 'God brought you here and gave us the chance to do something good. Something useful.' She smiled. 'That hasn't happened in a long time.'

Mai looked at each of them in turn. Whatever took place, she knew they wouldn't leave her. Their eyes were calm, infused with kindness.

But now they were saying goodbye.

'Turn off the lights and stay in the car.'

They had stopped just in front of the bodies.

Ahmed got out and stood listening for a moment. The wind had dropped. He hadn't expected the damp stillness that had settled over the area.

He knelt down on the track, extracted a small flashlight and turned the corpses face up.

For a second, he didn't recognize them. Their expressions, angry and rigid in life, were now relaxed, almost benign. The cheeks still warm.

From their pockets he removed the mobile phones and threw their weapons into the darkness.

'Who were they?' The contact re-started the engine.

'They came from Zarqa.'

'You knew them?'

'You ask too many questions. How far is the schoolteacher's place?'

'Half a kilometre – no more.'

'Then we go on foot. Turn the car round and lock it.'

The contact did as he was told.

Ahmed looked him up and down. 'You're ready?'

'Of course.' The man was shaking. 'It's not the first . . .'

But Ahmed had turned away and was already sprinting, head down along the rough farmland track. He wouldn't have chosen the contact to go with him. The man was capricious, emotional. Killer one minute, spoilt child the next. But there hadn't been anyone else. You took your decisions as best you could – and then you lived and died with them.

*   *   *

She heard the sounds way before the others. She had been trained to listen and assess. Trained to plan for all the worst eventualities. And now they had arrived. But she couldn't locate the plan, couldn't clear her head to find it.

They had gathered around her on the makeshift bed, the schoolteacher with his old rifle, rusty and unusable, pointing at the floor; Lubna, eyes tight shut, biting into her lower lip, the baker's wife holding her hand.

Mai held the gun and felt her own hand tremble – not from fear, but from the pain that rushed at her from all directions. She could no longer feel her legs, and didn't know if she could aim straight through the haze that had descended into the kitchen. For the first time, the coldness seemed to lie deep inside her, spreading out across her abdomen and into her chest.

It won't stop now, she thought. It'll go all the way and take me with it.

Perhaps she had closed her eyes for a second but when she focussed again, she could see the two figures standing in the doorway.

She tried to stretch out the gun but in that moment she couldn't lift it.

Sam looked at the message on his mobile.

'We've found the Russian's car . . .'

Margo snapped. 'What do you mean we – who's we?'

He made a face. 'Colleague of mine. Trailed us from Amman.'

'Now you tell me.'

Sam threw up his arms. 'What? What's the matter? You're one person trying to do this on your own. God knows why. So I thought, maybe a little insurance . . .' His voice trailed away. 'Jesus, you Brits amaze me.'

Margo shut her eyes, ran a hand through her hair. 'How far away is the car?'

'Very close. Seems likely they'll come this way. Maybe right past us.'

She took a deep breath. 'If there's trouble . . .'

'There will be trouble.' Sam shrugged. 'Seems there are others out there tonight. I saw two people a while back – could have been a border patrol but I don't think so. Looked like they were digging in.'

'Why didn't you tell me before?'

'I wasn't sure.' His self-deprecating smile had disappeared.
'And now you are?'
'Maybe.'
'Jesus, God, Sam – whose fucking side are you on?'

The Jordanian colonel didn't like Brits; thought they'd fucked up the
Middle East for all time when they'd redrawn the Arab borders a
century before and done their shady deals with the tribes. He glanced
at Manson and decided he was typical of the crowd London always
sent – a pushy bastard who wanted it done his way, gave orders as
if he owned the country and didn't give a toss about anyone else.

When the message had first come through, he had wanted to say
no to the whole operation. But the phone calls had kept on coming
and the squawking, high-pitched voices from the ministry in Amman
had by turns become angrier and more threatening.

According to his chief of staff, the minister had asked to be kept
informed of events throughout the night.

In other words, screw it up at your peril.

The colonel told Manson he was going for some fresh air, slid
out of the Land Rover and headed into the icy darkness.

What he disliked most about the mission was that, if it all went
to plan, his men would be shooting on sight a female American
agent, probably unarmed, almost certainly exhausted and running
for her life.

However you spun it, this wasn't going to be the unit's finest hour.

She could see the victory smile on Youssef's face, the sweat pouring
from his forehead, the tiny child-like hands trembling with excitement. But she felt no fear. The scene in the little kitchen was
darkening, the movements getting slower, voices fading in and out.
She was drifting beyond his reach.

She caught the rough guttural Arabic of the man who was with
him. 'Do it, brother. Why do you wait? Take her and kill the others.
What are you waiting for?'

But the words meant nothing to her. And the silence that fell
around her seemed to confirm that it was over.

'You remember me?' The nose, sharp and glistening was just
inches away from her. 'I knew I'd find you again.' Youssef began to
laugh. 'You thought you could run, thought you were cleverer than us.

Maybe you imagined your friends would rescue you. But now you will die at my hands. Do you know that now, American whore?'

The voice, soft and even. Syrian Arabic, she thought. The best, the most correct . . .

His face turned away from her, towards the others – the schoolteacher, the baker's wife, Lubna, their faces expressionless.

Mai could feel them close to her, sense their calm.

Youssef knelt down beside the schoolteacher, laid a hand on his shoulder as if to comfort him. 'You are the oldest, my friend. So perhaps I should kill you first. I shall try to make it last a little longer so that we can all enjoy it. What do you think?'

His hands fixed around the man's throat and his fingers began to bite into the arteries.

Neither Youssef nor the commander saw the gun that killed them, they were far too busy exalting in the capture of their prey, the certainty that they were invincible; the pungent, thrilling jab of a kill.

So they hadn't heard Ahmed's entry into the smashed and broken building, hadn't seen his sure-footed advance across the rubble and into the corridor that led to the kitchen. He had stood for a moment and listened, without emotion, to the rantings of Youssef and the curt commands of his companion and given no thought to the lives they had lived or the road that had led them to the schoolteacher's house.

They were problems to be put aside, obstacles to be surmounted, the means to whatever end Moscow had decreed. It was routine, nothing more, checking the line of fire, deciding the order of the two targets, pumping the two soft-nosed bullets into the back of each head with precision and economy.

Youssef was dead by the time he had hit the floor, the commander took another bullet before he too stopped moving.

Ahmed bent and checked for a pulse on both men, replaced the gun in his pocket and looked back at the faces of the living.

'It's over. Don't be frightened.' He glanced quickly around the room and pointed at Mai. 'I've come to take her home.'

The contact had been sent back down the road to collect the car. By the time he arrived and they had lifted her onto the back seat, Mai was unconscious.

Ahmed turned to her three companions who stood motionless beside the half-ruined house. The baker's wife and the girl held hands. Beside them the schoolteacher stared straight ahead into the darkness. The wind tore at his straggly hair and the sleeves of his shapeless jacket.

Three people, he thought, who did not expect to live till the morning.

'You need to leave here,' he told them. 'Now. There's not much time. People will come looking for those men.'

'Where will you take her?' asked the baker's wife.

'I can't tell you.'

'Then go quickly,' she said. 'She needs urgent care. And when she's better, tell her there are three people in Syria who will not forget her.'

Ahmed took the driver's seat and guided the car slowly and without headlights along the rough track.

He felt troubled but it took a few minutes before he realized why.

So many years since he'd heard words of kindness from gentle people. People who looked out for others, who took no part in brutality or execution, who would always give more than they took.

They seemed to echo from a distant world he had once visited many years before – and to which he had never been able to return.

Margo led. A black woollen balaclava covered her blonde hair. In her right pocket she clutched the automatic, its silencer already in place.

She remembered smiling the first time they had handed her a gun in training. Didn't want it, didn't need it, she had told them. And they had shrugged and told her to do as she was told and learn how to use it. Such early days, she reflected – long before reality had broken down her door and stolen all the silly ideals. She had wanted to believe that intelligence was more about brains than bullets. But as she rose in the Service, the bullets came back into fashion. Colleagues left London in planes and returned in coffins, apparently unprotected by their brains.

Sam tapped her shoulder and pointed to a car, caked in filth, abandoned on a farmtrack. An old Mazda with local Jordanian plates.

He tried the doors but they were locked. 'This is the Russian's car. No doubt about it. If he makes it, he'll come back here.'

They crouched in the shadow of a small hedgerow close by.

Margo thought she felt snow. The cold seemed to have locked itself around her.

'It'll be light in less than an hour.' Sam gestured towards the east. 'He'll have to hurry.'

Two hundred metres from the border, Ahmed ran the car into a ditch. He heard the figure on the back seat move and turned to look at her.

'Can you hear me?'

Mai coughed. 'Yes. Who are you?' The voice was barely audible.

'I work for the Russian government. They told me to find you and deliver you across the border to your friends from America. I know nothing more.'

The contact touched Ahmed's arm and jerked his head at the border.

'I'll take a look outside.'

'There may be patrols.'

The contact nodded. 'I know this place.'

He slid out of the car and was lost in the darkness.

Mai tried to clear her throat. 'Talk to me . . . please.'

Ahmed stared straight ahead. The windscreen had misted and he opened the side window to let in air.

In the driver's mirror he caught sight of Mai, her eyes now shut. He didn't know if she was still conscious. In any case he reckoned she would die soon. Perhaps that made it easier to talk.

He started haltingly, as if choosing foreign words from an un-familiar book, his hands and fingers in constant motion, plucking and tugging at memories, long since abandoned.

He told her of a young Moscow boy, beaten often by his father, spoilt and idolized by his Jordanian mother; of the gangs he had joined and the victims they had chosen, of cruelty and power on the streets, of a tramp battered face-down in the snow, of fresh blood frozen where it had spilled.

Of guilt and shame.

Of the men in uniforms who had sought him out because he was good with his hands.

A story he had never told – to a listener who had never existed.

Mai opened her eyes. 'And you've been here . . .'

'. . . for years.' He didn't look round. 'Since the killing began.'

'But how have you survived?'

'By force.' He shrugged. 'All I can do is create incentives for them not to kill me.'

'Has anyone tried?'

He could see now that she was fully awake. And yet her ragged breathing told him it wouldn't last.

'Of course. It's normal in this part of the world.'

'What happened?'

'Russian special forces came in and eliminated the man who attacked me.'

'That's it?'

'Not quite. They killed him after killing his children, his wife and his grandmother in front of him and posting it on the internet. Even in this region, with its quite exceptional levels of brutality, people sat up and took notice of that.'

She didn't say anything. He realized she was using him to help her stay conscious.

'So they left me alone after that. The odd stray bullet. An accident here or there. But everyone avoids me if they can. They fear the Russians more than anyone else.'

She coughed for a few moments, tried to sit up. 'You ever think about Moscow . . . what it was like there?'

'Moscow? So different from here.' Ahmed grinned. 'If you want to do something in Russia, the first answer – automatically, instantly, without a second's hesitation – is no. And then if you're very clever – or rich – you get around the no and start pushing for some yeses.' He shook his head. 'Here, as you know, the first answer is always "yes". Yes, of course, *Habibi* – my dear – it is the most wonderful idea in the world and it will all be agreed by tomorrow, I swear to you.' He stopped and spread open his palms. 'And then nothing. The man never calls and never contacts you again. So the project dies. Perhaps it died in the exact second that he gave you his approval and swore on all that was precious and sacred to make it work. You see? That's the Middle East for you and for me.' He fell silent for a moment, before turning back, trying to read her expression. 'It's a land of beautiful promises – broken in the same moment they are made.'

WASHINGTON DC

Harry knew there would be no sleep that night. Once again, as he had done every hour, he checked the battery on the unlisted mobile phone in his pocket.

It was the last of the devices Grigory had given him – to be used only for the final message.

They would hear it, the moment it was used. *They* would hear everything, sitting even now in the anonymous grey or silver van, parked at the end of his road. But they'd have been told to wait for orders.

No one would touch Harry Jones until the White House said so. This was the president's call. And no sweaty-handed, gilt-badged subordinate from local law enforcement would get to press the button and bring him in.

He wondered how the president would feel when the time came – but it made no difference. The two of them would never meet again. Once the machine kicked in, the process would be ruthless and unstoppable.

It was odd to think of such things, surrounded, as he still was, by the normality of his own house and its green and pleasant neighbourhood.

In that moment, he was still free to do as he wished, to read or eat or play music – or to climb the stairs and sit beside Rosalind, sleeping in her sickbed, watched over by the night nurse.

Choices which would be taken from him within a few hours, before the sun came up over the eastern seaboard.

He tried to imagine how the handcuffs would feel on his wrists and whether the cold steel would bite deep into his skin.

Only then did the sadness and the sense of loss settle over him.

Harry looked at the phone, laid it on the desk beside him and shut his eyes.

He would never again know peace and privacy and the right to decide how he lived his life.

In a little while Harry Jones would be a case file, on its way to a grand jury and a courtroom.

A problem, about to be terminated.

LONDON

At three a.m. the prime minister's wife had brought them coffee in the study.

She had asked if 'everything was all right' and had left without receiving an answer.

But the set of her husband's jaw and the silence between the two men had told her all she needed to know.

When she'd gone the prime minister poured the coffee and took a cup over to Sears. 'I want to know her name, Wally.' It was an order.

'Whose name?'

'Don't fuck me about. The name of the MI6 agent who's in Jordan right now, trying to protect this country from enemies and allies alike – while we sit around pretending it's nothing to do with us.'

Sears seemed about to object but the prime minister's expression changed his mind. 'Her name's Margo Lane. She's forty-three, single, born in North London, read Modern Languages at Oxford.' He sipped the coffee and looked up at his boss, on the other side of the darkened room. 'You want to say a prayer for her?'

BORDER

In the cramped rear of the Land Rover Manson heard the colonel's radio burst into life and the short guttural exchange in Arabic.

The Jordanian turned to face him. 'Patrol says someone's moving out there. Single figure so far. Come with me.'

'Wait.' Manson leaned forward, hissing at him across the seats. 'I made it perfectly clear: no one gets through tonight. Your men have orders to terminate whoever is crossing the border illegally . . .'

But the colonel was already outside the vehicle, moving stealthily across the freezing field. Manson caught up and tugged at his arm. The Jordanian shook himself free. 'Listen to me. Sometimes children cross this border. Not many. Sometimes women. You want me to execute them in cold blood, whoever they are? I won't do it. Nor will my men. Understood? You've two choices: go back to the Land Rover or come with me and stay silent. You're in Jordan – you do as I tell you.'

The contact thought he'd been careful, thought he could find the way through, but he knew they had seen him, heard the shout and saw the movements a hundred metres to his left. Two, maybe three figures . . .

Stupid to have gone out there to recce – they might have been lucky and got across first time. But arrogance and bravado had got the better of him. Now he could sense the footsteps getting closer, knew the men would be younger and fitter and faster . . . and he couldn't hold them for long.

He began to run. An old reflex. But it was pointless. He knew already there was nowhere to go. Only one thing left to do.

In his haste, he fumbled his mobile and sank to the ground to retrieve it. Just a second to dial Ahmed's number.

Lying on the ground, face up, he saw the figures closing in on him. 'Go now,' he shouted into the phone, 'go now . . . I'll lead them away . . . go now.'

From his pocket he removed his favourite Glock pistol and wondered if he could buy the Russian a little more time.

Ahmed didn't hesitate. Straight out through the driver's door and from the back seat, he scooped Mai up in his arms, barely noticing the lightness of her body, face inert, eyes shut.

He wasn't young but he was fit enough to do it. A fireman's lift put her over his shoulder, her head down across his back, the long black hair, cascading towards the ground.

A final look back at the car and he caught the headlights skittering in the distance, moving rapidly towards him. Two sets at least. But it no longer mattered. Someone would have found the bodies at the schoolteacher's house and would guess where he was heading. There was no way back.

He ran as best he could, bent double at the waist, like a strange primeval creature, eyes scanning for trouble. The ground was uneven, treacherous, and he skirted boulders and low fences. Despite the cold he could feel the sweat falling from his forehead, but he couldn't wipe it. His left hand secured Mai to his back, the other was locked on the gun.

He was driven only by the mission, oblivious to risk, no star to guide him, no God to summon, skirting the frozen fields across a border that stood in name alone.

The living didn't see him and the dead let him pass unhindered.

The line from a Russian poem dropped into his mind, repeating over and over again.

At the brow of the hill he stopped, heart heaving, and straightened his back. Turning, he could see the first light of day in a starless winter sky, the dawn seeping in over the path he had taken.

A moment later he heard two shots in quick succession and realized that the contact had paid the price for his journey.

Manson pulled out a flashlight, examined the body and swore under his breath.

He turned to the colonel. 'How could you fuck it up this badly?'

For a moment, the Jordanian didn't answer. Behind him, Manson glimpsed the men in black emerging from the darkness.

'This is your doing.' The colonel went over to Manson. 'You wanted assurances no one would get across. There was no time for any identification.' He jerked a hand at the body. 'This man had a gun and he refused to drop it.'

'Did he?' Manson snorted. 'I doubt he was even given the chance. Now there's no way of knowing who he was and what he was doing here . . .'

He backed away angrily. 'We have no idea what happened here tonight. You realize that? While you were chasing the wrong person, the woman might have got through.' He threw up his arms. 'What the hell? You don't give a fuck anyway.'

He stared in turn at the blackened faces of the Jordanian soldiers, but no one spoke. Manson could feel their anger, their loathing.

'I'm finished here. I need to get back to the airport.'

The colonel took the wheel of the Land Rover and drove in silence to the runway. Only when Manson had got out, with no goodbyes or thank yous, and was striding towards his plane, did he wind down the window.

'Get out of my country,' he shouted. 'Every time you people come here, you destroy us a little more. Always have. Don't come back to Jordan. You'll never be welcome here. I'll make sure of it.'

* * *

She told herself she wouldn't forget the sight: a lone figure, silhouetted against the dawn sky, with a body across its back. Like a hunchback emerging from the darkness of an alien world.

The realization that all the betrayal and the killing had come down to this – and there was now a decision of her own to be made.

She was close to the hedge but she moved slowly forward where she thought he would see her, knowing the risk, the gun held tight in her jacket pocket in case it didn't go well.

'I'm Margo Lane from British Intelligence.' Her voice sounded soft and weak, even to her. 'I know who you are and I've come to help with the American officer. We've no quarrel with you.'

In that instant she saw him turn that practised turn, with the gun rigid in his hand – the executioner's swivel, fast, easy, a movement so liquid, so precise and faultless – but he didn't fire.

For a few seconds, they stood immovable, staring at each other . . .

Carefully, Ahmed put away the pistol, lifted Mai down from his back and laid her on the ground. As Margo approached, Sam emerged from the other side of the hedge and the three of them stood looking down at the body.

'We can take her now,' she told Ahmed. 'And we need to do it fast.'

He stood up. 'You're too late. She's dead. She was badly tortured. Died about twenty minutes ago before we crossed the border.'

'You knew that as you came over?'

'Yes.'

'But you still went ahead and did it.'

He shrugged. 'Those were my orders.'

She drove with Ahmed through the ramshackle town, past the deserted sports ground, out towards the cemetery he had come upon just a few hours before. Sam's car stayed close behind. As they stopped she could see a shepherd herding sheep through the grey-lit fields, up into open country. Across the graveyard snow began falling, blown in from the east, from Syria.

They lowered Mai's body as gently as they could, took turns to shovel the piles of earth, left by the graveside.

When it was done, Ahmed pulled Margo to one side . . . 'You weren't here to help her, were you?'

'Why do you ask?'

'No doctor, no medical team, no CIA special treatment.' He cleared his throat. 'You were going to end it here. Right? That's the truth, isn't it?' His hand tightened on her arm. 'Only she saved you the trouble.'

Margo said nothing.

Ahmed bent down and started pulling a few stones around the makeshift grave. 'I make it look decent, OK? Because I think she deserved it.'

Margo pulled up her collar against the wind.

'Did she leave any message?'

'You mean for the Americans? No. Why should she? She knew where she was going.'

He finished arranging the stones and stood up, his voice barely audible. 'I will tell you this . . . in case we ever meet again. If she'd been alive, I would not have let you take her.'

Margo returned his stare. 'And I would not have let you leave.'

She watched till his car was out of sight. 'We'll wait a few minutes,' she told Sam. 'If there are any patrols out there, I'd rather they dealt with him instead of us.'

'Was he right?' Sam stared down at the grave. 'Would you have killed her?'

She didn't look at him; didn't even register the question.

She had expected a sense of relief; no doomsday choice to be made between duty and conscience. No guilt or shame to carry forward. But there was nothing to celebrate about a woman, tortured out of life, buried in a grave no one would ever visit.

In a while, she thought, the living – whoever was left – would wake up and pass by and the town would limp into another day. And the only visitors would be the dead or the dying from across the border and the grief they brought with them.

'We better get going,' she said.

Ahmed sent his message from the car. He had done all he could. Moscow would make of it what it wanted.

But there was also the issue of the contact. When things had calmed down in a week or a month, he would visit the man's widow and leave her some money. It wasn't often that he felt bad about violent endings. Normally, the people he dealt with seemed uniformly determined to live down to his worst expectations. But not this time.

In truth, he hadn't rated the Syrian. Worse, he'd judged him a poser, a petty crook – never had the slightest expectation that he'd sacrifice himself in a fight if the need arose. Why would he?

And then, out of nowhere, the man had produced a flash of quite exceptional courage.

Made you think.

Ahmed wondered if he'd have done the same.

He took a deep breath and kept his eyes firmly on the icy road to Amman.

Once out of Israeli airspace and over the Mediterranean, the pilot asked Manson if he wanted to send any messages.

He didn't.

For the first time in his career, he had no idea what to say. His part of the operation had ended in failure. Even now there would be angry protests from the Jordanians, sleepless, spluttering ambassadors pulled from their beds in all sorts of capitals and large helpings of injured pride at the Foreign Office.

In the days to come Whitehall would resound with the noise of it all, and a whole bunch of important people would tell each other in angry phone calls from unlisted numbers to 'go fuck themselves'. And some might even do that. But after a few months when the prime minister would have promised a full investigation, with no intention of delivering it, a good and faithful servant of the Crown would pick a dark, rainy night and chuck whatever paperwork there was into the Thames.

He hoped.

Perhaps, he told himself, Margo Lane had after all 'finished' the entire, wretched business and would, if fate had willed it, be on her way home in the morning.

He didn't know – but as the plane headed north over Europe, he conceded grudgingly that she was one of only a handful of officers who could have pulled it off.

At around four thirty a.m. the prime minister left the study and took the stairs to the flat.

Sears would call when there was news.

Obviously, things had not been simple.

He sighed. When were they?

After a few minutes he lay down on the sofa, closed his eyes and heard the mobile ring in his pocket.

He didn't answer immediately, didn't want to hear bad news, knew that nothing good was ever communicated in the middle of the night.

'I'm coming up.' It was Sears.

The prime minister opened the front door of the flat and beckoned the man to come in, but Sears shook his head.

'I'm not staying. Just wanted to tell you it's done, finished. That's all I know. I'll find out more in a few hours. The agent's on her way home. You can get some sleep.'

He closed the door, but didn't go back to the bedroom. He felt no sense of satisfaction. The woman he had sent to Jordan had survived the night – God only knew what she had been through – but someone else would have died.

Perhaps Sears had been right. There might have been another way. He could have talked to the president, warned him that Britain wouldn't tolerate . . . Only, even as the thought surfaced, he knew it wouldn't have worked.

How many times had he gone to Washington, talked himself silly and flown home with a bagful of platitudes? A slap on the back. A 'great to see you, fellah'. And they'd ignored everything he'd said.

Couldn't happen again.

Nobody would ever thank him for it.

But this time there hadn't been a choice.

Harry let the phone ring three times before he answered.

In the distance, on a bad connection, he heard Yanayev's dismal voice, like a priest intoning at a funeral.

So mundane, he thought. So matter-of-fact. A simple one-line ending to such a complex production. And then – curtain down. Audience gone home. Bad reviews all round.

The blazing clarity of failure.

Strange how he felt outside of it all. The sense of watching it happen to someone else; of sitting in the empty theatre with the lights extinguished.

He got up, tripped on the table leg, half fell against the sink. The pain brought him back to reality and the tears that he could no longer hold inside.

'I'm sorry, my friend. She didn't make it.'

The words of the Russian ambassador. They weren't much of an epitaph.

As soon as he reached the Residence, Yanayev called Lydia to get her coat. They walked in silence for a moment across the grand white garden, their boots crunching on the hard snow. It was peaceful, he thought, in a way that Moscow never had been. Peaceful because people left you alone. Because you were free to think.

He didn't look at her. 'They've recalled me,' he said quietly. 'I knew they would. Nobody returns my messages. I'm history. They all know it by now.'

'I don't understand . . .' She took his hand. 'None of this was your fault.'

'This isn't the issue. *I* was the one who took them the plan. If it had worked it would have been a spectacular coup. We'd have had a lever on one of the most powerful figures in the American government – think of it! Their imagination went wild.' He swallowed hard. 'Now they are inconsolable. Their promised toy isn't coming for Christmas after all. So someone will have to pay for the disappointment.' He pulled out a handkerchief and blew his nose. 'The someone is me. I know how their mind works.'

'We'll get through it. We always have. I'll be there at your side . . .'

'No.' He pulled his hand away. 'That's out of the question. I've no idea what they'll do and I don't want you in Moscow when I find out.'

'Please, Vitaly.'

'I said no.' He stopped and turned to face her. 'You leave for Paris in the morning. There's no discussion. From there you buy a plane ticket in cash and go somewhere safe. Best is Jerusalem. I'll contact you there. American Colony Hotel. They'll keep letters if you're nice to Reception. Don't try to reach me . . . please, my dear, I need you to be strong.'

He walked on, taking her arm again. 'Who knows if anyone is watching. We must act normal for now. First thing tomorrow, you'll go out for a walk, take nothing with you and get a taxi to the airport. Buy what you need in Paris. Just be careful.'

He squeezed her arm, felt her weight and her warmth against him. 'We're Russians,' he whispered. 'Life is shorter for us than for others. You know that.' He put his arms around her. 'We've always known that.'

*   *   *

They had monitored Harry's call from the mobile command centre, overheated, overcrowded, parked next to a supermarket. They were nervous, all of them, throwing anxious glances at each other, checking and re-checking that the microphones in the house were live and working. Because this went way too high to screw up.

Parked beside them, a man in a blue Chevrolet read the transcript twice and put it in his pocket.

He phoned a Washington DC number, recited the single line he'd seen and was told to stay where he was.

They'd get back to him.

Reclining the seat, he switched the radio back on and let the gentle jazz fill the car.

Didn't matter if they used him or not. He'd be well paid any which way. Cash, of course. Went without saying. When the government really wanted you, they wouldn't be stupid enough to leave a trail of forms and figures.

And they really wanted him. Especially tonight.

Delayed by fog, the BA plane stood for an hour on the runway at Amman airport, with Margo Lane asleep in row fifteen.

Before leaving, she had sent an encrypted snap from the embassy, thrust the gun, wrapped in newspaper into the hands of the First Secretary, still in his bright blue pyjamas, smiled at his 'goodness me!' and taken a taxi out of the city.

Catch a quick glimpse of her that morning and she could have been a tourist, roughing it through the Middle East in jeans and sweaters, a guidebook and a map, sticking out of her bag. But look more closely and there was nothing casual or relaxed about her. Margo Lane didn't saunter and didn't idle. You would always know that she had a place to go and a time to be there.

And somewhere to leave in haste.

Even as she shut her eyes, she had the story straight in her mind, the version she would give to Manson, the questions she would answer, and the one she would leave on the shelf.

They didn't own her. Never would.

Harry didn't know if she could still hear him. She lay motionless in the quiet white room, next to the daffodils that would outlive her.

And her silence condemned him.

Like an old man on a darkened path, his words tripped and stumbled, slowed, then picked up speed again, a litany of regrets and confessions; he wished, he wanted; he begged; if only he had done and not done all the things that could no longer be corrected.

Somewhere in the middle of his monologue she died, but for several minutes he seemed not to notice.

And when he did, it was with the knowledge that whatever she had taken away with her through that uniquely one-way door, the serious baggage was still in the room. He could see that now.

What she had done was to remove for all time the power she alone possessed – to forgive him. She had made sure to take that with her.

Only the silent, bitter accusations had been left behind.

London dripped, locked in a cold front that would push on eventually towards Germany but not soon enough.

This time there was no one to meet her at the airport. It's how you always knew that an operation had ended. They've moved on to someone else, somewhere else; other nails to be bitten; other lies to be constructed and spread. So go join the queue and get the bus home.

Nobody looked at her on the journey. Nobody, she thought, looks at anyone in London. We just don't want to know anymore.

Certainly not about a woman who just a few hours earlier had carried a silenced gun along the Syrian border in readiness to kill for her country.

Made no sense at all.

And if she tried explaining it to the faces opposite her on the Number 13 bus, would they call the police – or a doctor?

Was she mad or dangerous? Or both?

The president opened the door to the Rose Garden and felt the cold rush in. But it wasn't important.

Much more important was to hold the conversation with his visitor outside the Oval Office and to ensure that no one else would hear it.

The two men stepped into the darkness. The president had known his guest since his days as a US attorney in New York. Southern district. Full of crooks in suits, who mostly got away with whatever they wanted. Nothing had changed.

As on previous occasions, the visitor's name would not appear on any official list and there would be no record of his arrival or departure.

After all, as the president was so fond of telling his closest advisers, open government had its limits.

He wasn't surprised by what Harry Jones had done. Not even disappointed. You couldn't work in the US capital and seriously expect anyone to live up to the crass and self-congratulatory rhetoric that echoed daily across Washington.

As long as politicians were born with backs, he reflected, there would be people in this city to stab them.

Loyalty, much trumpeted, was a favour to be offered and then withdrawn. It always carried an end date – you just never knew in advance when it was.

So Harry Jones was no worse than most of his colleagues – none of them, in time-honoured tradition, would dream of lying until they opened their mouth. And that was the only certainty you ever got.

The visitor leaned towards the president and spoke quietly in his ear. There wasn't much to tell. Endings don't take a lot of time in Washington.

The president opened his mouth wide, sucked in the cold air and folded his arms across his chest.

He thought he should feel *something* – anger at Harry, sorrow for his wife – but he felt no emotion of any kind, no sense of occasion.

'Finish it,' he said quietly. 'Do it now.'

'Harry Jones?'

The man wasn't dressed for winter. Just a shirt and jacket. And gloves. Always gloves.

'I'm . . .'

'I know who you are. You'd better come in.'

Harry turned and led the way into the kitchen. 'I'd offer you coffee but you're probably in a hurry to be on your way.'

'No, coffee would be good – thanks.'

He was just as Harry had expected. The perfectly forgettable face, devoid of landmark or blemish. The quick, practised smile; eyes that were Arctic blue, wide open but so very disinterested.

Harry put the coffee on the table and pulled up a chair. 'I'm gonna make this easy for you but I'd like to know what you have in mind.'

How odd his voice sounded to him. So normal, so mundane.

'I put something in the coffee and you'll fall asleep quite quickly.'
The voice was measured, almost gentle. 'And then a quick injection.
Very peaceful.'

'I see.'

The man raised an eyebrow. 'Is there something you need to
finish? I . . .' He stopped suddenly. A car had drawn up outside the
neighbour's house, doors opened and slammed. A young woman
called out happily, 'Bye, guys'. And then the silence returned.

Normal life had come home and gone to bed.

Harry loosened his top button. 'No, nothing to finish. I'm pretty
much set.'

The man took a tiny vial from his pocket and poured a couple
of drops into Harry's cup. 'It's tasteless. You won't notice.'

Harry picked up the cup, drained it and sat back in his chair.
'You do many of these?'

Perhaps everyone talked to their executioner. He didn't know the
etiquette.

In any case there was no reply and the easy smile had gone.
Business was almost complete.

Harry shut his eyes. It took only a few seconds for him to know
that the man had lied. As the acid coursed down his throat he thought
he could taste his own death in slow motion, as if a long, sharp
blade was gouging out his life from deep inside him, silencing the
scream that no one could hear.

'You buried her where?'

'You want a postcode?'

Manson turned his chair and stared at the river below. 'Somehow,
I don't think anybody's going to ask for it.' He thought for a moment.
'Fucking hellhole the Middle East, isn't it?'

She said nothing.

He clasped his hands under his chin and watched her carefully.
'You know that Harry Jones died last night?'

She raised a single eyebrow. 'I didn't.'

'Surprised?'

'Why would I be surprised? People die all the time. I wasn't
expecting it today.'

'His wife died overnight – he committed suicide shortly afterwards.'

'And you know this from . . .?'

'Something as secret as a White House press statement.' Manson made a face. 'Implication being that he died of a broken heart.'

'How convenient.'

'Except for him . . .' Manson got up. 'Anyway, we're told the president is devastated to have lost such a close and trusted member of his team . . .'

'But you know better . . .'

'I do.' He held open the door but stood, blocking her path. 'By the way . . .' He allowed a few seconds of silence to tick past, opened his mouth to speak but seemed to change his mind.

'You have something to say?'

'It can wait.'

She closed the gap between them. 'Let me help you on this one. You want to ask if I'd have carried out your order to kill the American woman – but you don't even have the guts to say it out loud. Typical, isn't it? You give illegal orders but you hesitate to spell them out in plain English.'

He turned away.

'So would I have put a bullet in her head? If she'd been standing in front of me, fit and healthy and wishing me a nice day . . . would I have pulled that trigger?'

'Get out of here, Lane.' He wouldn't look at her; had nothing to say; knew he'd been played.

'We've been piecing together a few unfortunate events here, Alec.'

The president's deep baritone was slower, more measured than normal.

Or was it the split-second delay on the transatlantic line? The prime minister hunched low over his desk.

'Go on, please.'

'We had an operation in Syria. Went badly wrong. Some collateral . . .' He hesitated. 'The fact is some of our folks crossed red lines. And some of those lines were yours.'

'Indeed.'

'Won't happen again, Alec . . .'

'It would be extremely damaging if it did. In all sorts of ways.'

'My understanding is that you were taking certain counter-measures of your own. Is that right?'

'I have no knowledge of that, Mr President. I can't conceive of a situation where I would order what you call "counter-measures". Our countries have a strong and vital alliance. It's in both our interests to keep it that way.'

There was a loud, insistent silence on the transatlantic line.

Much to be said, thought the prime minister. No wish to say it.

'Goodbye, Mr President.'

'Goodbye, Alec.'

Sears came in from the outer office where he'd been listening but he didn't sit down.

'You sent your signal, Alec. Clear and unequivocal. Just as you wanted. He got it.'

'Did he?' The prime minister bit hard into his lower lip. Always dangerous to revisit decisions when it's too late to change them. 'Think they'll do it again?'

Sears stood for a moment in the open doorway. 'Course they will. You know that as well as I do. It's who they are.'

The overnight guest in the White House replaced the handset and turned to face the president.

'The man lied to your face.'

The president shook his head. 'Not exactly. He was 3,500 miles away at the time. Besides . . .' He paused for a moment. 'If allies ever told each other the truth, they wouldn't be allies for very long.'

Lydia stood for a moment and took in the magnificent stone courtyard, the sprawling creeper, the candle-lit tables along the thick, rough walls. At each of them she could make out the lined, worn faces of East Jerusalem's Palestinian elite – the talkers, always outnumbering the doers, the caring and the plotting, the dark, silent figures who came just to watch all the others or to tell their fortune from upturned cups of coffee.

Once, long ago, the American Colony Hotel had been in Jordan, only Israel had expanded its borders, the way you did in the Middle East, and the proud building with its metre-thick walls, had woken up in 1967 to find itself in a different country.

She remembered the last time she had seen him – could still smell the airless, summer afternoon in Moscow's Park Dubki, the fumes from the filthy buses, wafting over the trees, the sweat on his face and the enormity of the fear etched in his eyes.

And even with thirty years gone by, his back to the doorway, she recognized the tight curly hair and the elbows on the little table, the way he had sat when he had introduced himself at the university.

Or had it happened to someone else?

Sam, Sam, Sam . . .

As he turned, she stumbled, glimpsing the hesitant, knowing smile, grabbing at the nearest table, steadying herself, seeing him open his arms wide in greeting.

And they both said it at the same time. 'A glass of tea in Jerusalem.'

A promise, undiluted by time and distance, now kept in full.

As so often when there is much to say, they said nothing; held hands, playing and replaying the silent memories between them.

The baker and his wife never spoke about *that* evening.

He never told her of his meeting with the commander – or the fear and the cold and the long walk home that had almost killed him.

And she, in turn, never spoke about the American woman, although she thought about her every day and wondered if she had gone home to Missouri or California, or somewhere else with a strange name.

She was glad of Lubna's company.

The girl had driven back with her and, as the days passed, never shown the slightest desire to leave.

She worked hard in the shop, learned quickly about making bread. She was clean and efficient but she seldom spoke. And the baker's wife had never seen her smile.

When they did talk, it was only about matters of the day. After all, both the past and the future lay in impenetrable darkness, best undisturbed.

To those of the townspeople who asked, Lubna was the orphaned daughter of distant relatives – two committed fighters, killed in a Russian airstrike. The daily reality of Syria. No need for explanation.

And the baker? He too had become silent, afraid to look in the wrong direction, say the wrong thing, speak – God forbid – to the wrong person.

He knew – because his wife had told him just once and so very quietly – that if he ever talked about Lubna to anyone, ever told or even so much as hinted at the real story, she would slit his throat.

* * *

Mum and Dad had gone to bed by the time she climbed the stairs.

Their door was open. Light from the streetlamps flooded onto the landing.

Margo sat on a chair in her old bedroom and tried to recall some happy moments.

But they wouldn't come.

Instead she saw the dark, winter fields on the border between Jordan and Syria and heard the shots that had echoed across the frozen landscape.

For all her misgivings, she had, when it came to it, been quite ready to kill.

She would have done it quickly and in silence, without emotion, crossing into the new world she had dreaded, closing the doors behind her.

It's who I've become.

And one day the situation would come again. On a desert road or a back-street in a European city. It didn't matter. Somewhere, sometime she would be required to pull the trigger.

As an officer in the intelligence service she was paid to catch rats in traps, deter them or despatch them back to their maker. The motive was paramount. So was the result. Everything else was secondary.

Margo shivered. Dangerous ground; her mind already finessing the moral dilemma, collecting excuses and justifications.

She replayed a far-off conversation with the Service's legal adviser.

In the darkness of the tunnel, he'd said, the rules are different; no one can see you or tell you to stop. You can live there for years, unencumbered by belief or principle. But when you return to the light, you should know that the world will no longer want you. Your place is with the rats you hunted. Out of sight and in the gutter.

People will know that.

In the distance she heard a bus draw up at the stop on the Finchley Road, caught the sound of a police siren, a car racing down the Hendon Way.

She closed her eyes and lay flat on the bed where she had slept away her childhood.

Perhaps I think too much.